A Rumble in The Attic

Mary Barr

A Rumble in The Attic

Vanguard Press

VANGUARD PAPERBACK

© Copyright 2024
Mary Barr

The right of Mary Barr to be identified as author of
this work has been asserted by her in accordance with the
Copyright, Designs and Patents Act 1988.

A CIP catalogue record for this title is available from the British
Library.

ISBN 978-1-83794-247-3

This is a work of fiction. Names, characters, businesses, places, events
and incidents are either the products of the author's imagination or
used in a fictitious manner. Any resemblance to actual persons, living
or dead, or actual events is purely coincidental.

Vanguard Press is an imprint of
Pegasus Elliot Mackenzie Publishers Ltd.
www.pegasuspublishers.com

First Published in 2024

Vanguard Press
Sheraton House Castle Park
Cambridge England

Printed & Bound in Great Britain

Dedication

To my many cousins, some I know and some I don't.
Especially Pamela Barker and Anne Hazle. And my
wonderful family, who I am very blessed to have known
for a short time…

About the Author

Mary Barr's literary journey unfolds as a captivating odyssey through the realms of imagination and creativity. Beyond her proficiency in diverse genres, Barr possesses a unique ability to breathe life into her characters, making them resonate with readers on a profound level.

What sets Barr apart is not just her storytelling prowess but the meticulous attention she devotes to character development. Each protagonist becomes a vessel for introspection, embodying desires, fears, and aspirations that mirror the intricacies of real-life individuals. Barr's commitment to authenticity ensures that her characters evolve organically, contributing to the immersive quality of her narratives.

Mary Barr's creative process is a fascinating blend of intuition and discipline. Each new book demands her immediate attention, a testament to her dedication to capturing the essence of the unfolding narrative without compromise. It's a dance with inspiration where the characters guide the steps, and Barr is an adept choreographer ensuring every move resonates with purpose.

Mary Barr's dedication inspires us all to unleash our creative potential, reminding us that the true magic of storytelling lies in the fearless exploration of the human imagination.

Why Ms. Barr wrote this book:

When Ms. Barr wrote A Rumble in the Attic, she wanted to challenge herself with a one-dimensional character and a single plot line.
Rumble's life came with many outdated perceptions, nuances and intricacies – most of which served no purpose other than in his mind. However – along with the voice in his head – they controlled his every waking hour and therefore ultimately his life. Rumble is proof that learned habits and behaviors are in us all, and they are extremely hard to change.

Ms. Barr knows it's essential that each genre she write remains fresh and exciting to both her, and her readers.
Ms. Barr hopes she achieved her goal in writing this book – what do you think?

Contents

Chapter One

He climbed the stairs slowly. With each step, his feet felt heavier. Gradually, as he climbed the narrow stairway to the attic, he became aware he could barely lift another foot. The stairs to the first and second floors were wider and with the outline of faded carpet barely visible on the edges of each worn stair; like the last stairwell; there was nothing but bear dusty wooden floorboards beneath his shoes. Maybe, these stairs had once seen a coat of varnish, but if they had, no remnants remained and Rumble knew that was many years ago, if ever. He was now climbing the tiny stairway leading to the attic and for him, home. The fourth stair was approaching, he knew the timbers would protest under his weight, and he waited for the noise – the deep mournful moan he heard each time he stepped on the stair. The sound was unlike the second to top stair that squeaked like an irate mouse once he pressed the timbers down with his shoe.

Each evening when he climbed the stairs, he thought that perhaps by treading to the side of the offensive stair, it would alleviate the dreaded noise, but each evening he was too tired from climbing the previous three flights of stairs – to be bothered, and he decided it didn't matter anyway. There was no one around – in fact, he had never seen another living soul in the entire house – so was it only he who heard the noise?

The high-pitched squeak alerted him, jolting him from his daydreams making him aware he was almost at the top of the narrow stairway. Above him, a long electrical wire hung down from the high dark ceiling with a single light bulb attached to end of the wire. It was completely unadorned by a shade, and Rumble thought it had always been so. How helpful some light would be as he climbed the narrow stairs – now the days were getting shorter. But search as he may, he had never found the switch that would turn on the light and illuminate the stairs. But, he reasoned, *What are the chances of the light bulb still working?* He knew the chances would be slim to none. And just who would climb up, up, up on the narrow stairway to replace it.

Unlike the other three flights of stairs, there was no railings but grimy walls and nothing more. Each floor of the house was much the same as the others except for the railing on the third set of stairs, which was dangerously loose. Once he had tried to hold onto it, but at his touch, it had wobbled valiantly and threatened to fall. It was a long way down to the murky entranceway from the third floor, so Rumble was always careful not to touch it, unless absolutely necessary. The only time he'd grabbed it was once when he was extra tired and had stumbled over and old nail that stuck out from the center of the seventh stair.

Each floor had a landing and the same ornate old

craved banister ran along one side – while on the otherside there were doors. They were tall doors, made of dark timber, once stained an even darker color, but any maintenance on the doors or the house had been forgotten many years previously. Rumble assumed that behind these doors the other tenants lived. There were three doors on the third floor and a single door at the end – probably a bathroom, Rumble assumed. The floor below, the second floor had four closed doors and maybe a bathroom at each end, or so Rumble assumed. The layout of the house like the house itself was old and boring. Its few furnishings were astir, dusty and the coverings crumbling with age.

Rumble put his free hand deep into his trouser pocket and extracted a large key. He thought the house, like the key, came straight out of the eighteenth century. He found the key bothersome to carry around. He owned only three pairs of trousers, but only one pair had pockets deep enough to accommodate the long heavy brass key, so he wore the same trouser every day and his other two pairs were never worn. Using all his strength, he pulled the door hard toward him like he always needed to do. He heard the familiar grinding noise as the rust covered key turned in the lock. Once inside, he closed the door and breathed deeply of the air. It was less musty in here as he had managed – since his arrival – to coax the small window into opening, with the help of some soap in just the right places. Every few days, he managed to open it slightly wider. He observed with great delight that it was now open about six inches. But six inches of space was enough to make the air smell fresher, at least in his room.

The old house had a distinctly clawing, clinging, unused smell – one he couldn't quite place. He had smelled something like it before many years ago when he'd visited an old people's home to do some sketching for the residence. It had been at the request of Cootes, of course. Rumble always called his boss 'Cootes' in his head and he was worried that one day he would forget to put the honorary title before his name and call him simply Cootes to his face, instead of 'Mr. Cootes'. Cootes wasn't much older than himself, but unlike Rumble, he commanded respect just by being who he was – nothing more, nothing less.

Rumble threw his worn black leather sachet into the corner – it was the same place he threw it every evening on his return home. Next, he removed his shoes – the odor in the room changed significantly from the smell of his unwashed socks. His room – like the house – comprised of very little furnishings and what it did have looked like they had been there since the last century. He had a small four-poster bed, one pillow, a down quilt and two mismatched flannel sheets. In the corner, was a wooden kitchen chair that showed traces of grey paints, so Rumble assumed it may have once been painted.

He had a small alcove that was missing its door and here he hung his few clothes. There was also a bathroom – it was tiny – with the narrowest shower Rumble had ever seen. Rumble was of average height; he had a rather slim frame, perhaps some might say bordering on boney, but even he, had to turn around in the shower and should he wish to do so, he must first get out of the shower stall, turn and re-enter. Rumble was most proud of his shower; he felt it was his greatest achievement. When he'd first arrived, the old showerhead was so rusty with age and neglect that only a dribble of water ran through the nozzle. Rumble wasn't one to complain, however, he had tried to contact Edwards his landlord because he needed to shower each evening, and he felt he was entitled to a shower that worked.

Edwards, a most difficult man, had explained that the house was full of tenants, and he couldn't possibly use another bathroom; he was getting very cheap rent and if he didn't like it. He should leave. As he had only just moved in at that stage, so, Rumble didn't like the alternative at all. Rumble didn't shower for several days as he pondered the problem. It was a Saturday when he was using the laundry facilities that were provided in the old house. They were located at the back of the house, through the backdoor and then left into the laundry room. Like everything else in the house, the laundry looked as though it had never been updated and the washing machines were the old type that Rumble hadn't seen since he was a child. These washing machines had the wringer attached to the machine and you must put your clothes through the wringer to get the excess water out. There were two washing machines side by side in the dusty laundry, but Rumble soon learned that one didn't work. Once you filled it with water, it would run out on the floor. While Rumble watched his few meager clothes churn around inside the washing machine he thought about his showerhead and just how he could get more water out of the shower nozzle.

He knew he must look for better accommodation, of course, but not right now. Rumble was, unless pushed, a slow mover by nature. It was then his foot pushed something on the floor, he looked down and saw a woman's' hairpin lying there. It was old and rusty. He looked some more. Slowly, he bent over and picked it up, he held it toward the light and turned it around in his hand. Here, he thought is the answer to his problem. This hair pin shall fix his shower nozzle.

Rumble used the old hairpin to poke out the rust in the holes of the shower nozzle; he worked patiently and diligently until the water ran freely. Monday morning was his monthly meeting with Cootes and Rumble was, for once in his life, he was happy to have a warm shower and clean clothes, before he met with his boss.

Chapter Two

Rumble never mentioned to Edwards he had got the shower working. It was the very first thing Rumble had ever fixed, and he felt a brief, momentary flash of pride in his achievement.

Edwards, his landlord, was a stout man of interminable age, he looked old but he could be older. He had snow-white hair around the edge of his balding, shiny head. Coarse long white whiskers perturbed from his ears, nose and eyebrows. With deep-set steely eyes and thin lips; Edwards seemed an intense enigma from another place and time. Edwards wore a ring on the pinky finger of his left hand; it looked altogether out of place on the old man. Rumble remembered staring at the heavy wide silver band with the fiery deep red ruby glinting back at him in the dim light.

Rumble knew nothing about jeweler or gemstones. He didn't own any nor did he have any interest in them, but he assumed the red stone was a ruby and the band was made of silver. He didn't know why it caught his eye, maybe it was due to the fact it was in such stark contrast to the way Edwards presented himself, or was it how the ring seemed alive with a life of its own. It shone brightly in the gloomy day, Rumble briefly thought this strange, but his eyes were drawn to the ring. Edwards was a strict, no-nonsense sort of guy and the ring looked totally out of place on his old wrinkly finger. Rumble knew he had always worn it as his chubby finger seemed too large for the ring and, over the years it had made a deep indent in his skin.

Edwards proved unapproachable and un-contactable and there was no denying the house rules for his tenants must be followed to the letter. And his rules were many. All lights must be turned off unless being used directly. All doors must remain locked at all times. Any tenant found nosing around the house would be immediately evicted.

Rumble was instructed to enter the house through the back door, move through the unused and outdated kitchen with the cobwebs covered appliances, to the entrance hall, with its high ceiling that spanned up to the third floor. There he must immediately climb the stairs directly to the attic and not stop or speak to anyone on his way up to the attic. That must be a joke Rumble realized; he had never seen or heard another living soul, so there would be no chance of him speaking to anyone.

He was not allowed to cook in his room and must not leave his room after dark. He was allowed the use of the laundry facilities once a week between two and three p.m. on Saturdays and any washing left on the clothesline after dark would be confiscated and not returned. Edwards was firm that he would enforce the house rules and they must be followed to the letter. Again, he said how the house was fully tenanted and with respect to the other tenants Rumble must not become a nuisance, if he was, he would be quickly evicted. Any complaints would also render an immediate eviction. Apparently, Edwards stated his tenants and Rumble were not allowed a radio, telephone or T.V. in their room either. Nor were they allowed any of these items in the house. No visitors or animals were allowed in the house or on the grounds.

Rumble, thought himself an easy-going man and not given to emotion.

He is of average height and build, with mousey brown hair thinning at the front and peppered with gray. He has small gray eyes, a long thin nose and pink lips covering good teeth except for the chipped one in the front. He has pasty white skin from never seeing the sun; this gives his nails a slight purple hue that Rumble thought was not a healthy sign. Why he thought this, he didn't know. Rumble is a thinker, a dreamer and a creative man, but never a doer. He thinks things through several times before he may move forward slowly and with purpose; he needs an understanding of where he is headed, or he doesn't move at all.

Rumble sat on his bed, thinking of his day, before slowly lifting the old chair toward the door. He removed the rusty key and placed the back of the chair at an angle under the door handle. He knew this would not make it impossible to enter, but it would make it harder and maybe the chair would break before the door fully opened. But what would he do then? Anyway, he was probably alone in the house, so why should he worry. He actually wished again he had never come here. But as usual Rumble had thought for too long and done nothing when he was asked to leave his last lodgings and time had almost run out before he began the search for new accommodation. They had given him two weeks and may have given him longer. In those two weeks, he had thought what he wanted to do and where he wanted to go, but he hadn't done anything about moving out.

That was when Rumble was renting a room from a delightful old couple. Mr. and Mrs. Millington were in their late fifties. They owned a tiny cottage in West Sussex not far from where he lived now but on a much nicer street. He'd lived there for over five years and hated leaving; it had worked well for them all. His room was outside the back door of the cottage, and he'd guessed that once it belonged to the maid. A small bathroom had been added, but compared to what he had now, it was actually a large bathroom, and the furnishings were cozy and comfortable.

Each weekend, the Millington's would drive to Woolpit and stay with Mr. Millington's elderly mother. So, Rumble would have the entire cottage to himself. All that was required in return was that he feed their cat. It was an old ginger cat with huge yellow eyes and long white whiskers. It had a way of sitting almost at eye level with Rumble and staring at him. Rumble felt the cat could read his very soul. Often it would meow. It was a soft meow of an older cat and its tail would flick this way and that. When this arrangement had first begun Rumble didn't like the cat. He had never had anything to do with animals; didn't understand them and didn't feel a need to.

Sykes, as the cat was called, soon formed a close bond with Rumble and they enjoyed being together. After a while, Rumble would buy him cat treats and their bond grew closer. Every weekend Sykes stayed close to Rumble. If Rumble sat in the love seat, Sykes would sit close beside him but never touching him. Rumble began to talk to Sykes, and Sykes would stare at him with his huge golden eyes and meow softly at just the right moment, so Rumble believed he was heard and understood. A part of Rumble knew Sykes was just a cat but gradually he was thinking of Sykes as his best friend. He spoke to Sykes like speaking to your closest confidant and he told Sykes everything. For Rumble, it was the first time in his life he had formed a bond with anyone or anything, and he cherished the weekends. Whether, they we talking or sitting watching T.V.; which was also a first for Rumble. Rumble felt like he had a friend.

He also valued the Millington's as friends, not like he thought of Sykes but each Wednesday they'd have him into the cottage for dinner and on Friday evening when Rumble arrived home he'd help Mr. Millington in the garden, before they left for the weekend. The arrangement worked well and five years passed in a flash. During his stay nothing extraordinary happened and time moved on. They celebrated each other's birthdays and exchanged presents at Christmas.

Rumble remembers the Monday evening well; he had just got home. He seldom saw or spoke with the Millington's on Monday, so when they knocked on his door, he knew something was different. In fact, he'd been feeling something was amiss all day, deep inside something had been niggling, although he didn't understand it. It was the same feeling he'd had when his mother died, and he hadn't understood it then either.

He was surprised to see Mr. and Mrs. Millington standing there. They didn't appear their usual jovial selves. They were a well-matched happy couple always joking with each other in a loving kind of way; he found their behavior reassuring but unfamiliar. Rumble learned a lot about life and love from them. They both entered his space and sat down on his small love seat without speaking. Rumble became concerned,

"Rumble," Mr. Millington began, "we feel just awful, Mrs. Millington and I, having to tell you this."

"You are like one of the family, Rumble," Mrs. Millington added.

"And we know Sykes adores you, he doesn't take to just anyone but he loves you, we can tell," Mr. Millington added.

"Oh, yes, we can tell, and we are so pleased he loves you," Mrs. Millington said.

"Oh, is anything the matter with Sykes?" Rumble asked concerned and then noticed him at the partly opened doorway, his tail held high looking in with his intense yellow eyes, he was staring straight at Rumble, and at that moment Rumble knew nothing good was about to be said.

"No, Sykes is fine," Mrs. Millington spoke as she got up from her seat and opened the door wider for Sykes. He ran into the room and sat at Rumble's feet staring up at him as only he could do. Rumble bent down and stroked him once slowly from his ears right down his back to his tail just like he preferred. Rumble knew to give him more than one stroke would make him move away.

"No, it's not Sykes, Rumble. It's Mother."

"Oh, I am sorry, will you be away longer than the weekend?" Rumble asked.

"Rumble, Mother is getting older, she's almost ninety, and she's rather frail. We travel a long way each weekend to be with her, only now she needs more care," Mr. Millington continued.

"Rumble, we need to have her here living with us," Mrs. Millington said, her eyes averting his, but Rumble still didn't understand. They had two large bedrooms inside the cottage after all and a smaller one they could use as well.

"She is deteriorating rather faster than we should have hoped. And Rumble we intend moving her in here along with her nurse. We're very sorry."

"Oh, that's all right," Rumble replied still not

understanding what they were trying to say.

"We can give you two weeks to find somewhere else to live, Rumble. I'm sorry it can't be more time, but she really is deteriorating rather rapidly, and we need her here with us, she's family and family comes first," finally, hearing Mrs. Millington's words, Rumble understood.

"We're so sorry, Rumble, really we are," Mr. Millington said as they got up and walked out the door, holding it open for Sykes to follow.

And just like that the very best part of Rumble's life was over. He felt crushed. He thought they liked him. He thought Sykes was his friend. And now, he was out. It had taken him over a week to process what they had said and understand that he must leave. During that time, he'd hardly spoken to the Millingtons. Although, they still had him in for Wednesday dinner, they never again asked him when he would be leaving. They had given him two weeks to find somewhere else to stay, and he knew, in the meantime, it wouldn't be mentioned. However, the next Wednesday, they did mention that the nurse would be arriving the following week and would be moving into his room.

That evening, he finally knew that this really wasn't his home after all, and he must do something about moving out. He needed to find somewhere else to stay. The next morning, he used the phone in his room to call Cootes and tell him he wouldn't be handing in any sketches for a few days, as he needed to move. Sadly, Rumble knew the

Millington's weren't his family after all. He heard his mother's voice in his head saying the same words he had heard his whole childhood. 'No one hears or cares what you say. The world doesn't want you, and neither do I. Stay invisible and maybe keep drawing.' Somewhere deep inside Rumble still refused to believe her, but this time she was surely right. He knew the Millingtons would contact him after he left, he just knew they would, and they did try. However, Rumble didn't reply, and soon they stopped trying. Now he knew he would never see or hear from the Millingtons again. It would be his choice. After all, they had abandoned him.

Chapter Three

With just a few days before he must leave, Rumble found himself walking aimlessly around the streets of West Sussex, buying newspapers and scanning the pages for a room to rent. He saw several but most were either more than he wanted to pay or not available in time for his imminent departure from the Millington's cottage.

A light drizzle forced him to find shelter under the nearest tree. He would have preferred to get out of this neighborhood, it gave him the creeps, and it was not the type of place to loiter. He wasn't sure just how he had managed to end up here in the first place, the address he was given now seemed, on a closer look to be in quite another street altogether; but the old map he was holding was telling him this is where he should be.

The drizzle turned to a heavy rain and Rumble pulled his coat collar up around his neck. He looked around at all the old rundown houses, the broken fences, the boarded-up shops on the corner and several scruffy looking children, smoking cigarettes and jumping in the puddles at the far end of the street. Then he looked in the other direction and saw several vacant pieces of land where a house had once stood but had, at long last, succumbed to the elements and crumpled back into the earth. He saw the old street with the bitumen cracked and rutted and the large gapping potholes like unhealed wounds staring back at him.

He was pleased, he didn't have a car because those holes could do some costly damage to any automobile, no matter how well sprung it was. He watched as a rusty red car slowly entered the street, inside were four youths. Greasy black smoke bellowed from the exhaust pipe, it hung in the damp air as the car moved on, like an evil entity unsure of its way. The youths inside the car, yelled obscenities from the open windows at no one at all until it rounded the bend and disappeared into a driveway further up the street.

The rain continued, Rumble was thinking of making a run for it, but where could he run? He must think further about his dilemma; Rumble hated being out of his daily routine, but he needed accommodation, and he needed it now. He leaned against the tree, and while he almost shielded the map from falling moisture, he tried to work out his exit route. Drops of water began to drip from the overhanging branches onto his map, and he reluctantly folded it back into its former creases and placed it in his pocket.

He leaned into the trunk of the tree and looked closer at his immediate surroundings. Something in the overgrown hedge of the house beside him caught his attention. It was an old sign. It had once hung from a post but the post had snapped or was pushed over into the fence

29

and the overgrown garden beyond. It had broken through the once white picket fence when it fell. But it wasn't the fence that interested Rumble; it was what he thought he saw on the sign. He moved from the safety of the tree trunk into the rain and reached over to pull the sign slightly toward him. Brushing away a few leaves, he realized the sign was not as old as everything around it. The paint was clean and appeared to have been written professionally. The sign read:

Vacancy – room to rent – call Mr. Edwards and there was a number. Rumble fumbled in the damp pocket of his raincoat for his pencil. He doubted it would write, but he needed to record the phone number. The pencil managed to write the number on the back of his moist map. And that was how he'd met the eccentric Mr. Edwards and was living alone in an old house that supposedly he shared with many tenants who he never saw or heard. Already, he had been in the dreary house for six long months and in all that time, he had never seen or heard another living soul.

Chapter Four

Rumble was preparing for his monthly meeting with Cootes his direct boss at the magazine brokerage. Rumble knew he had been fortunate to meet Cootes. It had happened by chance when he was attending school with Cootes's youngest sibling James Cootes. James was now a successful architect, happily married with two grown children. Although, they had little in common apart from their childhood; they remained friends and would meet at least once a year at the coffee shop by James's office.

It happened quite by chance when Rumble first met Cootes. Cootes was James's elder sibling while James was the youngest, so, Cootes was twelve years older than James and Rumble. Many years ago, as Rumble sat in James's living room sketching while James and his brothers raced around the house. James older brother, whom Rumble now addressed simply as Cootes, had recognized Rumble's early talent as a sketch artist. At that time, Cootes had recently been appointed junior editor for the Country Life magazine. Later, he joined a magazine brokerage where he was offered a partnership. It was about the time Rumble and James attended university. Soon, Cootes sort out Rumble, who was now in his second year at university taking art and design.

Rumble jumped at the opportunity when James mentioned the possibility of getting paid to just sketch without the need to study. Soon, James, on the insistence of Rumble, had set up an interview with Cootes. All Rumble had ever wanted to do, was sketch. He just wanted to be left alone with a large sketchpad and pencils, and perhaps, occasionally, some watercolors, to create life in his etchings and pencil sketches. After the interview with Cootes, which Rumble thought he'd blundered through, he was offered a meager job with the magazine.

So, began his employment with Cootes who was now a partner in a small brokerage company. Over a short amount of time Cootes was promoted as the brokerage grew. Now Cootes was the senior illustrations broker and editor to several country magazines. Under his banner he supplied, *Country Life, Country Living, Horse and Hounds, Birds of the Countryside, Birds of a Feather and Hunting with the Gentry.* There may possibly be more but these were the main ones Rumble knew and the ones that helped pay his meager wage each fortnight.

Long ago, Cootes had suggested Rumble change his name, nothing major he'd said, but something catchy was required. Soon, Cootes suggested Bumble instead of Rumble and a picture of a small bumblebee under his signature. Rumble didn't wish to change his name to Bumble but he did use the idea of the tiny bumblebee under his signature. He'd used the bee in the bottom right corner of his sketches as his nom-de-plume ever since.

However, Rumble had never seen any of his work in magazines or his signature of the bee at the bottom of the page. He knew his sketches were in the magazines, but he never knew which of his sketches were used. The magazines were too costly for him to afford, and he felt guilty standing at a news-stand flipping through the pages. Last time, he'd tried to stand in the corner of the news agency and flip through the pages in order to find his work, the clerk had quickly approached and asked if he intended to buy. He should have purchased a copy then even at the prices they changed, because soon after, all the magazines his work was featured in, were wrapped in plastic wrap and you could no longer open them without purchasing. On his pay slip, each week was printed the names of the magazines in which sketches were displayed, although, he never knew which sketches had been chosen nor if they mainly printed the pencil sketches or the pencil and watercolor sketches.

Rumble bought his thoughts back to the present and tomorrow mornings meeting. He sat on the end of his small four-poster bed and flipped through his work of the last four weeks. He was relatively happy with what he saw. He liked the varied collection of etchings and sketches. He thought the watercolors looked professional although, as watercolors often do; he thought they looked washed out and not nearly as vivid as the subjects he had captured. One day, he would visit the art shop and discuss with the old gentleman who owned it, the possibility of finding some watercolors that had more brilliance and depth. But nothing needed to change this month. Rumble didn't like to do anything in a hurry, he would think on it a little more; there was no rush to change what he did or how he did it. And there was always tomorrow.

At exactly seven thirty the next morning, Rumble finished dressing; he had the same trousers on as he always did and a clean shirt, one of the four he owned. He had already shaved and brushed his teeth, and he now ran the comb through his hair exactly three times, once on each side and one down the middle to the back. Then he got down on his hands and knees and reached under his bed to retrieve the toaster and electric kettle he kept hidden there. Once he had eaten a piece of dry toast and drunk his tea, he threw his sachet over his shoulder and holding the large key in his hand exited the room, pulling the door toward him hard enough to turn the key. Placing it into the deep pocket of his trousers, he walked down the steep narrow stairs to the next landing. He heard the loud squeak on the second stair and anticipated the mournful sound of the stair at the bottom.

Once on the third floor landing, he saw a murky sun filtering through a window somewhere below it cast a ghostly hue into the house. Now, he noticed for the first time the heavy layer of dust, it coated everything, even the banister. Looking down he saw the only area free of dust was where he walked each day. How then, did the other tenants in house move around without disturbing the dust?

He moved several paces along the banister toward the first closed door. He knew no one else was in the house by the amount of dust he now saw everywhere. He didn't know why he detoured along the landing, but he knew he was completely alone in the house. He also knew of Edward's rules, but how would Edwards know if Rumble explored a little unless he saw his footsteps in the dust.

Rumble walked toward the banister and looked down the two flights of stairs to the entranceway below. The house was deathly quiet as it always was, not a creak or a murmur he heard, nothing stirred, no breezes, no movement, just quiet, a deep bone chilling silence of nothing. For a few seconds, Rumble felt routed to the spot where he stood as the loneliness of the house seem to wrap around him and blanket him in its desperation of nothingness.

Rumble quickly shook himself and the little voice inside his head that often spoke to him when he was scared or confused, bounced into life, *this is crazy it's just a house, how could it feel desperate, how could it feel anything?* 'Okay,' Rumble replied, 'you are right again.' He was still a few feet from the nearest door, but again he remembered Edwards rules and feeling slightly guilty as though he was trespassing he resumed his walk down the three flights of stairs through the entranceway and then left through the kitchen and out the back door.

The weather was fine and clear but there was a crispness that told him autumn would soon be knocking.

As he rode the bus to the center of Essex and Cootes office, he couldn't shake the feeling he had experienced in the old house when he gazed down to the entranceway from the landing on the third floor. A house cannot evoke a feeling in a person. It is not a living thing, and logically he knew what he felt was completely ridiculous. The rational voice in his head told him. He looked out the window of the bus for the rest of his journey and watched the world go by. People were everywhere doing many things. Children were running, late for school; parents were going shopping or to work.

"Rumble, you're five minutes late, not like you. I can usually set my watch by your arrival. Bus late, was it?" Cootes asked, greeting Rumble as he entered his office. He moved toward the same large chair, where he always sat, directly opposite Cootes wide desk. It was a well-used overstuffed brown leather armchair, he would never consider sitting anywhere else.

"Lingered too long in the old house where I live. I still think it's a weird place. Lonely, no one else lives there."

"I thought you said the landlord, whatever his name is, told you it was fully tenanted?"

"Oh, he did. I'm beginning to think Edwards is just as strange as the house."

"Maybe, the tenants are there during the day while you're out. Rumble you're always out and about sketching and things, aren't you?"

"I am always out, yes, but there's no one else there.

I'm sure of it. And I don't intend to stay there much longer either."

"How can you possibly be so sure no one else is there? It's a big place and knowing you; you keep to yourself. I doubt if you even wander around the place, not your style. I've known you too long Rumble, you're not one to make friends with strangers."

"No, I'm not, you're quite right. But today, I noticed the dust. It's everywhere, thick dust from years of being vacant; it covers the entire house apart from where I walk. I see it floating in the air where the sun penetrates the gloom."

"All rather mysterious, I must say. Maybe, you should go exploring the place, not your style I know; you don't like getting out of your routine. But it's the only way you'll find anything out, Rumble."

"Maybe time I looked for a new place, Mr. Cootes."

"Oh, Rumble that will take you a while, you know how slowly you move."

"It's just who I am, Mr. Cootes."

"You must be able to afford something a little nicer than where you are surely. You earn a decent wage now, in fact you have done for some time, not huge but better by far than the average person. Maybe, it's time to let the moths out of those deep pockets of yours and live a slightly better existence."

"Mr. Cootes, my mother always told me to save every penny I earn for a rainy day, because she said, there's always one lurking just around the corner."

"Quite the pessimist your mother, Rumble. Even our mothers are not always right. I believe it's more a situation of knowing when to save and when to enjoy life a little. This place where you're staying is by far the worst place you have ever lived I would say. Or from what you're telling me anyway," Mr. Cootes added scratching his chin.

"I must agree with you there, it was only meant to be temporary, and I still believe it is. Although, without a phone it does make it rather hard to search for new accommodation."

"That's another thing that's rather strange Rumble; the many unusual rules of the house; most strange indeed. I've arranged for Lucy to get you another mobile phone, local calls only are covered on your expense account, same as your last mobile phone, Rumble. I doubt it will work inside the house but you're only there to sleep anyway. This time do report to Lucy if you lose or misplace it, don't be shy, these things happen. Anyway, you're totally un-contactable at present, and it really won't do Rumble, it really won't do, at all."

"Thank you, Mr. Cootes, a mobile phone shall make my life rather easier at present."

"Pick it up from Lucy on your way out, she'll give you the run down on how it works, and she has already programmed in the main numbers you'll need as well as internet access etc."

"The Internet is rather a strange, unknown creature to

me, Mr. Cootes."

"Do try and master the internet, Rumble. I know it's not who you are, and you will probably need to add it to your very rigid routine, but simply everyone uses it now days. Anyway, you can get some wonderful images to sketch on it, just change them slightly, due to copyright rules etc. Save you visiting the library all the time," Mr. Cootes chuckled softly again, and Rumble as usual had no idea why.

"Something new, oh my. Quiet frightening, really, Mr. Cootes, and you're right it is not who I am."

"We must all go with the tides of change Rumble or we get tramped over in the process."

"Yes, I suppose you're right," Rumble said slowly about to quote something his mother often said and then thinking better of it.,

"Okay, Rumble, let's get back to work. What do you have for me this month?" Cootes asked, eager as always to see what Rumble had created since they last met. Rumble opened his sachet and handed Cootes a selection of etching and sketches.

"Good work, Rumble, I see you've been to the library. These horses have movement, perfect for the next edition of *Horse and Hound*."

"Thank you, Mr. Cootes,"

"Rumble, we have a new sketch artist on our books, bright young chap, reminds me of you when you were younger. He uses watercolors, as you do, but his are alive with vibrancy of color, where as yours often look washed out. More like just a hint of color. This young chap has travelled the world. His portfolio is full of exotic interesting places and things. Maybe, you should consider doing the same. I could ask around our magazines. I feel sure one of them would sponsor your travels. Follow your adventures and print them as you captured the images of your adventures on paper."

"I've never had a yen to travel, don't think it's quite who I am, Mr. Cootes," Rumble added looking perplexed at the mention of something new and outside his realm of thought.

"Yes, quite so Rumble. But it really is food for thought, and I know you think a lot, so, maybe add the thought of travel to your many hours of thinking," Cootes replied with a chuckle to himself which Rumble didn't understand.

"Perhaps, I shall give it some thought, Mr. Cootes. It has certainly never occurred to me before now."

"Indeed, Rumble, I'm sure it has not. Anyway, be that as it may. More importantly, I would like you to consider using the same colors as this young chap uses, very bold and modern. Then, I know I could get your work on one of our magazine covers."

"Oh, a cover, Mr. Cootes, well now…" Rumble's words trailed off to nothing; he was unsure of what exactly he was expected to say.

Cootes quickly continued. "It has been a long time coming but you deserve a cover, Rumble, you certainly do," Cootes said flipping through his work and pulling several sketches and watercolors out and placing them on the top of the pile.

They discussed just what was required for the magazine issues during the coming month, over a cup of tea bought to them by Lucy, Cootes long standing secretary. After Rumble had spent some time with Lucy and picked up his new mobile, it was lunchtime when Rumble finally left Cootes' office. As Rumble always did after his visit with Cootes he headed toward Reeds fish shop, he would enjoy fish and chips for lunch; it would be his main meal of the day as lunch always was.

Rumble slowly ate relishing each delicious flavor as he always did, although today his mind was thinking over what Cootes had said about the vibrancy of his watercolors. Rumble would love to see some of his work on the cover of a magazine. He hadn't thought about it in years, but it was something he once hoped would have happened years ago, and so far, it hadn't. Maybe, there was still a chance, it would certainly put his bumblebee into the big time and get his work noticed. Just the thought made Rumble smile; just the slightest of smiles.

But then, he thought of changing the watercolors he used. He would certainly have to give that idea a lot more thought. He crumpled the paper where his fish and chips had previously been and walked toward the same garbage basket as he always did to dispose of the greasy newspaper. High above him several gulls glided on the wind, up and down round and round they glided occasionally their mournful squawks could be heard as they circled or dipped in the air. Yes, thought Rumble this afternoon he would capture them on paper gliding on the wind…

Chapter Five

Rumble was later than usual arriving home that evening. He had done several good sketches of the gulls and captured some workers backs, sitting talking in the cafes on the side of the street after work. He didn't like sketching people, but he enjoyed having parts of them in his sketches even if he wouldn't give any of them to Cootes. He'd tucked them away in the back of sketchbook. He was getting quite a collection of sketches just tucked away in the back of his book, he needed to take them out and leave them in his room.

Then, he had stayed on where he was and thought. He knew he had a lot to think about, and he also knew that too many thoughts would cloud his creative abilities. He didn't like having things that needed to be thought about, considered or worst of all, resolved. Resolution was certainly not something he liked. Action had never appealed to him unless he was sure of where he was going, very sure. But before he got to that place a great deal of thinking was required. The rush hour traffic was at its peak now, so he would wait a while longer, no point in standing up in the bus all the way home when he could sit comfortably later and hopefully have no one beside him.

It was almost dark as he let himself in the back door.

He seldom came in this late and wasn't familiar with finding the light switches. It didn't matter, he knew the house, he didn't need the light even though it was darker in the house than outside. He could find his way. The Kitchen was the worst as it had one grimy window above the filthy unused sink. He walked through the kitchen toward the patch of weak light where he thought the door to the entrance hall would be. He started up the stairs, one foot in front of the other, his sachet over his left shoulder as he held onto the banister with his right hand. He began up the stairs relatively quickly, and managed a good pace until he came to the third floor. He was careful not to touch the railing as he continued to climb; he feet were beginning to feel heavy, his sachet weighing down his shoulder. He changed shoulders, taking the sachet from his left shoulder and placing it onto his right. Each night, it seemed like more stairs had been added since the morning, and he grinned slightly at his foolishness. He continued on until he came to the landing on the third floor. He paused; at the exact same place he'd seen the dust in the weak sunlight, this morning. Only now he saw no dust, in fact in the looming darkness he saw very little, just outlines of the lonely, empty house.

He stood for a moment on the landing, there was no sound, not a whisper of anything, again he felt the loneliness of the house begin to wrap itself around him. He shivered and turned to continue up to the attic. He legs were weary now. His feet felt heavier with each step.

Maybe, he would side step the noisy stair tonight. Yes, he would do it, and he was excited at the prospect. As he approached the step he moved to the side, the staircase was so narrow that stepping to the side was not hard to do. He was careful not to touch the grimy walls. He placed his foot on the very edge of the stair closest to the wall, and then something caught his eye. Something he hadn't seen before. Looking down he stopped…

There must a be a small gap between the step and the back of the stair because he thought he saw a pale glimmer of light; no, he was sure, he saw a glimmer of light. He stared at the sliver of pale yellow, seeping from between the stairs, and as he watched, it faded slowly until there was nothing. Nothing but darkness all around, but he remained standing on the stairs. He stood for some time, staring at the exact spot where the sliver of light had been the brightest. He stared his eyes unblinking. Did he expect the light to return to prove to him he'd actually seen it? Or was he staring because he didn't believe what his own eyes had seen?

Rumble didn't know how long he stood there, but by the time he moved up the last stairs to his room, carefully avoiding the one that squeaked; it was pitch dark. He had to feel the walls while his foot found the next step. At the top, he turned and looked down into the darkness the way he had just come, but he saw no slice of light between the stairs, he saw nothing but blackness below. He fumbled with the heavy key in the darkness. Dropping it twice, he fell to his knees to feel for the key. He was about to put the key in the lock that he had located with his other hand when he heard a single knock. It was a sharp sound, perhaps like metal on metal. He stopped. The hairs on his neck rose. His palms began to sweat. He needed to get into the safety of his room. It seemed to Rumble a lifetime before his trembling fingers managed to maneuver the key into the lock, pull the door toward him, and turn the key. It ground reluctantly as it always did.

He almost fell into his tiny attic room; he slammed the door behind him, placed the key back into the lock and turned it into the locked position, then he leaned against it, before grabbing the old wooden chair and propping it under the round brass doorknob. He stood in the center of his tiny room and breathed deeply of the fresh air. Then inside his head he heard the little voice, it had been with him his whole life, but he only heard it when it wanted to speak and that was usually when he was scared or in danger, '*are you aware you're shaking, every part of you is shaking,*' it said, and he replied, "I'm not shaking violently, but, yes, I admit, I'm definitely trembling." He felt his brow and found tiny beads of sweat clinging to his hairline. He wiped his palms on his khaki trousers as they too were sweating, no wonder he'd dropped the key it must have slipped right through his fingers.

'*You have to get a grip; are you going crazy. It was just a single noise and tiny strip of light. Or maybe, it wasn't, perhaps, it wasn't anything; maybe it's all in your imagination?'* The voice was challenging him again; he hated it when it did that. It should know it wasn't in his imagination, yes, it really should know. 'Oh, do shut up,' he replied aloud to the voice and it did. Dusk was a scary time of night at best and maybe his imagination was playing tricks on him. He'd have a shower and go to bed and think about it. And so that's what he did. Then he remembered his new cell phone and Lucy's words, "be sure to charge it over night the first time, Rumble, I know I can rely on you not to forget," she had said. He got out of bed took out the box, removed the mobile phone and charger, threw the box in the corner by his sachet and plugged it into the wall socket, then he returned to bed. He didn't fall asleep until after midnight, after finally coming to the realization that he was lying there listening. Listening to house, listening to the silence, and listening to the fear in his head, as it went around and around looking for logical answers when there probably weren't any.

Even after, he thought he'd quieted his mind subconsciously he was listening to the house. Listening for a noise. Listening for anything. He didn't want to put the light out in case he saw it again, perhaps, it might appear in his room this time, that thin sliver of pale yellow, it must have come from somewhere below. But where? In his mind, he slowly went over the layout of the house as he knew it… but he quickly realized he had no idea whether they were actually bedrooms behind the closed doors. He had only assumed from what Edwards told him… but why had he assumed they were bedrooms? Now, he was questioning everything he knew about the house. Finally, as time moved into the small hours of the morning, he decided he'd seen nothing and he hadn't heard anything either. Finally, the voice spoke, *'can you just stop thinking over and over and go to sleep, it's almost morning.'* Rumble didn't like being told off by the voice so he quietened his mind and tried to sleep.

Rumble slept badly before morning fully broke. Half of him seemed to be awake and alert, ready to spring out of bed if he heard a noise. Although, what he'd do then he didn't know he was in an attic after all. Sometime later, the wind increased and Rumble became aware of a scratching noise outside his window. It was only faint and only occasional, but it was there, and it was a scratching noise, perhaps like Sykes would have made had he been trying to get in. Before dawn chased the night away, Rumble heard nothing but quietness, like he was used to. He fell into a deep sleep. So, it was much later than usual when he finally a-wake.

He suddenly sat upright in bed; he'd heard another noise. It was soft rustling noise from somewhere close by. Or maybe, it was the mournful noise of the stair outside his room as it moaned when under stress. Maybe, he'd heard both noises, or maybe he'd heard nothing, he didn't know. The room was bright with daylight and upon searching for the time Rumble was surprised to see it was nine-thirty a.m. He had never slept so late. He was shocked at himself, why had he slept so late? This would surely throw his daily routine out by several hours, and he couldn't have that at all; just the thought of his daily routine being interfered with, scared him into a state of high anxiety. But the question in his mind was simply, what had caused his routine to be thrown out? Was it merely a couple of usual noises and a strip of light under the stairs? In the light of day, they didn't seem nearly as scary as they had last night. Maybe, he had imagined them after all.

Rumble, leaped out of bed and then realized just how tired he felt and hungry also. Maybe, he would change things around and have his toast and tea before his shower. He felt positively indulgent with the change he was proposing with his routine, but his stomach ruled, and it was growling loudly. He sat on the side of his bed in his pajamas and tired not to think of anything at all. Then, his eyes moved to the door. Sitting on the floor just inside the door was a yellow sheet of expensive writing paper – it was folded once in half, and it lay there. How did it get there? Had someone pushed it under the door? But surely, there wasn't anyone in the house.

Rumble felt talons of ice trickle down his spine; all thoughts of his toast vanished; he sat and stared at the paper on the floor. With his teacup poised halfway to his mouth – he stared.

Chapter Six

Rumble had learned over the years that if you ignore things that aren't really there they often disappear.

As he entered the house on his return he had glanced up to the top floor, the interior of the house seemed vaguely lighter. Rumble thought he saw the light in his stairwell go out, but this couldn't possibly be, firstly, there was no switch and secondly Rumble doubted it had been used in years.

He told himself he hadn't seen a light and it had only been for a split second anyway. He was just tired from his meeting with Cootes.

The next morning Rumble needed to use the same philosophy. He pretended the yellow piece of paper on the floor of his room, wasn't there at all. He continued to drink his morning cup of tea as he tried to look anywhere but at the floor. Again, as he sat there he heard the soft scratching noise. He turned; it was coming from his window. He placed his cup down as his palms began to sweat again, so he knew he would no longer be able to hold the cup anyway. He moved toward the window and there it was again, a soft scratching sound, as he looked he saw a small branch of the gnarled old apple or was it a peach tree, brush against his window.

He almost laughed with delight, it was nothing but a branch, caused, he guessed by the fact he had recently pushed opened the window another inch. So, it was now almost touching the branch. He wiped away some grime from the inside of the window, just a small circle with his fingers. He peeped down at the twisted gnarled tree that was starved of nourishment and water. He marveled at how it still clung to life. It was a tall, spindly tree, probably many years old, Rumble doubted if it still bore fruit or if it ever had. Then he fetched the soap from the bathroom and applied it to the rusty sliders of the window and opened it a little more. He knew the scratching would happen more often now, but he didn't care and once there was enough of a gap to get his hand through he would snap of the offending branch anyway.

He focused his thoughts totally on the tree. A good tree to climb he thought; immediately his mind drifted back in years, back to the time he was a young boy, playing with James and his three siblings. They had all crowded around him, laughing when they'd found out he had never climbed a tree. So, they had taught him. He found being high up off the ground rather frightening at first but once they showed him how to use crabapples in his slingshot, he forgot about the height. Soon, the boys were firing crab apples at each other up in the tree. By this time, his fear of heights had completely vanished, he was enjoying himself immensely. It was the first time he had played with other boys, and he loved it. Now, so many years later he recalled those times as some of the best times in his life. Cootes's siblings who were all much younger than Cootes; Cootes himself was of course, too old at that time to join in the kids' games, so his playmates always remained James and his three older siblings.

Rumble remembered the time he was hit by a rotten crab apple and how it stained his shirt. He knew he would be in trouble with his mom from that stain, but he didn't want the Cootes boys to think he was baby and know how concerned he was.

He knew they would think it was nothing, he also knew they had plenty of shirts. The Cootes boys were relatively well off by Rumble's standards. They had two parents and a nice house, plenty of free time with a large garden to play in and many tall healthy trees to climb. So, he kept on playing until he could excuse himself to the bathroom. By that time, the stain had set and no matter how much water and soap he put on his shirt and how hard he rubbed – it wouldn't budge. Now, he not only had a crabapple stain on his only shirt but most of the front of his shirt was dripping with water. He'd made a quick excuse and ran all the way home. He didn't think the Cootes boys ever knew anything was wrong, and he was glad about that.

His mother saw the stain immediately on his arrival home, and as expected she was furious. She called him irresponsible and dirty; she said he was turning out to be just like every other man. Then she told him how she had once trusted a man, just once, and look where it got her – you're the result – 'I never wanted you and neither did your father,' she yelled.

"Who is my father?" Rumble ventured boldly for the very first time and immediately knew he shouldn't have.

"He's a waste of my time, that's who he is. He ruined my life, and I hope you'll never discuss him again, go to your room," she yelled, he didn't need to be told twice. He never did get that stain out of his shirt; however, by the next summer it was too small for him anyway and another secondhand shirt was purchased.

James Cootes and his brothers had not only introduced him to the delights of climbing trees and using crab apples as ammunition in his slingshot; they had also introduced him to the only girl he had ever been out with. He easily recalled her name, and he could imagine her quite clearly sitting with him in the back of James's brothers' car. Her name was Jeni Lorington. She was taller than him by several inches, he had only been fourteen at the time, and she was almost fifteen. James said girls always grow faster than boys. Jeni had large buckteeth encased in wire braces and ears that stuck out and could match those of any boy. She had freckles and a dimple in the middle of her chin.

But what he remembered most was the rest of her, the bouncy blonde hair and lively blue eyes. She also had long shapely legs that went on forever, under her tiny mini-skirt with the large deep pink polka dots that clung to her tiny waist. Rumble recalled that above her waist was also quite delightful; probably the best part of her. Jenni had curves in all the right places. Once she had accidently brushed against him and he'd felt such a rush of something, it scared him so much he thought he might wet his pants. Even now, thinking back, Rumble had the very same feeling, and he didn't understand it now any more than he had as a fourteen-year-old boy.

Rumble stopped his thoughts there and decided he'd try to reach out through the small opening in the window to break off the thin branch that was making the scratching noise. But the gap of the window was still too small, so the branch would have to wait. He turned around and faced the door hoping the paper on the floor had disappeared. It hadn't.

He felt slightly braver now, but as he looked at the sheet of good quality paper all the questions he was trying not to think about came again in to his thoughts. How did it get there? Who had delivered it? When had it arrived?... and so on. Rumble took a deep breath, then reached down and retrieved the paper from the floor with trembling hands. It was folded simply in half, and Rumble opened the sheet and recognized Edwards' heavy, old-fashioned writing immediately. It read:

The terms of your tenancy agreement need to be strictly adhered to. Please, read over our agreement again so you fully understand it. Entering the house after dark is strictly forbidden, last evening you came close to ensuring eviction. I bring this to your attention. This courtesy will not be extended to you again. This time it is a warning only. Be aware, I seldom give warnings. The rules are for your safety and those of your follow tenants.

Edwards

Rumble folded the paper neatly in half and placed it in the corner on the floor. Most strange, he thought, most strange. Then Rumble remembered his mobile phone. Cootes had said it would probably not get service inside the house. But maybe it would. However, Cootes was right there was no service in his attic.

Then Rumble remembered the rule of no phones in the house. But, he reasoned, his mobile phone didn't work in the house anyway so surely that couldn't be counted. Rumble placed the charger back in the box and hid the box under his bed. Then he placed the mobile into the pocket of his crumpled khaki trousers as they lay on the floor. What Edwards doesn't know won't hurt him; he thought as he headed to the shower.

It was almost eleven o'clock by the time Rumble locked the door to his attic room and headed down the stairs. Again, he stepped to the side of the one stair that moaned, he smiled slightly at the thought that he had overcome a mournful stair. It wasn't much of an achievement but to Rumble it was something. Then the thought occurred to him that if he sidestepped the offending stairs perhaps others could do the same. Had anyone else ever been up to the attic? That thought bought chills to his spine, and he continued on down the stairs.

Again, today the sunlight penetrated the depths of the house, although this morning the time was later than yesterday, thus the angle of the sun was completely different. Again, he stopped on the landing on the third floor. He listened to the silence, the utter silence of the house. He felt the loneliness, the desperate loneliness, creeping toward him, creeping, creeping in the shadows to where he stood. He turned to look at the closed doors. Today the sun's rays penetrated the front of the door closest to him, and he saw again the dust particles heavy on the once varnished surface. The doorknob also was grimy with age; although it may once have been a shiny brass, it was now a greenish black.

Some of Cootes conversation came back to Rumble as he stood there. It was the part about exploring the house. Maybe he should. Rumble thought his routine was already ruined for the day, so maybe… But no, he thought of the terms of his tenancy agreement and the overly strict rules, one of which concerned trespassing into the rest of the house and disturbing the other tenants. That rule must surely be a joke; Rumble thought and then realized Edwards was not a joking man, so he rephrased his thoughts to 'ridiculous' rather than 'joke'.

The first closed door loomed only about six feet away, not far at all. He only needed to take the steps toward the door, turn the handle and… then what… would there be someone sleeping in the bed… would someone be staring back at him… or maybe pointing a gun at him. He shivered at his last thought.

Scenarios went around and around inside his head as he considered doing something so very daring like turning a door knob. Although, Rumble knew it was daring only for him. Even considering this, was so far from his realms of normalcy that his heart was racing. In his mind, perhaps, he had already done it... taken a few steps to the first door... opened it and gone inside. But then, he returned to the present and knew he was gripping the banister much too tightly.

Here he was standing on the third-floor landing in the dusty old house that was presently slightly illuminated from a single ray of sunlight. He was standing here contemplating... what... trespassing. But was he trespassing? He lived here, or at least he rented a room in the house, he had a key and was allowed entry. So, how did one define trespassing? He had signed a tenancy agreement, a very strict and ridged tenancy agreement, he had read it, understood it and signed it. And what he was proposing to do was against everything he had agreed to, trespassing being one of them.

How long Rumble stood there, contemplating, he didn't know. But he was aware how the sun had shifted and was no longer directed on the door. Perhaps, the house was trying to tell him something as it illuminated the door. But that was crazy it was only a house. It can't speak or evoke feelings or emotions. Well, maybe he was going crazy also? '*You can't stand here forever,*' the voice in

Rumble's head told him. He knew he couldn't. So, *'why not be daring and walk to the door and turn the door knob, do it, do it, do it'*, the voice encouraged softly in his head. Rumble now turned fully toward the door, he stared, he thought, and he stared some more.

Then, as if in a trance he took, first one step then another, but they were not in the direction of the stairs leading downward, they were toward the nearest door. This was crazy he kept telling himself he shouldn't be doing this. Then, he took another step, and another, until he was standing directly outside the door. He turned and saw his footprints clearly in the dust on the old wooden floor boards behind him. He could now reach out in front of him and touch the door. This was ridiculous, he needed to turn and leave, this was not who he was. His head told him to turn around and walk down the stairs and forget any thoughts of trespassing in this lonely and forgotten place; but there was a little voice that was louder than reason, and it was telling him to

'turn the doorknob, just turn it,' it kept saying. *'Do it… do it… do it…'*

And then he did.

He reached out with his trembling right hand, and grasped the doorknob firmly. His palms were sweating. He felt the grime, gritty with dirt and age adhere itself to the palm of his hand. Nothing happened. So, he used more force and tried to turn the knob harder. He was sure it wasn't locked as it moved, just slightly. He tried again and it moved again, a little more until he had almost turned the old knob all the way round.

So, intent was Rumble on his task that when a distance knocking came from perhaps the front door, he let go of the knob and almost leapt off the ground. What was that? Where had it come from? Was it coming from inside the door?

In a flash and walking much faster than usually. In fact, Rumble almost ran to the attic stairs and then bolted up them two at a time; in moments he was able to retrieve his key from his trouser pocket and unlocked the door, the knocking sound came again. Only this time, he was sure it was coming from somewhere below, probably the entranceway.

There was a large solid front door there, with stained glass across the top. Several locks kept it secure against intruders on the inside. Rumble had never contemplated opening it and after all these months in the house he was hardly aware of its existence; until now.

Who would be knocking? Maybe one of the tenants had forgotten his key? What tenants? Rumble thought, more convinced than ever that he was alone in the house. Or perhaps, a passer-by simply wanting to gain entry, or speak to the owner, or rent a room, yes, he thought, that was it. Someone was simply knocking on the door, nothing unusual or scary, about that.

It was not until Rumble wiped the sweat from his eyes that he realized just how anxious and frightened he was.

Then he noticed his hands, they were black with grim. He moved to his bathroom and saw the greenish black stuff was now over his face where he had wiped away the sweat. Quickly, he threw water over his face and then washed his hands with soap. But the grime did not give up easily. He needed to use soap on his face and then use his small nailbrush on both his face and hands before he was clean again. Rumble detested being dirty.

Once his nerves quieted, he sat on the corner of his bed and checked the time. It was already after three o'clock, too late to start sketching today. But he had to sketch something it was what he did.

Slowly, he retrieved his sketchpad and pencil from his sachet and opened the door to the attic. He walked half way down the stairs and sat on the middle stair. Then he did what he was good at. He began sketching all he could see before him. In thirty minutes, it was finished. He tore out the sketch and added it to the others at the back of his sketchbook.

Again, as if in a trance, he returned to his room threw the sketchpad and pencil on his bed, grabbed several tissues from the box in the bathroom and moved slowly down the stairs avoiding the ones that squeaked. Now, he knew or thought he knew the doors to these rooms weren't locked, so he didn't feel like he was trespassing, although he knew, he actually was. At the bottom of the stairs, he stopped and listened.

He listened to silence just as he expected to do. To the

nothingness of vacancy, to the desperate emptiness that was the house. Although, it felt heavy somehow, like it wanted to attach itself to him. He moved slowly along the hallway, half way between the banister and the wall. Soon, he saw his own footsteps in the dust and walked in them, only because he could.

Then he was outside the door again, staring at it, challenging it as if it was alive and blocking his way. He didn't open it, but instead walked to the next door, again turning to see his and only his footprints in the dust behind him. This time he didn't hesitate; he gripped the tissues he was still holding wrapped them tightly around the doorknob; he used more force than last time to turned the knob. He had hoped this door would open more easily, but it didn't. Using the tissues, as this doorknob was as grimy as the last; he kept pressure on the knob as it reluctantly moved, little by little until again he felt like it had turned all the way round.

He pushed, there was movement, but the door didn't open. Then he leaned against it and he felt the top half of the door give way under his weight. Still gripping the knob and turning it fully he moved his shoulder away from the door and then heaved his weight into the part of the heavy door closest to the knob, just like they did in the movies, he thought.

It moved again, but still seemed to be stuck at the bottom to the doorframe. He heaved again, until he heard a slight creak, like old thirsty timbers awaking from a long sleep. Rumble looked over his shoulder, he didn't know what he expected to see, he knew he was alone but he looked anyway, as if anyone was in the house they may have heard the noise he was creating in the stillness.

Several more heaves were needed until the timbers creaked again. This was a very solid door Rumble thought, although, he knew he had no experience with doors at all.

Rumble's shoulder was aching, but he would try once more. This time it moved and finally opened a few inches. It felt like a weight on the other side of the door was holding it closed. Rumble pushed with all his might and managed to get the door open just enough for him to squeeze through. Inside there was nothing but darkness, heavy forgotten darkness and a smell – what was the smell? Disuse? Despair? Desperation? Or maybe, just dusky forgotten furnishings. He wanted to believe the latter. He should have bought a torch with him, but he hadn't thought that far ahead. He hadn't thought, not nearly enough, that was the problem. He almost turned and left the room. Almost.

Now, inside the room, the door managed to automatically close to half the width so the room was almost pitch black. He stood where he was and listened, not a sound, not a movement. The air was heavy. He waited for his eyes to focus in the darkness and after a while they did. He could just see outlines of furniture, large heavy furniture and as he stared directly in front of him he saw the tinniest glimmer of light. He walked careful toward it, hands out in front. Something at his feet almost caused him to fall face first onto the floor, but he managed to catch himself just in time and he continued toward the thin sliver of light.

He touched what he assumed where drapes probably covering the windows, heavy drapes, some sort of velvet or brocade maybe. He felt his way to the center of what must be the window where the strip of light was barely visible. This must be the center of the drapes. He reached out and took one old dusty drape in each hand before pulling them apart. They grumbled to the floor under his attack, covering his shoes as they disintegrated from his touch. Light flooded the large room through tall grimy windows…

Chapter Seven

Rumble turned and stared. He had been looking down at the drapes that once covered the windows. Now Edwards would know he had been in here. But then Rumble was sure no one had been in here for quite some time.

The room was large with high, rough beamed ceilings, and a huge four-poster bed straight out of the 18th century. It had a rumpled faded yellow chenille bedspread thrown over the bed and several large pillows haphazardly tossed on top. An ornate chaise covered in faded reddish brocade occupied one corner of the room and tall lamps with glass or maybe crystal shades stood on each side of the bed. They were, like everything else covered in cobwebs and a rather thick layer of dust. The three drawer bedside cabinets were also ornate and definitely antique. Each drawer had brass knobs these were now badly corroded with age. They were big and sturdy and Rumble could tell they had once been highly polished. A tall chest of drawers that appeared to match the night tables stood solidly against the other wall. On top of it was an old oval mirror inside a stand. However, the mirror was now murky with age and had blackish lines running down it. In front of the mirror stood an ornate water jug and large washbowl, like the type you used to wash in.

A wide chest sat at the end of the bed, long ago it had a padded seat on top but the padding appeared to have since, like the drapes, disintegrated. Rumble could vaguely see the outline of a large rug that may have been covering the floor, but for some reason it was no longer here. Rumble moved toward the lamps beside the beds, they had crystals hanging from the shades. Rumble reached out to touch one and it came away in his hand, the thin wire that held it to the shade was rusted through.

This was a wonderful room Rumble thought, so much bigger than his own, maybe he could ask Edwards if he may move in here. He placed the crystal carefully on the bedside table and as he did, so he looked closer at the lamps. He was astonished to realize they were not electric lamps but the old oil burning kind, which needed filling regularly.

Not for the first time, Rumble felt as if someone was watching him, watching him from above. Turning his head, he stared up at a life size painting on the far wall between the bed and the window. It was hung in a heavy elaborate wooden frame and on closer inspection; Rumble felt the man sitting on the old-fashioned chair and dressed in breaches and lacy shirt, slightly resembled Edwards. This man however, had dark eyes and hair and his eyes seemed to follow Rumble around the room. He had been captured on canvas as a foreboding, fierce looking gentleman, one Rumble instinctively knew couldn't be trusted.

The man was judging him, summing up his worth, working out his punishment, for this intrusion. Rumble's eyes couldn't help but notice the man was wearing a ring on his pinky finger, it had a solid silver band and a sparkling red stone, he had seen that ring before he knew, but he couldn't remember where. The ring like the man looked alive, angry, menacing from inside the frame.

But no, that was ridiculous, it was just a portrait and only its size was daunting. It didn't have any thoughts or feelings, and it wasn't capable of punishing anyone, it was just paint and canvas, nothing more. With an effort, Rumble tore his eyes from the portrait and focused again on the room. Rumble wanted to straighten the bed, but he was afraid it would fall apart; he had done enough damage for one day and hadn't properly thought about the consequences of his actions.

Tentatively, he reached for the nearest pillow and, just as he had anticipated, it dissolved into a lump of feathers and cotton under his touch. Something shiny caught the light from the window; it had been under the pillows. It was something a little more solid Rumble thought; he reached out and brushed off the feathers that had drifted downward and covered the object.

It was a silver rattle, the kind used by babies. It looked rather old fashioned with tiny angels carved into the silver. As he shook it, he heard a small tinkling sound. Rumble held it up to the window and turned it around and around. The name 'Baby Sarah' was engraved on the handle in old-

riting.

realized he was no longer trembling and, in was almost enjoying himself. He thought it was just like Christmas discovering this new room and all its treasures. Looking at the dark wooden floor with the wide solid floor boards locked together, he again knew there had certainly once been a rug covering the surface, you could see the outline of where it had previously laid.

It had been a square rug; as the floor was darker, shinier, less scuffed and scratched within the outline of the square. Then Rumble's eyes moved to the door, it was partly shut, there he noticed for the first time a heavy rug rolled up. It had been placed hard up against the inside of the door. But how could it have been placed there and then the door shut from the outside. It simply wasn't possible; however, it explained why the door was so hard to push open when he tried to enter.

Rumble walked toward the half-closed door and listened... nothing... nothing but silence came from beyond the door. He really needed to move the rug away from the door. It was loosely rolled up, and Rumble thought it would fall apart at his touch. Rumble had never been a physical man he hated sports at school, and he had never had any desire to do anything more than sketch. But the rug didn't look heavy, in fact it looked old, quite thin and very worn and the pattern was fading, so just how heavy could it be? Maybe, if he pulled it back into the center of the floor, he could unroll it in the place it obviously belonged. And the door would open freely.

Rumble bent toward the rug and firmly gripped the rolled-up end with both hands. He pulled as hard as he could but all he heard was a slight tearing noise as the binding on the end of the rug gave way. He hadn't thought an old rug could be so heavy. Next, he decided to pull the end of the rug closest to him the part that lay slightly unrolled. Again, it started to tear. Maybe, he should just unfold, as much of it as he could, where it lies and then drag it into the middle of the floor.

So, very gently he pushed the edges of the rug back toward the door until a small portion was unfolded. The rug was indeed almost threadbare and Rumble couldn't understand why it was so heavy to drag across the floor. Carefully, he unrolled it, little by little, not wanting to cause any further damage.

He'd managed to unfold nearly one feet of rug, but he had no more space because of the door, which was now shut. Pushed closed tightly by the rug. Maybe, the inside of the rug would prove more solid. He held it tightly with both hands not on the edge but on the first fold of the rug. He pulled, it hardly moved. Why was it so heavy? He pulled harder. He felt the drops of sweat on his brow, and he tugged again, pulling backwards with all his strength.

This time it moved almost three feet, as dust particles from the rug floated up into the air. Now he moved around behind it to the inside of the door, he thought if he pushed the rug into the center of the room he would do less damage. He could feel the threads under his hands were about to tear at any moment.

So, he pushed the rug, it was still very heavy, but it was moving and little by little he moved it back to the center of the room. Slowly, he straightened up, caught his breath and wiped his sweaty brow. Until finally, he bent down again and carefully began unrolling the rug back into its former position. He had a quarter of the rug unrolled when he looked at the remaining rug and noticed it looked lumpy as if something was inside. He gingerly touched the lumpy part, and it felt reasonably solid.

He resumed his task until gradually, he felt something begin to unroll with the rug. He had no idea what he expected to see. And when he saw it he still had no idea just what he was looking at. It appeared to be several long thin bones and instead of stopping his task Rumble gave the rug a hearty push and more unrolled before his eyes. The smell in the room seemed to change. It was an acidotic arid smell that burned in his nostrils. Rumble hardly noticed, so intent was he on his task.

In front of him on the floor, on the newly unfolded rug, lay bones, long bones and short bone and scraps of blackish fabric were in heavy contrast to the colors in the rug. Rumble stood where he was he didn't know or understand what he was seeing.

Then he felt something touch his trouser leg and looking down he saw the long skinny bones must have moved and was touching him. The light from the window caught something red that sparkled and looking closer Rumble saw laying under the long thin bones a silver and ruby ring, the light made it sparkle and Rumble again thought this room was like Christmas, so many presents, he thought bending down to retrieve the trinket. *'It's not like Christmas'*, a voice in his head warned, *'don't touch anything else'*, the same voice in his head commanded. Rumble had heard the voice before over the years, it seemed to talk to him when he was in danger, or scared. So, why was it talking now he was neither of those things. He looked again at the ring; it seemed to blaze with a life of its own. Then, he briefly looked again at the portrait on the wall, the eyes were still watching him, and, yes, he was sure, this was the same ring as in the portrait; Just laying here on the floor at his feet.

The moment his hand made contact with the ring, it seemed to flare into life with a brilliance that filled the room. The portrait behind him crashed to the floor but remained upright. The man in the picture glared back at him.

The door slammed shut with an intensity that shook the walls. The old lamps flared into life, brighter and brighter the room grew in brilliance. The drawers in the bedside cabinets and dresser flew open and then shut loudly several times. Rumble turned toward the painting that lay on the floor and in the light from the lamps he saw smeared on the wall where the painting had previously hung, in red ink, or was it blood, the words 'You like the dark, we kill the flame'.

Rumble felt a scream of terror gurgle from deep inside him. He dropped the ring he was holding and in seconds the bright white light died and turning he saw the room had returned to normal. The huge portrait again hung on the wall exactly where it had been. The lamps remained shrouded in cobwebs and the old worn rug lay at his feet, partly rolled.

Rumble had always been slow to react and as he stood there he was unsure of what had just happened. He knew he was trembling all over, he felt the sweat on his brow and palms. And somewhere deep inside, he understood what he had just witnessed and felt was nothing short of sheer terror.

He had to leave this room, he had to get out; he had to leave now. He needed to move. His feet were frozen like lumps of lead and disconnected from his body. He had to make them move, he needed to leave this room. He needed to think. He didn't understand.

He looked down at the ring at his feet, lying on the rug under the bones in the exact same place it had been before he'd chosen to pick it up. The ring glowed with a brilliant intensity; it seemed to shimmer as if it was alive. It glowed up at him teasing, taunting him. Should he reach down and retrieve it, again.

It seemed to want his attention. Then he thought of taking it from under the bones, and he shivered. Should he pick it up, would the same thing happen again, had anything happened at all? Maybe, he would take it with him, it sure was sparkly and maybe it's worth something.

The little voice he'd heard earlier said, '*Do it, do it, do it.*' Rumble almost did, he wanted to, but he was shaking with terror and he needed to leave. He turned toward the door, which was again open several inches. He willed his legs to move him in that direction. At first, they wouldn't move, couldn't move. Then terror overcame Rumble and in an instant he bolted for the door. Pulled it wide and leaped through it like a drowning man into the dreary interior of the familiar house, before he heard the door slam shut behind him.

Chapter Eight

Rumble moved as fast as his heavy legs would carry him along the landing to his stairs leading up to the attic. He took them two at a time avoiding the ones that squeaked. He fumbled in his pocket for the key as he arrived at the top of the stairs only to see the door to his attic room was standing wide.

Rumble stopped, he stared, he always locked his door. Had he forgotten to do so, in his haste this time? Or had someone been in his room while he was trespassing in the forbidden room below? He slammed the door and grabbed the old chair propping it up hard under the door handle. He couldn't stop the trembling. He couldn't stop his body from shaking, his palms from sweating. He felt the sweat from his forehead trickle over his eyebrows and into his eyes. It stung, burning his eyeballs with its salty wetness.

Then gradually, he became aware of his shoulder aching, deep, heavy slow aches rolled through his upper body and rippled down into his lower back. Why was his shoulder aching? Was it all the dragging of the rug he had just done?

Then he remembered slamming into the door over and over as he tried to force it open. That had not been a smart thing to do. What was he thinking? His actions had been so unlike him? Was he going crazy? He didn't know but what he did know was that his recent behavior was not who he was, not who he was at all.

Rumble lay back on his bed still aware of the sweat running down his face as he tried to control the trembling. 'Why wouldn't it stop?' *'Take some slow deep breaths'*, the voice said *'and count slowly'*. The voice instructed so he took several deep breaths and still he trembled then he took several more; slower this time and he counted to ten before releasing his breath. That seemed to help a little.

He closed his eyes, he was exhausted, he actually closed his eyes without checking the time, and he'd never done that before either. He fell immediately into a deep sleep, only to get images flash before him of the room. The bright white light as the lamps flared into life. A life they couldn't possibly have; he reasoned even as he slept. The thumping of the drawers, the door, the portrait falling, the words, 'You like the dark, I kill the flame', the brilliant red stone in the ring the wide heavy silver band, the bones...

His eyes flashed open, he bolted up right, the sweat was dripping in his eyes, and he was shaking again.

It was only a dream.

'More like a nightmare.'

Had it really happened?

'Had what really happened?'

The bones... oh the bones.

Then he asked the question he knew had been lurking at the back of his mind. *'What did the bones belong to? Or*

Who? Probably a dead dog or cat,' he assured himself as a small voice inside his head told him, *'don't be so naive.'*

No, it hadn't happened, nothing had happened. Nothing.

Still without looking at the time he tore off his damp clothes and headed for the shower. He stayed in there until the water went cold. He was trying to wash away what he had just seen, the images, the visit to the room and what had happened the moment he touched the ring. It hadn't happened, it wasn't real. If he didn't think about it then it wasn't real. He'd block it out completely, that's what he intended to do.

Tomorrow, he would get back to his normal life; he enjoyed his life. He had all he wanted and he needed nothing more, not a bigger room or a larger bed or anything, he was totally happy just the way he was, right now.

And so, Rumble tried to sleep, he tossed, he turned, he pretended he was sleeping; he even set an extra alarm on his new mobile phone so he wouldn't over sleep. It sounded at seven-thirty a.m. precisely.

Rumble pretended he had been sleeping and once the alarm sounded he followed his usual routine. Firstly, he prepared his cup of tea and dry toast. Then checking he had all he needed in his sachet for the day and pocketing his key and mobile phone he headed out.

The house was silent, silent as a tomb, just like always, or was it even quieter. Was it waiting for him, listening for his step on the stair? Was it deciding his punishment? But for what? He'd done nothing he kept telling himself.

On the third landing, he tried to focus on the next flight of stairs but try as he may he had to sneak a quick look sideways, at the door, the first and second closed door on the landing. They were still closed tightly so, Rumble hurried on letting out the breath he wasn't aware he was holding.

He didn't look back up the stairs as he descended, although he wanted to. He wanted to focus on the door until he was out of the house. But he looked straight ahead and kept telling himself over and over in his head, that nothing had happened, he had never opened that door. He had seen nothing. Nothing had happened.

Once outside, he breathed deeply and then trying not to feel as tried as he was, he strode with a fast pace to the bus stop. The bus was just arriving, and he managed to get the last seat at the rear.

Today he was sketching a recent foxhunt for the 'Horse and Hound' magazine. He could now get the images on his phone, and he knew that's what he'd do, he didn't need to sit inside the stuffy library, but he needed to be around people even if they didn't talk to him. He needed his usual routine as he always did; only today his normal routine seemed like his lifeline.

There was a Nando's chicken store beside a water feature. It was peaceful, and he could have lunch when he was ready. It was not a place he visited often, but he had been there before. By noon, he had several sketches from the images captured of the hunt on his mobile phone.

He liked the idea of the phone more and more. Just as he had taken the last mouthful of his chicken burger and was wiping his fingers on the paper napkin, his phone rang. It was a loud sound and one he couldn't mistake. Lucy, Cootes secretary, had said she had the volume turned all the way up as she knew he got engrossed in his work.

"Rumble, here," he said hoping he had pressed the speak button and not already cut the caller off. He was relieved to hear Cootes unmistakable voice speak to him.

"Rumble, where the devil, have you been. I know you may not get phone reception where you live, but I tried you all day yesterday. Where the dickens where you? Or didn't you have your phone turned on?"

"I've just done two rather nice sketches of last weekend's hunt, Mr. Cootes. I'm liking the fact I can get the images off the internet, most pleasing," Rumble replied without answering Cootes questions.

"Glad you're enjoying your new technology, Rumble. Guess the battery ran out, you have to watch that you know. Got to keep the phone charged Rumble that you do."

"I understand, Mr. Cootes, and I shall endeavor to do so from now on."

"Wanted to give you the heads up and a flying chance

to keep up with your stiff completion, Rumble. Do the decent thing and all that."

"Yes?"

"Well, Lucy texted you the address of this art shop that sells the vivid water colors that your young competitor is using so aptly on his sketches. Yes, wanted to make sure you'd been to the store and picked up some supplies for your work. Otherwise, Rumble the newcomer in our midsts will make next month's cover. His work is fresh, bright and exotic. He's talented Rumble just like you are, but unlike you, he's modern and uses all the up to the minute tools at his disposal. Tell me you were busy shopping yesterday, Rumble; now don't let me down, you know I've always been on your side." All this was too much for Rumble; he was being pushed outside his comfort zone. Too many new expectations were happening too fast. But he knew he needed to answer Cootes, the silence was due to him not Cootes. He would love to finally make it onto the cover, any cover, so he swallowed hard and replied,

"Just on my way there, now, Mr. Cootes."

"Jolly good, Rumble. I'll call you later to make sure you found the place. You are after all, the biggest procrastinator I have ever known and without me always pushing you forward heaven knows where you'd be now. Goodbye, Rumble, put your best foot forward and get moving." And before he could answer the line went dead.

Too many new things. Rumble urgently needed his

routine today; he needed it like a drowning man needed a life raft, and now this. He felt the sweat break out on his brow. His lunch break was definitely over.

Rumble checked his phone and soon found the text from Lucy. He knew the place, he had never actually been inside its doors, it looked too fancy and expensive, but he'd gazed in the window and admired the organization within.

Rumble threw his sachet over his shoulder and moved in with the pedestrians as they walked the pavement all in a hurry to get somewhere. Well, Rumble was also in a hurry to get somewhere, but for him it was not somewhere he wanted to go. Up ahead a music shop blasted loud unconventional music into the ears of anyone in the vicinity. Then the music stopped and a deep throaty voice began speaking words Rumble hardly heard.

Until, the deep raspy words made Rumble stop. He stood frozen to the spot, unable to move. Did he just hear what the singer, or rather talker was saying, or was his mind playing tricks on him, again. No, he had heard it and then he listened although it was too loud not to. There. There it was again the words, deep and throaty, and there was no mistaking, the words. 'You like the dark, we kill the flame.' The very same words there could be no mistaking. Rumble felt ice run down his back, his palms became moist and he began to tremble. He hadn't moved. He couldn't move. Some of the passersby were giving him strange looks. Those words, they were the same. No mistake. Get a grip, Rumble told himself, get a grip. He had to move he couldn't remain standing in the middle of the pavement forever. Who was saying the words? He had to know.

Finally, Rumble was able to tell his heavy legs to move forward, move forward into the shop. Moments later he was leaving the shop. It was Leonard Cohen the woman told him, no mistake they were his words. The woman behind the counter was sure; she said she was a big fan. She knew his words were creepy and often told of violence, but she thought Leonard Cohen was wonderful, 'Just the sound of voice,' she said.

Now as Rumble walked blindly forward he wondered just who this Leonard Cohen was and why he had been saying the exact same words that Rumble had seen blazing on the wall behind the portrait when it fell? No Rumble told himself firmly it hadn't happened, he hadn't been in the room, the portrait hadn't fallen from the wall, he hadn't seen the ring and the lamps had not blazed into life. None of this happened. And he definitely hadn't seen the words...

He was out and about living the life he loved. Nothing else had happened. The voice inside his head spoke to him severely in a tone much like his mother often used moments before she hit him.

'*Nothing had happened. He'd seen nothing. He'd read nothing, He'd been nowhere.*' Gradually, he believed it. As slowly the sweating stopped and the trembling subsided. Rumble was uncomfortable with anyone looking at him; he was not use to being noticed. He enjoyed blending into the background. He liked being invisible it had always been so. His mother had often told him he was nobody and therefore of no worth in life. He believed her, so when passersby stopped and looked at him he felt uncomfortable and compromised.

His heart was slowing and he quickened his pace to the speed he normally walked. The art shop was not far.

He would take the shortcut down an alley and arrive there quicker. But why was he here at all? He didn't want any new art supplies? He was happy with what he had. Why was he even headed here anyway? Then he thought of his work making the cover of the next issue of one of Cootes magazines. Yes, he'd like that; he'd like that very much. Now his focus was again firmly on his work, he felt lightness in his step. He emerged out the other end of the dim alley into the busy street. A light rain was beginning to fall. He would stop and retrieve his rain jacket from his sachet; he was almost at the art shop.

The shop was bright airy and modern. Large overhead lights illuminated the space and as Rumble browsed he realized he hadn't seen so many new and exciting art supplies in years.

He thought of the small shop he always went to. The same old man had owned and operated it for many years. It was dingy and dusty, and it was hard to see into the corners. But the old man was cheerful and very helpful.

Rumble looked around at the young hippy looking characters with their white aprons over their jeans and the shiny orange nametags attached to the top right-hand pocket of their shirt. Just how could they possible have any experience in the art world? They looked like they had hardly finished school.

Rumble was wondering aimlessly around the shop not looking at anything in particular when a young assistant approached him.

"Can I be of any help?" he asked politely, blocking Rumble's way. Rumble didn't want help, he didn't even want to be in the shop at all and now, he was cornered; the sales boy blocking his path.

"No, not really, I'm just looking."

"What interests you in particular, in the art world," and just like that before he could think of a suitable answer Rumble was caught, sneered in the young man's grasp. Rumble looked at his large orange nametag. Was the boy's name really Rolly? Modern look, modern name; Rumble guessed as he answered.

"Perhaps, some watercolors, that have some depth and brightness... Rolly."

"Are yes, planning on doing some drawing then are we?"

"Perhaps."

"Well, you're in quite the wrong area for watercolors, follow me," replied the young man with the orange nametag. Rumble thought about turning and walking out of the shop and if Rolly hadn't begun talking again Rumble may have made a run for it. Rolly told him how he was putting himself through university and majoring in art history.

He was still talking as they entered the watercolor area. It was well set out and many of the watercolors had been used on a card above the color, so you really saw what they looked like. Rumble hated to admit it, but he was impressed.

Thinking Rolly would leave him now he began in earnest walking the rows. He had the name of the watercolors he was supposed to buy, and soon he saw them. The colors were gorgeous far better than Rumble had expected, but so were the prices. Reading the back of one of the boxes he also learned they were made in France; Rumble only purchased goods made in Britain. So, he couldn't possibly...

"Can I help you make your selection," Rolly said, scaring Rumble half to death. He thought the young boy had gone elsewhere, but looking up he saw he was right beside him and in his hand he carried a small yellow plastic basket.

"No, thank you, you see they are much too expensive," Rumble replied turning and walking away in the direction they had just come.

"But..." Was all Rumble heard Rolly say as he blended in with the other shoppers.

As he stepped outside, he recognized it was raining

now more than a drizzle. He would get his plastic rain jacket out from his sachet. Then his mobile made its presence known.

"Hello, Rumble here," Rumble answered thinking he sounded very professional.

"Rumble, good chap, I see you're enjoying the mobile after all," Cootes cheery voice came from the other end of the phone.

"Yes, indeed it makes life easier,"

"I've just been on the phone with Hector Oliver the store manager at the art shop. Told him to look out for you. Have you got all you need now, Rumble?" Cootes asked, Rumble hated lying but the prices were more than he'd ever paid for art supplies, and he thought they were far too extravagant. Rumble paused not knowing what to say, and then he replied as diplomatically as he could.

"I'm at the art shop now, Mr. Cootes just making my decision."

"Glad to hear it, Rumble. Ask for Hector Oliver and you'll get a discount, I know how every little helps; and I also know how deep your pockets are."

"Yes."

"Well, happy shopping Rumble, watch out for moths," Cootes said chuckling as he hung up. Rumble replaced the phone in his pocket and searched in his sachet for his rain jacket.

It was then he felt the hand on his shoulder. It was a large hand with a strong grip. Rumble first thought was not to turn around; maybe it was Edwards, had he been found out? Rumble shivered he was not use to being touched.

"Mr. Rumble?" An accented voice inquired and Rumble breathed a sigh of relief it definitely wasn't Edwards. Rumble spun around and came face to face with a tall good-looking black man. He wore a white apron and a large plastic orange nametag. Rumble looked at the name, Hector Oliver, it was red and unlike Rolly's tag, the writing was in gold lettering, under his name in smaller black print was the words Store Manager.

"Yes," Rumble replied turning.

"Yes, I thought it was you from the description Mr. Cootes your editor gave me."

"Oh."

"Welcome to our store. Glad to have caught you on your arrival. I am most familiar with your work Mr. Rumble you have quite a talent."

"Thank you," Rumble mumbled quite unused to compliments.

"Follow me, Sir, we have a discounted section, not available to the public. I think you'll find everything to your liking, both price wise and the selection of range." Rumble spent several hours in the discounted section, and he found Hector Oliver's knowledge to be very helpful.

Once they were headed toward the cash register Hector asked, "Mr. Rumble, if I may ask a favor of you please?" Rumble nodded and Hector continued, "From time to time we get celebrities such as yourself in our shop and it is an honor to have you here, Sir. Could I ask you, before you leave, to sketch me your famous Rumble Bumblebee, so we may place it on the center of our wall for all to see. It is an honor indeed having you shop with us, Sir." Rumble was amazed by Hector's request; he was astounded that anyone knew about his signature bumblebee. He was happy to oblige.

Rumble had never felt like a celebrity or been called one before nor did he have any idea that his signature bumblebee was so well known. Once it was sketched, Hector invited him to color it using a brand-new line of watercolors' that only arrived in the shop yesterday. The new water-colors' were the best Rumble had ever used, and he was pleased to try them out on the large bumblebee he had just sketched. He then looked at the price tag of the new line of watercolors and knew he would never be able to afford to own any of them himself. Rumble's bumblebee looked better than any of his other smaller signature bumblebees ever looked. At the request of Hector Oliver, Rumble signed the sketch 'Rumble Bumble' and then watched Hector expertly frame it and place his Bumblebee in the very center of the display wall. It hung amongst many other famous artists who frequented the same art shop.

Later, Rumble exited the bus; he still had a small smile on his face. As he walked home that night, his shoulder continued to ache but tonight his sachet was much heavier than usual. Hector had been right the prices were more attractive in the back room plus he also got a further discount.

Although, he hadn't planned on spending any money at all, he was pleased with his purchases; he was also pleased that he wouldn't have to lie again to Cootes. Rumble felt a tingle of excitement at the thought of trying something new. He hadn't felt that feeling for many years, since he was a teenager in fact. He would be busy coloring tonight and just maybe he would make the cover...

Chapter Nine

Rumble quickly discovered he liked the new watercolors very much indeed, and he worked later into the evening than ever before. It was the tinkling of the silver rattle as he retrieved something from his sachet that made him aware of the time.

The sound was so unlike anything that was familiar to his world that he stopped and sought it out. The rattle had rolled from his trouser pocket he supposed and due to the unevenness of the wooden floorboards it had stayed on the lowest part of the floor until Rumble disturbed it. Holding the rattle, the thoughts of where he had found it came flooding back.

But tonight, he wanted to focus on his work so he placed the tiny silver rattle carefully in the back of his only cardboard and tried to erase the sound and image from his thoughts. Soon, he was completing the last of his recent sketches; he held one at arms-length and admired it, he loved the realism the colors added to his work, yes, he was pleased with the result.

His work looked alive, almost lifelike. It had a certain color flow and movement that it hadn't had before. Yes, thought Rumble, I am good, aren't I?

He was turning out the light when he heard the first

thump. It was loud and heavy and coming from somewhere below. What was it? Who was it? Loud noises didn't happen by themselves. Rumble was immediately alert, awake; his senses heightened as he sat up in bed in the dark and listened intently. Silence nothing but silence. But he had heard it he knew he had. Why would he imagine a noise like that? Why he wasn't even thinking of anything but his art, he couldn't have imagined it, he couldn't?

He sat stone still exactly where he was hardly breathing and waited. He was waiting for the next thump. He knew there would be one. But how did he know? He couldn't possibly know. Maybe, he hadn't heard it after all? However, Rumble had just had a most successful day, he was feeling good, braver and stronger than usual.

So, he waited some more and took in a little more breath. Then, he slowly moved to the head of the bed and then, keeping close to the wall he put his bare feet onto the cool wooden floorboards. He knew they didn't creak when he walked close to the wall, so that's what he did and keeping one foot closely in front of the other he crept the few paces toward the door. Quietly, he lifted the chair from under the handle and placed it at the foot of the bed.

Then, he stopped again and listened. Nothing, not a sound, just the silence reaching out to him. He had just inserted the key and gently turned it, and he was feeling proud of himself for yesterday using soap on both the lock and door hinges, so they moved easily and silently, and he was just about to grip the door knob, when another loud thump, just like the last one, made him freeze.

He felt icy droplets run down his back and damp sweat moisten his palms. He took a deep breath and then pushed his ear hard against the door. He thought he heard, something, what was it? A scraping noise perhaps? No, no it was something being dragged, something heavy. He pressed his ear harder against the door and listened. But the noise ceased and silence came from beyond the door.

Again, he gripped the knob, his palms sweaty on the cool brass. He turned it slowly, silently and opened it just a creak at first. He peeped through the opening, but he saw nothing, nothing but the darkness of the night beyond. He opened the door a little more, and a little more, until he was able to put his head out. He stared, nothing but darkness, although, although, was there mist in the house coming from the floors below. Yes, it looked like a pale grey mist moving slowly upwards. He stared into the mist, focusing hard as if he was trying to make it into something solid. As he stared, he thought he saw in the distance the outline of Edwards, his white hair around his shiny bald head, his square jaw and intense eyes, he was dressed in a pale colored shirt and light-colored trousers and Rumble thought he saw the red stone in the ring flash, just for an instance. He peered deeper in to the darkness; yes, it was Edwards, was he raising one arm in the air?

Then Rumble took his focus off the center of the mist that he thought was Edwards and realized he was staring at the mist that was in the center of the hallway below, high up off the floor. It couldn't be Edwards, it couldn't be. Because if it was it would mean he was just hovering, hovering in the air, there was nothing below him apart from a sheer drop to the floor of the front entranceway. But it was so dark, he couldn't be sure. What he was sure about was that his mind was playing tricks on him, cruel evil tricks. He knew that seeing a misty image of Edwards hovering inside the house wasn't really possible.

He was about to move back inside the door when he saw it. His eyes had now grown accustomed to the gloom of the darkness. It was just sliver of light, hardly visible at all. He moved forward on to the small landing at the top of the stairs, and he looked down. Down those familiar steps one at a time. And there it was a thin sliver of yellow light in the creak at the back of the stair, in the same place he had seen it once before. Yes, it was in the same step, he hadn't been imagining it. He stayed where he was feeling relieved he wasn't going crazy. He kept his eyes fixed on the thin line of pale-yellow light coming through the crack at the back of the step. And then, right before his eyes it went out. It was gone and nothing but darkness and silence surrounded him.

He felt strangely vulnerable outside his room in his old pale blue pajamas with the faded navy stripes running down them. He felt like he was being watched. The tiny hairs on the back of neck seemed to rise, and he was aware of them doing so. But watched by whom? He knew he was alone in the house.

But if he was alone, who had turned off the light? Where was the light coming from? He was about to turn and move back into his room, when he heard the faintest sound, only unlike the thump this one was unmistakable. It was the sound of a door quietly being closed, somewhere below. He wanted to race down the stairs to the landing and look, he wanted to see who had shut the door and which door they had shut.

But his feet were heavy with fear and all he could do was turn and head back inside his room. Lock the door and place the chair under the handle. He moved back into bed the way he had left around the edge of the room. He made not a sound as he climbed back into the warmth of his bed. He sat waiting, listening. Fearing another noise, yet wanting to hear it, waiting, waiting as the silence also waited.

Then he did what he always did, he tried to pretend he had heard nothing. Only this time it was harder. He was a natural pessimist and a born thinker, he needed answers, and he analyzed everything, so he could get an answer. Tonight, his mind wanted to do just that. Although he knew there were no answers and he worried his mind would drift to the forbidden room he had entered, and he couldn't afford to analyze that, not at all.

That must be locked away in his thoughts, locked away and forgotten. The noise of tonight must also be locked away and forgotten. Nothing happened, he had heard nothing. He would go to sleep now he had heard nothing. But the other voice in his head kept on arguing that he had heard something and it had to be made by someone, someone real, a living breathing someone had made the sound. It had come from somewhere, and he knew it was somewhere inside the house.

Finally, Rumble had talked himself into believing he had heard nothing. He had taken several deep breaths and his heart had slowed, he steadied his trembling body, and he was ready for sleep. But sleep wouldn't come, he lay on his back his eyes open looking into the blackness.

Was this what death felt like, he wondered? Then, he stilled his mind, almost completely. Before he fell asleep, he promised himself he would find new lodgings, better lodgings, although almost anything would be better than this.

He also promised himself he would never live in a place like this again. Cootes was right he could afford much better. Then he heard his mother's voice telling him to save his money for a rainy day, as one was always just around the corner. So, he forgot about living somewhere grander and merely promised himself he would move, just as soon as he got around to it.

He knew that staying here was not good for his mental health and his stability of life. Maybe, he could purchase his own small place perhaps a tiny studio apartment or something, after all he did have quite a large nest egg and at present it wasn't giving him any quality of life at all. Then he realized he was dreaming grand thoughts, thoughts about his future. This was not like him at all. This was not who he was. Finally, he fell into a deep sleep.

The next several days passed uneventfully. Although, every morning when he walked down the stairs he stopped and stared at the first and second closed doors on the third-floor landing, his mind again remembered what was inside the door. He would immediately stop the thought and think instead of something else. His shoulder and back still ached slightly even though the deep throbbing had gone.

He knew the pain was very real, and he knew exactly where he had got it. Once he had healed, he would be able to forget completely, or so he thought. Also, now as he arrived on the landing of the second floor he would stop and look at each door and the floor directly in front of them. He wasn't sure just what he was looking for until one morning he thought he saw it.

From the landing where he stood he saw the heavy dust on days when the sun was shining through the grimy windows and inside the house. This morning he searched the floor and thought the dust at the far end of the landing in front of the door furthest from him, had been recently disturbed. He squinted his eyes, as he didn't want to move off his usual path or get any closer to the doors. He thought or maybe imaged that he could see a path in the dust where something large and heavy had been dragged. Maybe, he saw it maybe he didn't, he couldn't be sure. Or maybe, he wanted to see it so his mind could reach a conclusion and still his analytical thinking.

Chapter Ten

However, there were many times when his analytical thinking would not be stilled. And as he headed to the bus that morning, it was one of those days.

The little voice inside his head kept asking him questions. Didn't he know what the bones were? Wasn't he curious about how they got there? How did the carpet rug get rolled up against the inside of the door? Where had he seen the ring before? Why was the room so old-fashioned? Shouldn't you be doing something about it? And on and on the questions went, until he almost shouted out loud for it all to stop.

His bus arrived on time, and he moved quickly to the back as he always did. The bus driver recognized him and gave him the slightest of smiles to which Rumble nodded, just the slightest of nods in return. As he walked to the rear of the bus, no one saw him, no one looked at him and no one recognized him. This was how it always was, and he preferred it that way. He had no desire to talk to anyone or even sit close to anyone. He liked being invisible, and this morning he was having enough trouble quietening the voice in his head; he didn't need any further distractions.

It was later that day, he had already had his lunch and Rumble was sitting on the pier sketching the sea birds as they soared and dived over the ocean, that he was startled to hear his mobile ringing. He fumbled in his sachet almost dropping it over the side in his haste to answer the call. Usually, he kept the phone in his trouser pocket but as he hadn't had any calls for a while he had thrown it directly into sachet.

"Rumble here."

"Ah, good chap, on the ball I see." It was Cootes, of course, who else would it be?

"Sketching sea birds today, Mr. Cootes, the wind is just right, and they're weaving and diving all over the place. Lots of movement, it's all in the wings I believe."

"No doubt, you're right, Rumble, you're the expert after all. Anyway, I haven't called to check up on you, in fact quite the contrary."

"Oh?"

"Perhaps, you will think this is good news and perhaps not, but once you think it over I know you will be pleased I called," Cootes paused, probably to put more impact on his words. Rumble knew he often did this, so he needed to say something. Although, he still didn't know why Cootes had called.

"Yes," Rumble replied because he thought he needed to answer.

"Well, Rumble I am calling to give you an opportunity, one you need but may not want. I was just speaking with an old school chum of mine, Ms. Epping, most efficient character, tried to write some articles for us on several occasions. Now she has a small column that we place once a month called, 'Ask Epping.' Anyway, all that is by and by. She owns and runs a small prestigious boarding house, not far from here, in a rather good neighborhood. She has boarders, or tenants as she prefers to call them, only four at a time and most stay with her for years. Well, she just now told me she has a vacancy. One of the girls has gone off to marry a Spanish sailor she met several years ago at a dance. Apparently, it has all been rather exciting for the other boarders. Anyway, Rumble I digress. The point is I've put your name forward," Cootes paused again so Rumble asked.

"For what, Mr. Cootes."

"Really, Rumble, sometimes you really are too slow."

"Oh."

"Rumble there is now a vacancy at the boarding house. It's what you need even though you may not want it you need to move out of that dreadful place you live in. This place is closer to everything, and you'll have other people around you." Just like Rumble, his immediate instinct was to reject change.

"Mr. Cootes, its very kind of you to think of me, but I am all right where I am, really I am. I also like my own company rather well," Rumble replied desperately trying to convince himself. He heard his own words and knew they sounded hollow and not at all convincing, even to him.

"Nonsense, Rumble, you are not quite all right where

you are, it's a dump and its weird to say the least, everything about the house is weird, it's not normal, and I for one would like you out. Once again, I have to push you Rumble, but this time you have no time to over think, or over procrastinate. Lucy has texted you the address and contact name, and they are expecting you at four-thirty today. I know exactly where you are now and it's not far from you, so you should have no trouble keeping the appointment. And Rumble, her rooms are very much in demand, so I suggest you take it, immediately. I've given you an excellent reference which I know will be good enough for her, and I've already basically told her you'll take the room. This is indeed your lucky day, Rumble." Cootes hung up and Rumble was left holding the phone and listening to nothing.

Just when life was getting back to normal and, now this – it was just too much, too fast. Just how could he get out of it? And by four-thirty, it was an hour and a quarter away. But then that horrid little voice in his head spoke again, just when he thought he'd quietened it for good or at least today. *'Do you really want to get out of it?'* It asked. *'Don't you desperately need somewhere else to live? Aren't you scared out of your wits most of the time living in the attic? You need to grab this opportunity with two hands? Where would you be without Cootes?'* Rumble wondered just whose side the voice was on, and he quickly came to the conclusion that apparently, it was not his. Did he really want to live in house with a woman? The answer was definitely no!

Rumble thought back to when he lived at home with his mother. Her mood swings, her angry tendencies and her violent outbreaks toward him. The time she had locked him in the bathroom for two whole days because he said the bread was moldy, and it had been. She was not much of a cook. He remembered the numerous times she had locked him out of house without so much as a warm jacket. He had spent the night outside, terrified, alone and freezing.

He was only a small boy the first time it had happened, she had attacked him for heavens knows what and beat him on the back and around the ears, she had then picked him up like a rubbish bag and thrown him outside. He was badly hurt, and the next morning after a horrific night spent alone outside he had taken himself off to kindergarten. He'd found the way and walked there. He must have only been about five years old, but he'd done it.

He'd seen the look on the teachers face as he'd entered the room. He was blooded and his clothes were ripped, and he was filthy from sleeping under the bushes on the muddy ground all night. Soon, social services were called, then a doctor. He didn't go to the schoolroom at all that day. The pretty lady had feed him and asked him lots of questions, and he had answered, truthfully.

His mother had told him never to lie. Although, it backfired on her that day. Soon, the social worker took him home and had a long talk with his mother. Once she left he knew his mother was furious and again she hit him for telling the social worker what had happened to him at home. Rumble learned that day how it was okay to lie to protect your mother, but you couldn't lie directly to her.

He remembered thinking it was a curious world, and he still didn't understand the rules. Just like living in Edwards's attic, the rules his mother imposed were many and could change at a moment's notice for no reason. He also learned the rules only applied to him. There were many more times when he was beaten and locked outside, but never again did he tell anyone.

So, he must lie now so he didn't have to live with a woman, a woman he didn't know, in a house he didn't know. Now what could he say to get out of this meeting? But all too fast the little voice was back talking to him in his head. '*I'm your savior,*' it began, '*and I'm the rational logical part of your brain. I'm the one you must listen to. I'm the one who speaks when you need help.*' Rumble held his hands over his ears trying to make it stop. He didn't want to hear it; he didn't understand it. He needed to make it stop. And then it answered him; or rather it answered his thoughts. '*I shall stop when you are no longer in danger. You must see the house and take the lodgings it is the only way you'll be safe. Go now, move forward read the address. Do it, do it, do it.*' The voice said the last three words loudly, before it added, '*I shall stop tormenting you once you are safe, but you must move out of the attic.*' This time Rumble replied, 'So, then you will leave me alone?'

'Yes, I will, so long as you do it, do it do it, and do it now.'

'Promise you'll leave me alone?' Rumble asked out loud as an old lady in a purple raincoat stopped in front of him and stared up at him before she muttered, "These newfangled phones, hard to tell if you're talking to someone or yourself," then she shook her blue dyed, over permed hair and moved passed him. The voice didn't reply for some time, and Rumble hoped it had left for good. Then it said, *'I don't promise, but once you are safe maybe I shall leave. Better get going Rumble or you'll be late.'*

'Promise you'll leave?' Rumble asked again still not moving... but there was no reply. Then it started to rain.

Rumble retrieved his plastic raincoat from his sachet put it on and read the contact name and address Lucy had sent again. Then he googled the address on his phone, he was indeed only a short distance from the house.

He walked briskly forward and after taking several more turns he found himself in a nicer part of town. The houses were neat, well maintained and some looked even rather rich. He passed a house with a gardener hard at work trimming hedges. He knew only a gardener who was being paid would be out working in the rain. He turned another corner it was a short avenue that went nowhere, and by counting the numbers on the letterboxes, Rumble knew it was the house at the end of the street facing him in the very middle of the turning circle.

What a difference this place was to where he lived.

Was he fancy enough to live here? Was he fancy enough to come home here every evening? Did he want to come home here every evening, to a woman? No doubt, there would be lots of rules, there was always lots of rules where women are concerned. But maybe, after living under Edwards roof, he was use to them. Could he live in a place called Rosemary Avenue? Maybe. It was after all only a name.

He walked into the middle of the road, so he could face the house directly. It was a large, cozy thatched cottage, rather modern looking for a cottage. The gardens were neat and expansive. It had a white picket fence across the front just like you would image, and a heavy purple front door with an elaborate handle. Above the door in small gold print was a plaque and Rumble thought he could just read the words 'Rosemary Cottage'. Now's the time to turn and walk away, Rumble thought, or run. '*No, now's the time to knock on the door,*' the little voice immediately responded but Rumble preferred his idea of running, better.

He took a few steps toward the front gate, looked for the latch and lifted it. The gate swung easily inward, no squeaking or resistance, obviously well used and cared for, thought Rumble. Now, it was only about a dozen steps to the front door. Only he couldn't take them. His legs wouldn't move. He swiveled around to leave the avenue and saw a pretty young woman with warm curly auburn hair clipped loosely on the top of her head. She was holding her handbag above her hair to try and shield herself from the rain.

She wore shoes with high heels and a short dress with a matching jacket in a grey check fabric. But it was the pale orange lipstick on her full lips that Rumble focused on as, half running, half walking she drew nearer. Now, he saw she had soft blue eyes under small-wire rimmed glasses.

"Oh, dear, the rain always gets on my glasses no matter how hard I try, most annoying, then I can't see," she said looking directly at him through rain smeared glasses. She came to an abrupt halt right in front of him. He was still holding the white picket gate open with one hand, and he soon realized he was blocking her way and she couldn't get past. Rumble found her enchanting, the way she smiled up at him, the twinkle in her eye and her bouncy auburn hair. He also liked the way she smelled, like a garden in springtime, the soft scent wrapped itself around him.

When he didn't answer, she said. "Hello, I bet you're Mr. Rumble, we've all been expecting you. I left work early just to be here before you arrived. And I can still beat you inside if I race you to the front door, I'll get home before you," she said her eyes twinkling with fun.

Rumble smiled at her mischievous comment, but he was not sure what to say other than, "Yes, I am Rumble."

"Well, glad to meet you. I'm Primrose Pringle. I live here also, if you let me pass, I have a key so you can come in out of the rain. Its dryer in there," she giggled trying to wipe her glasses with the back of her free hand, again. Rumble hadn't moved he remained blocking her way.

He was wondering now if he really did want to run. If this were the woman he would be sharing the house with, why would he? She was nothing like his mother.

Primrose Pringle he thought, how delightful and just like that he moved aside holding the gate wide and followed her up the front path and onto the porch of the cozy cottage. While she searched for her key in her dripping wet handbag, Rumble turned to survey the garden. Even with the flowers and shrubs drooping and heavy with rain, it was a picturesque garden, the perfect cottage garden. Rumble knew he must capture it on paper one day. Yes, he would sketch it and record its perfection forever, and perhaps the beauty of Miss Primrose Pringle also, he thought smiling.

"There, I found it, it was right down the very bottom of my bag, again. It always ends up there no matter how well I place it," she said looking up at him the mischievous twinkle still in her eyes. Then the door swung open, it opened easily without so much as a squeak or grind; Rumble was impressed. He thought of his battles with the heavy old neglected kitchen door that he used each morning and evening on his return to the house.

The way the huge key seldom turned without a fight. He'd feel the door resist, until he had to place his sachet on the ground and use both his hands to pull the door toward him, so he could turn the key. It was the same old-fashioned key he used to open his attic door and he often thought that maybe it was the wrong key.

"I found him everyone. I found Mr. Rumble," Primrose called upon entering the house.

"Really, Miss Pringle, I doubt the man was lost, so you could hardly have found him." Came a rather chastising arrogant female voice from a room close by. Rumble couldn't see to whom it belonged but already he didn't want to meet her.

Then down the stairs came a mature slightly overweight lady, although she was still quite elegant. She had short dark wavy hair, small hazel eyes and today she wore pretty pink lipstick that matched the scarf she had wrapped around her green woolen dress. The dress came below her knees, and she wore fluffy dark green slippers on her feet. Her smile was warm, and she greeted Rumble kindly.

"Mr. Rumble, what a pleasure. Sebastian, your editor speaks most highly of you, and I am so pleased to finally meet you." She offered him a neatly manicured hand with clear shiny polished nails. Her hand was warm and soft as he took it in his cold wet hand and shook it gently.

"Sebastian?" Rumble questioned, not thinking fast enough to work it out for himself.

"Yes, your editor, why I've known him for many years. I only started calling him Sebastian once we were adults, because I didn't like him calling me by my childish nickname, so I stopped using his. It worked, no one has called me that ridiculous name in years," she finished, as she stood beside him in the front entranceway. She was much shorter than he was, so she looked up at him. Rumble liked her she seemed genuine.

"Nice meeting you, Mr. Rumble. I'll see more of you once you move in properly." Primrose added moving past him and along the hallway until she opened a door and disappeared inside. Rumble smiled at her as she passed breathing deeply of her scent. He thought she was the prettiest woman he had ever seen, and then he returned his focus to the lady in front of him.

"I'm Ms. Epping, if you haven't already guessed," again Rumbled nodded, he was feeling rather overwhelmed by all the new people he was meeting. But he was trying to take it all in and wasn't allowing anyone to see just how anxious he was really feeling. All he wanted to do was run. But he couldn't, he simply couldn't. Ms. Epping was now holding his arm and saying, "Mr. Rumble let me show you around the house. We are at present four. I like to have no more than four boarders, that way I always have a spare room just in case. Once you move in, we shall again be five," she continued as he nodded. They were now entering a large kitchen at the back of the cottage; it was well appointed and the appliances were white and gleaming.

Yellowed chintz curtains surrounded the two small windows and matched the tablecloth that covered the small wooden kitchen table. It had four wooden chairs neatly placed around it. But there was a fifth chair where a well-dressed lady sat tapping urgently at the keys of her Apple laptop computer.

She looked up briefly and nodded, "This young lady is Ms. Simons," Ms. Epping said and then paused if she expected Ms. Simons to stop what she was doing and at least look at them. When she did not, Ms. Epping spoke to the young woman with a different tone in her voice than she had been speaking to Rumble.

"Ms. Simons, where are your manners? This is Mr. Rumble who may soon be sharing this home with us, please at least be courteous enough to acknowledge him."

"So, you're the man Primrose thought was lost in the rain, you hardly look the type to be lost anywhere, silly girl I think she thought she was your fairy godmother because she rescued you or something." The woman replied and Rumble recognized her voice as the one that had spoken to Primrose when they first entered the house.

Rumble was about to say that Primrose had indeed rescued him when he saw she had returned to her laptop and was again paying them no mind. She was a haughty, birdlike creature. With dark hair that was pulled tightly back from her face, thin nose and lips and hard eyes. The type of eyes his mother had, there was no softness or kindness there and Rumble thought he knew exactly the type of woman she was. That was the type of woman he could never like, but fortunately there was Primrose…

"Come, Mr. Rumble we are not all bad mannered in this house," Ms. Epping said addressing Ms. Simons who didn't so much as look in her direction.

"Anyway, Mr. Rumble, you will have your own shelf in the pantry and fridge and also a space in one of the cupboards for your things, you can cook in here anytime of the day or night, but I do encourage my tenants to clean up after themselves and keep the kitchen in an orderly clean manner. Most everyone is clean and tidy in the house, more or less," she said and Rumble thought she was again addressing the young woman on the computer.

"All the shelves are named so there can no mistaking which is your area. I shall have everything ready for you before you move in, Mr. Rumble," she said holding his arm and guiding him out of the kitchen. Rumble was seldom touched, but he didn't mind her gentle touch at all in fact he found it comforting in these new surroundings. They walked back into the hallway and turned right. This time they were in a small sunny room with a floor to ceiling glass window along one side.

"This is our conservatory, not large I know, but if the sun's out, this is the place to enjoy it." Rumble noticed it was pleasant room with several large comfortable chairs, some antique side tables and a long coffee table against the far wall. The walls were heavily lined with artwork and several healthy plants stood on pedestals around the edges.

There was also a large T.V. and Ms. Epping must have seen Rumble eyeing it as she said, "This room is for the use of my tenants or boarders whenever they want to relax and have some quiet time. The T.V. is seldom used, but it is here should you want to watch it." Rumble wondered just why they hardly used the T.V., it was the biggest screen he had ever seen. Then he watched as one of the large brown leather chairs began swiveling around to face them.

"Are, Major Tyme, meet Mr. Rumble," Ms. Epping said as the phone rang somewhere in the house, and she excused herself, "Jolly pleased to meet you, young man," when he stood up from the chair, he was a hulk of a man, as square as he was tall. With thick brown hair, large lively pale blue eyes and a wide mouth with a solid chin, in fact Rumble observed the entire man was solid. His shoulders were broad and as Rumble observed, so was the large meaty hand the Major was extending, he realized he was indeed, very solid.

"Major Winston Bloomington-Tyme the second. Quite a mouthful, I know, so everyone simply calls me Tyme or Major, or maybe both," he said happily placing an elegant wooden pipe between his teeth and sucking deeply.

"She who must be obeyed doesn't allow smoking, so I just suck on it and wait until I can light up when no one's around, usually in my room but it's not allowed there either, jolly woman, still she's a good sort," he said releasing Rumble's hand. Rumble felt like it may have been crushed, so he slowly moved each finger in turn and was relieved to find they were all still working.

"Rather looking forward to having another chap around the place, Rumble, must say I am. Smoke, do you?" he asked slapping Rumble so hard and so unexpectedly on the shoulder that he almost fell flat on his face, the Major chuckled heartily at Rumble's amazement.

"Jolly good, not a well-built chap, are you? In fact, rather slight, if I may be so bold. Guessing you weren't a soldier, not enough of you is there, Rumble."

"No, Major, there is not, and no, I do not smoke," Rumble quickly replied taking several steps away from the Major. He was hoping he could avoid another slap or hand shake for that matter.

"Hunt, do you, old chap?"

"No, Major, I do not."

"Maybe, fishing's more your style, don't mind it myself on occasions."

"No, I do not fish."

"Well, I'll definitely get you on the golf course, bet you don't mind a round or two, you're built more for the genteel sports I would say myself."

"Sorry, Major, don't golf either," Rumble replied feeling rather inadequate and hoping Ms. Epping would soon make her appearance. He glanced slightly toward the door as the major continued talking in his booming voice. It seemed to bounce off the walls as he spoke.

"Well, I must ask again then, military man are you, Rumble, army, navy air force? I hold no prejudices, all as good the other. Now I'm army myself, of course, being a Major. Retired now many years, but somehow the name stuck. So, which is it, Rumble?"

Rumble was sure the major had asked him the same questions not so long ago, but he simply replied, "No, Major, I have never been in the military."

"No, I can understand that, why there's simply not enough of you to make the grade, you're a rather scrawny fellow aren't you Rumble? But nothing wrong with that, can't all be built to lead."

"No, Sir, indeed we can't," he didn't know why, but he knew the major commanded respect, and it came easily to him.

"Well, I'll have to make you my pet project then, old chap, after all we men must stick together. Now I've handed over the reins of the business to my two sons and sold the houses in London, my times my own. All rather daunting at first, Rumble – indeed it was – but now I'm rather enjoying it. I can go where I want when I want and do exactly as I please, all rather pleasurable, if I may say so," the major said satisfied, as he lifted a small cut crystal glass to his lips and took a long swallow.

"Err, forgive me Rumble, where are my manners, take a seat if you please, now are you a whisky man, I am myself, don't mind a little snifter any time of the day. But one can only drink beer in the evenings, my dear old mother always said. Beer is for men alone, not a very sociable drink and too rough for ladies of breeding," he chuckled loudly at what he had just said and then continued, "Yes, that's what she always said, yes, she did, god rest her soul. What'll it be, Rumble, I keep a well stocked liquor cabinet here, and I invite everyone to help themselves, although I'm sure it will mainly be you and I. Can't tell you how delighted I am to have another male under this roof. I love the female sex don't get me wrong, but with a man we can understand each other. What do you say, Rumble? I think we'll get on just fine, just fine indeed." Rumble finally heard Ms. Epping enter the room so he turned to move toward her. He didn't mind the major, but he found him rather overpowering; he knew it would take him time to get use to this solid, tough military man.

"Ah, my dear Ms. Epping I was just about to offer Rumble here a drink, care to join us, or is too early for you?" The major said getting to his feet. Rumble noticed he was shorter than he expected him to be, but he was just as wide as he'd first appeared.

"Thank you. No, Major, now so long as you are only offering Mr. Rumble a drink and not encouraging him to smoke. I have no objection, after all the liquor cabinet belongs to you," she said kindly then turning to Rumble she said.

"I have a no smoking policy in the house, what you do out of doors is your own concern. But I don't allow smoking in the house, and I would prefer my tenants to adhere to the rule," she said glaring at the major who pretended not to hear. "Mr. Rumble, you are welcomed to join the major for a drink before we continue our tour."

"Thank you. No, Ms. Epping, I believe I would prefer to continue my tour of the house."

"Another time, Rumble old chap." The major replied and before Rumble could move away the major had slapped him on the back so hard Rumble felt his bones rattle.

Rumble happily followed Ms. Epping out of the conservatory and as they entered the hallway they almost collided with Primrose. Rumble felt his heart skip a beat, but he didn't know why.

"Hello, Mr. Rumble, still here, are you?"

"Just having the tour, Miss. Pringle."

"Primrose, please."

"Primrose."

"When will you move in, Mr. Rumble?" she asked.

It was Ms. Epping who answered, "We haven't yet signed the tenancy agreement, Primrose. I think you're rushing the man, he may not even like us."

"Oh, I just know he will. Especially once you show him his room why it's the best one in the house, other than yours, Ms. Epping." Primrose bubbled as she moved passed them,

"I think I'll just take you straight to your – soon to be – new room, and you can see the rest of the house once you decide when you're moving in." Rumble was delighted with her decision, he knew the night was drawing in, and he also knew it would soon be dark. He remembered Edwards did not like him arriving home after dark.

The room he was to tenant was light and spacious, with a bay window looking onto the street. A small sink, a tiny fridge, a toaster, electric jug and TV. It had its own bathroom, which was about as big as Rumble entire attic room. The wardrobe was huge; Rumble's few clothes would quickly get lost in there. There was a loveseat by the bay window, a desk and chair and large queen size bed, with a soft feather duvet and fluffy looking pillows. Rumble loved the room and knew he wouldn't even need to see the rest of the house. He felt a ripple of excitement about living here in this cozy cottage; sadly, he knew it would cost him more than he was prepared to pay. Why hadn't he asked the price first and maybe not have wasted every-one's time.

"Mr. Rumble, is there something you don't like about your room?" Ms. Epping asked looking concerned.

"Oh, no, it's perfect, thank you."

"I almost forgot, we have a lady who comes in every Thursday. She does your washing, your sheets, towels and anything else you want washed and ironed. You need to have all your dirty washing in the basket..." She pointed to a large wicker basket in the corner of the room as she continued, "...By Thursday morning. She doesn't make up your bed or enter your room. So, leave the basket outside the door, but she will do any ironing she thinks needs doing. Once everything is washed, the wash basket will be left outside your room by five p.m. She will also vacuum and dust when required, but she needs your permission to enter your room. I hope this is suitable, Mr. Rumble? "

"Oh, yes, most suitable, thank you."

"If you need anything more just ask, and if I have it or I can get it, it shall be yours. I like my tenants to feel comfortable and happy. Most of them stay a very long time, Mr. Rumble, and that's how I like it. They become family. Except Ms. Simons, of course, who will be moving back to her own place once the renovations are complete on her apartment. I do think if she were a little easier to work with, they would have been completed long ago. Anyway, Mr. Rumble, what is it that's concerning you?" She asked kindly. Rumble was unused to anyone showing concern for him, and for a moment, he was unable to speak. He briefly wondered how she knew he had any concerns at all, but she was right he was concerned about the rent she would charge.

He didn't want to ask the price, as they all seemed so nice, but he couldn't just take the room without knowing. After all, there was always that rainy day, just around the corner, the one his mother always spoke of. Although he was forty-nine years old, and he hadn't had a rainy day yet. He must ask the price. He shouldn't have come here; he couldn't afford it, and he knew he didn't deserve it.

"Mr. Rumble, is something wrong?" Ms. Epping asked sounding more concerned than ever. He needed to just ask, he hated seeing her concern for him on her face.

No one ever showed concern for him. '*Or maybe she is just worried you won't take the room, although he doubted anyone would be glad to have this room,*' the little voice in his head said while the other voice the one that was him replied, 'but I can't afford it,' '*yes, you can, just ask*', the little voiced replied, and Rumble said, 'what about the rainy day?' '*What rainy day*'? The little voice said and Ms. Epping broke into his thoughts.

"Mr. Rumble?" she questioned.

"Oh, I'm sorry, I was just wondering how much the room rents for?" There he'd said it. He was surprised with the answer; it wasn't much more than what he paid now, and he would be getting so much more value in return.

Too many changes, Rumble wanted to run, he liked the room and the house, but so much was happening too fast. He would have run also, if he hadn't seen Primrose again as he walked down the stairs behind Ms. Epping.

Soon, the tenancy agreement was signed. Rumble noted that there were far less rules than Edwards had imposed. It was decided he would move in Saturday afternoon.

It was still raining as Rumble walked from the bus back to his dreary attic room. It seemed drearier after leaving the brightly lit happy cottage; the comparison was too great. Rumble was trying not to think of all that he must do in the next few days, although he didn't have much to pack. He was walking along the side of the road in the half-light of the late evening when an old battered blue truck drove slowly toward him. The back of the truck was full of youths, and by the language and noise, they were making, Rumble knew they were drunk and up to no good. He was almost at the house now. He heard the engine slow behind him, but he kept on walking and didn't look back. Then a beer bottle whizzed by his head hitting a tree and shattering, he turned his head to avoid the splinters of glass hitting his face.

"Hey, Pops, stand still so I can hit you." Another beer bottle smashed to the ground just inches from Rumble's legs, splashing him with the beer from the bottle.

"Yeah, Pops passed your bedtime, ain't it?"

"Want a beer, Pops?" Rumble kept on walking as the car slowed beside him, and the boys covered the end of the beer bottle and shook it vigorously before spraying him with beer. Rumble felt the wetness on his face and the smell in his nose, but he kept on walking as another bottle almost hit him in the head. He turned into the pathway that led to the backdoor of the house as they kept on yelling, laughing and cursing, "Hey, Pops, no one lives there," one of the boys yelled after him.

"Yeah, the place is haunted everyone knows that."

"Don't fucking go in there, Pops," they called as he fumbled with trembling hands at the back door and the old key. As usual he needed to leave his sachet on the ground to pull the door hard toward him, so the key would turn. He felt the youths in the old car watching him, he felt their eyes on his back and hoped they wouldn't throw another bottle in his direction at least until he was inside.

"Hey, Pops, don't do it, don't go in, come on, let's get him." Rumble heard them saying, and then, he heard the engine stop. Finally, he opened the door, grabbed his sachet, and almost fell inside. He quickly locked it just as they tried to turn the handle and then began pounding heavily on the door.

Rumble knew how secure the door was. As he walked through the grimy kitchen, he couldn't help thinking of the other kitchen he had just been in. The loud pounding on the door continued as they yelled for him to open up.

Rumble was shaking when he finally climbed the last of the attic stairs and entered his tiny room. Too much was happening; too fast. And he had signed the tenancy agreement, what was he thinking? It was all too much. And he was supposed to be moving in this weekend. Rumble went into his tiny bathroom and sank to the ground. He leaned into the toilet bowl and vomited. It was all too much...

Then he vomited again, the last of his lunch he supposed. He sat where he was on the floor of his bathroom for a long time. Trying to quiet his trembling and stop the voice in his head. He didn't need either, his clothes were soaked with beer, and he had no washing time until Saturday. He would need to wear different clothes tomorrow. The back of his hand was bleeding where he had obviously been hit with glass. Gradually, the trembling stopped, but the voice continued. '*So, what are you so scared of? The boys didn't really harm you they just scared you. And you're moving into a nicer place, a safer place. You'll have to pack. You'll need to write Edwards telling him you're vacating the attic. Not before time. All this is good, so why are you so upset'.* The voice went on and on. Until Rumble, still sitting on the bathroom floor said aloud, 'You wouldn't understand, you never have before, and you don't understand now. So just leave me alone,' and the voice replied, *'not until you're safe'.* 'Well, I'm moving, aren't I?' *'Maybe you are and maybe you're not but I hope so',* replied the voice. Strange answer Rumble thought as he replied, 'Will you go away once I'm out of here?' Rumble asked in his mind. He was waiting for an answer when he heard the squeak of the stair outside his locked door. Someone was out there? Someone was on his stairs. Rumble felt the icy talons of fear trickle down his spine. He heard his own breath, short rasping sounds from deep within his lungs; his heart also, was beating faster. Instinctively, he wiped the wet tears from his cheeks, he wasn't even aware he was crying. He stayed where he was; crouched on the floor by the toilet, and listened... the voice in his head was silent also.

Chapter Eleven

How long he remained on the bathroom floor, listening, he didn't know. He had no lights on in his room and, it was now shrouded with the shadows of pre-darkness. Soon, it would be completely dark. It was the little voice that startled him back into consciousness, his little voice of reason and logic, the one he didn't want to hear. *'Get a grip and, stop crying. Nothing has happened, nothing. You heard a sound, and you've heard nothing more. Stop crying and calm down.'* It said, before it continued, *'I told you this place scares the wits out of you, and there's the proof because, it just did.'* Rumble replied back to the voice in his head, he was actually glad of the distraction. It was not just the voice. 'It was everything, everything. Too much of everything, and it's all happening too fast.' *'Well,'* replied the voice, *'if it doesn't happen fast, you could procrastinate your way right out of anything ever happening. This is the best way, the only way, so get a grip and get up off the floor, you're a grown man not a little child.'*

Once the voice in his head ceased talking, he slowly stood on shaky legs and listened intently a little longer before he moved out of the tiny bathroom and sat on his bed. He removed his shoes, they made way too much noise and silence was his friend. *'Silence your friend?'* the voice began, *'indeed it is not, you abhor silence, it scares you half to death, and you're always listening to it. Who listens to silence?'* "Oh do shut up," Rumble said aloud, closing his eyes tightly and placing his hands over his ears, as if that would block out the voice in his head.

He stayed like that for a while, and the little voice was quiet also. Rumble was sitting on the end of his bed with his head bent forward, his eyes shut, and his hands firmly over his ears. He was almost enjoying the silence. When had the voice first started? He thought thinking back. Yes, he remembered, it was long ago, the very first time he had been beaten and made to sleep outside, that was when he'd first heard the voice. It soothed him, told him what to do, kept him calm and told him everything would be all right.

Well, that was years ago, when he was a child. But when he lived with the Millington's, he had never heard the voice, never. And now, it was back, why? He asked himself and the little voice answered immediately, *'You know perfectly well, why?'*

Slowly, Rumble swiveled on the bed until he'd moved his legs over the side. Then he gradually opened his eyes and removed his hands. The trembling had almost stopped. He reached over and turned on the tiny bedside lamp, it belonged to him, and he kept it plugged into the wall socket and pushed under the bed. The room filled with a dull pale-yellow light, not enough to light the shadows in the corners but enough to challenge some of the darkness within.

Then he let out the breath he hadn't known he was holding. Everything is all right, he told himself. I am all right. He was trying to convince himself as he told himself it was time for bed. Slowly, he undressed and put on his old pale blue pajamas, the same ones he wore every night the ones with the faded navy strips.

He folded his clothes as he did every night, but as the smell of beer wafted into the air, he decided to place them in the bathroom as far from the bed as possible. In the morning he would need to find different clothes to wear. It was then he turned to walk the few paces back to his bed.

He stopped.

He stared.

He froze exactly where he was standing.

He felt the sweat again break out on his palms.

His heart began to beat faster.

Lying on the floor just inside the door was a folded piece of paper. It was folded neatly in half just once. Rumble recognized it as the same writing paper as the last letter.

Did Edwards now know he had trespassed into the room? Had he been seen coming home too late at night? Did someone know he was looking around the house? Was he about to get evicted? He asked himself all these questions and more as he stared at the folded sheet of paper lying on the floor. The little voice answered him. '*So what. If you're afraid of eviction and you're already moving out,* *you may just have to move a couple of days early and either ask the kind Ms. Epping if you can move in early or stay in a hotel. So why are you so upset again? Get a grip and read the letter. Read it. **Do it, do it, do it** '.* The little voice said with emphasizes on the six last words. Rumble hadn't moved. But he knew the little voice was telling him the truth he should just read the letter and stop all this agony. He was, as usual thinking the worst. But living in this house, how could he think anything else?

'Yes, I shall just pick it up, unfold it, and read it?*'* Rumble thought still staring at the letter and not moving. Someone had been on his stairs? Someone had put the letter under the door? That meant someone else was in the house? A real live flesh and blood person, not like the bones... Rumble shuddered, his legs went weak, so weak he thought he might fall to the floor. But there was the little voice again. *'Get a grip; focus on the sheet of paper. What is the worst it can say? Maybe it is an eviction notice, or maybe not?'* Rumble knew the little voice was the closest thing he had to sanity and it was speaking the truth.

Only now he thought of the bones he couldn't stop, he knew they were not animal bones. *'*Animals seldom wore heavy silver rings with red stones. Nor do they live in a locked room with a silver baby's rattle – Baby Sarah,*'* he thought and shivered.

Poor Baby, Sarah. Had her bones also been lying just below him wrapped in a rug? Maybe, they were... no, no more, he must stop thinking of the bones and pretend he

122

hadn't seen anything in the room. He hadn't seen anything, he hadn't, he told himself over and over. He hadn't even been in the room. Then, he took a step toward the paper lying on the floor.

With sweaty trembling hands, he bent down and gingerly picked up the folded sheet of paper. He held it in his hand and looked down at it, not really wanting it at all. To Rumble, it was like holding a hot potato he didn't want it nor was it something he wanted to hold. *'Read it,'* the voice said, *'unfold it and read it. Do it, do it, do it.'* Rumble knew he must, he felt the paper vibrating in time with his own trembling. All he had to do is open it, that's all.

He needed to sit down. So, still holding the paper gingerly, he moved the few paces to his bed. His knees and legs felt weak, weak with fear he thought.

And then he did it. He sat on the bed, and slowly carefully as if it may crumble into thin air he unfolded the heavy sheet of cream writing paper. Staring back at him from the page was a single word. It was written in exactly the same writing as the last letter in pale blue ink. It simply said, OBEY. Edwards.

One word that was all, but it was enough to make Rumble shake with terror. Did Edwards know he had visited the room, opened the curtains, seen the bones… Rumble shuddered. Or, began the little voice, *'is Edwards merely referring to you arriving home later than usual and almost breaking one of the rules? That's probably all it is, otherwise he would have evicted you. So, calm down get into bed and have a good night's sleep.'* The voice concluded, but Rumble wouldn't let it go; he replied, 'but there was someone in the house, on the stairs, outside my door, someone real, someone else here in the house.' *'So, what?'* The voice answered, *'so what, it's not your house or your stairs and Edwards has never said you are alone, it is only what you think. So, forget it and go to sleep. Tomorrow will be a glorious day, and soon you will be moving ... moving away from this hell.'*

'A glorious day, when have I ever had a glorious day,' Rumble replied, then he continued, 'it may be easy for you, but I am the one who physically has to move, do all the work and then live in a house with other people. Ones that talk, like major, what's-his-name, Clock, no Tyme, yes that Major Tyme. I don't know if I want to be slapped hard on the back regularly, and if I live there, it may happen quite often, I'm just not built of that stuff.' *'This is what you need,'* the voice said, *'you will get use to the Major, you said so yourself'.* 'I'm sure, I said, I might get used to the Major,' Rumble corrected.

'So, be it,' the little voice continued, *'just think of who else will be living in the house?'* 'Who?' Rumble asked still speaking out loud and feeling, confused, *'Ms. Primrose, Rumble, the beautiful Ms. Primrose'.* 'Oh, yes,' Rumble replied, and he knew he was blushing, 'well, I don't understand any of that either. I don't know why my heart beats faster, or skips a beat completely when she's around; nor do I understand why I find her attractive, she

is after all, a woman. I generally don't like them, not my kind of creatures at all. Just the thought of a woman makes me think of mother.' *'Your mother'*, the little voice said, *'your mother, you weren't thinking of your mother when Ms. Primrose was looking up at you, now were you? And as far as not understanding, I'm sure you do, you're forty-nine-years-old, you must have some idea why your heart beats faster, and why you want to be around her?'* 'Well, I didn't and I don't want to think about it.' *'Okay then so go to sleep, you've calmed down nicely and it's past your bedtime,'* the voice said. 'Why are you being so bossy, who are you? My mother,' Rumble replied annoyed pulling back the bedspread, then the sheets before he climbed between them.

Then he bent down and turned off the lamp and placed it further under his bed again. Primrose's, face danced before him, her lively eyes and her glasses streaked with rain and the mischief in her voice, he could hear it all rather clearly, too clearly. He didn't want to think of Primrose she made him feel strange. *'Oh, just go to sleep then,'* the little voice said none to kindly, and Rumble finally went into a fitful sleep and didn't wake until the morning when his alarm told him it was time to get up.

'Rise and shine, it's another glorious day', the voice said, 'oh, do shut up,' replied Rumble as he headed to the bathroom to complete his morning routine.

Rumble enjoyed his early morning cup of tea and piece of dried toast. He dressed in clean clothes that didn't

125

have pockets deep enough for the large key, so he would have to keep it in his sachet. He closed and locked the back door exactly the same time as he always did.

He walked briskly in the fresh crisp early morning air and arrived at the bus stop as the bus came to a stop beside the curb. Most of the seats were occupied, but as he neared the rear of the bus, he saw one seat was vacant. It was the one beside the seat where he usually sat. A small round man in a bowler hat and reading a large newspaper sat in his seat. Rumble hated change, but he reluctantly sat down next to the round little man and told himself he must be glad he had a seat at all.

Moments after he alighted the bus, it began to drizzle. Rumble wondered what would catch his eye today, and just what needed to be captured on paper. It was all just a feeling; he loved the freedom to draw whatever he felt he needed to draw.

Cootes gave him few guidelines, usually none. So, he could go where he liked and capture anything he wanted to capture, and the best part was he got paid for doing so. He did indeed have a great life. He had only walked a few paces when his mobile vibrated.

He stopped to look at it and noticed it was a text from Lucy instructing him to draw some galloping horses, dressed for the hunt. Rumble smiled a small smile; now he had a purpose for the day. He crossed the road to the park with a light step and a small smile on his face. He didn't feel the drizzle in the air. It had almost stopped anyway, so he didn't need to stop and retrieve his raincoat.

Rumble found a wooden bench under a large oak tree; he had sat there often before, he found this a quiet peaceful place, a serene area where he could contemplate his work. He loved the need for total focus when he was drawing; it took his mind off everything. Everything like the house and all the people where he is about to move into, the awful place where he is about to move out of and the voice, which he didn't need to hear.

He shouldn't have thought of it, he waited for it to say something, but it didn't. Soon, he was looking at photos of horse, all kinds of horses running cantering, jumping. But he knew the kinds that were required and the images only gave him inspiration of movement, nothing more.

Several hours later, Rumble had created four life-like sketches, he knew they were good, he always knew when he'd done good work and he was feeling it more and more lately.

His stomach told him it was lunchtime, so he carefully replaced everything in his sachet and headed to the little cafe on the far side of the park. The food was homemade and delicious. Rumble knew there would be a queue and that tables were limited, but the wait was worth the lunch. He then returned to the park with the thought of drawing again, but as he began walking across the park toward the bench where he always sat, he noticed in the distance a figure had occupied his park bench in his absence.

Rumble swallowed hard, the annoyance at having to

break his familiar routine, he knew this person had surely ruined his day. From now on, nothing would go right for him because of a stranger who had decided to sit on his bench. The one he always occupied whenever he was in the park.

Reluctantly, he turned and headed to another bench. But it was enough to throw off his day and his creative flow. Rumble focused on his annoyance at having to sit on another park bench. He tried not to, he took several deep breaths, he tried to enjoy the beauty of the park, but his eyes kept wondering across the park to the stranger sitting on his bench. And he knew it was that person whose face he couldn't see and whose name he didn't know, who was responsible for ruining his day. How inconsiderate?

He sat and waited for an answer but the voice in his head said nothing, not a word, silence, just when he needed to talk it through. It was always the same; it was never there when he wanted it...

Thirty minutes later, he had his sketchpad on his lap, but it remained blank. Then over the far side of the park, he noticed the figure on his bench, get up and walk away. Rumble quickly packed up his things and walked briskly toward the bench. He sat down with a look of satisfaction on his face as he removed his sketchpad and pencils.

He was looking around the park at nothing in particular, but in his mind, he was thinking of his imminent move to his new lodgings. Then he began sketching. It was another forty-five minutes before he actually thought about just what he was sketching and when finally, he really looked at his work he was horrified to see the laughing face of Ms. Primrose Pringle looking back at him, rain streaked glasses and all. Rumble didn't draw people at all, never had, although, he could. He especially didn't draw women. What was he thinking? He tore out the sketch and was about to crumple it up when he looked at it again. A small smile played on his lips. Briefly, he remembered how beautiful she was.

He knew his face was burning and his heart racing, just at the thought of her, but why? Again, he was about to crumple the page, but he stopped and looked at her face once more, tracing his pencil lines softly with his index finger. Then he added her sketch to the back of his sketchbook and tried to think of horses.

His mobile quickly vanished any further thought of work.

"Rumble here," Rumble said thinking how professional he sounded and knowing it could only be Cootes, "Rumble, just been talking to Sybil, glad to hear you made the right impression, old man. Wouldn't want you to let the side down, to say nothing of my good name or the excellent reference I gave you."

"Who, Mr. Cootes? Who have you been talking to?"

"Oh, Rumble, do stay with the conversation there's a good chap, Sybil, you know, Ms. Epping."

"Oh, yes, of course, didn't know her first name, Mr. Cootes."

"Well, probably no need, Rumble, no need at all. But you surely didn't expect me to call her by her last name after all these years now, did you? After all, we were school chums and all that."

"I understand, Mr. Cootes."

"She's working on your room now, getting it all ready for you, says you are intending on moving in Saturday afternoon?"

"Yes."

"Not procrastinating or anything, are you, Rumble? Can't have you getting out of it and letting Sybil and myself down in any way."

"Of course, not, Mr. Cootes."

"Glad to hear it, I know how you talk yourself out of anything, Rumble, and this is golden opportunity for you."

"Yes, indeed, Mr. Cootes," Rumble replied, wondering how Cootes knew him so well.

"I've been doing some research on the old house where you're living, Rumble, most interesting, most interesting indeed. I'll give it to you at our next meeting. Or once you're safely away from it, wouldn't want to scare you or anything, Rumble."

"Oh," said Rumble as he felt his palms sweat.

"Anyway, Rumble, take Friday off if you're not doing so already and get yourself packed. I know you don't have much, but best be organized. As I said, Sybil is expecting you first thing after lunch on Saturday afternoon, Rumble, so don't disappoint." Rumble was listening intently to the sound of Cootes's voice and it took him several minutes of listening to silence to realize Cootes was gone. Now Rumble was thinking about his conversation with Cootes. Just, what had he discovered about the house? What exactly was it that might scare him… he couldn't stop the ripple of fear that ran through him…

Chapter Twelve

Rumble did not want to move. He hated change. Hated the thought of moving into a house that was new to him. Hated all the strangers he must interact with. '*Even Ms. Primrose?*' The voice asked loudly in his head startling him back into the present, and Rumble replied immediately, 'Yes, especially Primrose.' '*You must not fear the unknown, often the unknown is better than the known, we subconsciously know what we need, if conscious we don't, or in your case won't. Don't fear the unknown unless it is the immediate unknown!*' the voice replied firmly and Rumble began to feel concerned when he said, 'and what is that supposed to mean?' Silence.

Even though Rumble was back on his favorite bench under the large oak tree, he was feeling anxious at all he must do. Then he noticed how the drizzle had turned to rain; he mechanically got to his feet and headed home. It was earlier than usual, but his creativity had vanished like the sun. Too many interruptions and too many thoughts of what lay ahead. Rumble simply couldn't focus.

The bus trip to his street moved faster than usual, it was only early afternoon, and the bus was nearly empty. No commuters or school children. As Rumble walked toward the old kitchen door and retrieved his key from his sachet, he wondered just why he was home so early in the day? Why had he broken his routine?

He thought maybe it was because he had too much to think about and so his mind had shut down and wanted to go to a safe place. *'This is not that place this is definitely not a safe place'*, the voice gently reminded him in his head, and he replied as he always did, 'well, maybe not, but I'm here now.' Rumble battled with the key in the old door until finally he took off his sachet and placed it beside the door, so he could use two hands to pull the door towards` him. Finally, it unlocked and resisted being pushed open as it always did. It squeaked loudly, it was mournful sound, but to Rumble it was familiar.

He had only just shut the door when he heard above him in the house, quite clearly, the sound of a door being suddenly slammed. Rumble froze; he knew it was a door slamming, a heavy door by the sound of it. There were no open windows, and the house was never aired, so how could a door slam, unless someone… *'Stop being a baby and see who it is,'* the voice commanded, while Rumble stood frozen to the spot. 'No,' he replied, 'no, why should I? I heard nothing?' *'But you did you know you did'*, it replied, 'no, I heard nothing' Rumble said out loud under his breath as he took several deep breaths and started moving toward the entranceway.

Out the corner of his eye, Rumble thought, he saw a movement on the second- floor landing at the very end, but he couldn't be sure, he only looked up briefly. But it was like his legs were moving on their own, he bolted up the stairs to the second floor and feeling bolder than ever before he began moving alone the landing.

He knew you could clearly see his footsteps in the dust on the floor but he didn't care. Then, before he knew it, he was standing outside the last door at the end of the row. A tall, solid door, much like all the others, although Rumble felt it was somehow larger. Although that really didn't matter either way, what size the door was.

Rumble looked down at the round brass handle, it was just like all the others in the house, but unlike the last handle he had turned on the floor above, this one was much cleaner. It was still almost shiny in comparison, although he could see a thin layer of dust had adhered itself to the brass. Perhaps, meaning no one had entered recently? 'Wasn't that what it meant?' Rumble asked the little voice, but it remained silent.

Slowly Rumble reached down and gripped the brass doorknob firmly in his right hand. He tried to turn it, but it was obviously locked. So, that was that. He couldn't go inside the room because the door was locked tightly. '*Look closely at the lock*', the little voice said in his head and Rumble replied; 'now you chose to speak,' the voice again said, '*look closely at the lock.*' 'Why?' Asked Rumble, 'it is just a lock; they are all much the same, large and old fashioned by today's standards. Anyway, I don't see a key around here anywhere.' Again, the voice said, '*look closely at the lock*', this time Rumble listened and looked down at the lock. It was just like all the rest, they were all the same, all exactly like the lock on his attic door. *'Yes'*, said the voice, *'now you're getting it'*. 'But I don't understand,' Rumble said turning to walk back the way he'd just come. *'Think, all the locks look the same'*, the voice persisted.

Then Rumble stopped. He turned back to the door. He stood in front of it and looked down at the lock. It was exactly like the lock to his attic. Then he said one word to the voice, 'smartass.' There was silence for some time; Rumble had expected an answer, but got none. Finally, the voice said, *'do it, do it, do it'*. In its usual annoying way. 'Do what?' Rumble asked confused, wanting to get to his attic now. *'Do I really have to tell you everything?'* The voice persisted, the annoyance obvious in its tone.

Rumble was beginning to feel vulnerable standing there on the second -floor landing, he knew he was trespassing; he shouldn't be here at all. Then the voice said, *'open the door, **do it, do it, do it**.'* 'How?' Rumble replied, 'I don't understand.' *'Perhaps, try your key in this lock; if all the locks look the same then maybe one key fit's them all.'*

Suddenly, Rumble knew what the voice was telling him. It was so simply he wondered why he hadn't thought of it, although he knew he usually looked for the hard way. Maybe, the voice was the silly one, why would the locks all use the same key? Wouldn't that defeat the whole purpose of locking doors? But he remembered the kitchen door and his attic door both used the same lock, perhaps the voice wasn't so silly after all. Anyway, he would try. All he wanted to do was go to his attic, but if he did that he knew the voice would haunt him, and he hated that thought even more.

He got the large key from his sachet and placed it in the old lock. It seemed to go in easily. Then he pulled the old door toward him as he did with the kitchen and attic doors and he turned the key. He felt it wanted to turn, but this time it didn't – quite. So, he pulled the door harder toward him until it reluctantly turned. 'How did you know?' Rumble asked the voice, but there was no reply.

The door creaked as he pushed it open. It was solid and old and it resisted the intrusion. It opened easier than the last door had, but Rumble didn't think of that for more than a second, he knew if he did he'd run screaming from the room.

Just like the floor above, the drapes were drawn, the room was in total darkness. Rumble wished he had brought a flashlight, although he didn't even own one, he knew he would very soon, they were so necessary in his world now. He stood still while his eyes became accustomed to the light, the light from outside the crack in the door, it became fainter as the door slowly closed to just a thin line. There must be curtains Rumble thought and with his arms out in front of him, he slowly walked toward where the window should be.

Something brushed against his face. Something was

hovering in mid-air. Rumble almost screamed. With his arms out in front of him, he turned toward what had touched him. He felt a light thud and then something touching his trouser leg all the way down until it hit the floor. He quickly walked forward, his body shaking now.

Finally, his hands touched fabric, heavy fabric, but not like the ones upstairs. These must be the drapes. Rumble grabbed a handful of fabric in both hands and pulled them apart. They didn't crumble at his feet, but they hardly opened either. However, it was enough, light to see the room. It was just like the other room the one upstairs.

Slowly, his eyes moved over the room. The old four-poster bed still draped with a sheer once white canopy. The yellow chenille bedspread with a swirly white pattern neatly covered the made -up bed. Beside the bed were two square bedside tables, solid wood and maybe once expensive maybe even still expensive. Rumble thought, 'they are probably antiques' now'. The same lamps adorned the bedside tables although Rumble could clearly see they had bulbs inside the shades, they were not oil like the ones in the room above. On the wall was the same over-powering portrait of the stoic man that bore a striking resemblance to Edwards. Rumble again focused on the eyes in the dim light, they seemed to be alive and watching him. He shuddered.

Turning a little more, he realized there was a rug under his feet and, to Rumbles horror laying on the rug, was a partly decomposed skeleton. It was crumbled on the floor exactly where he had been standing. Rumble tried not to scream. Then he looked upwards and saw the old frayed rope. Rumble realized the skeleton had been hanging from the rope and only fallen when Rumble bumped into it.

Rumble stared, his eyes wide, his palms sweating as icy talons of fear crawled down his spine. He couldn't move. He stared at the person lying on the rug, half curled up. He could see she once had light colored hair, long and curly, some of it was still attached to her skull. Her face was touching the rug, so he was thankful he couldn't see it. What little of her clothing remained was a long ornate dress with frills on the sleeves and around the skirt, it was probably a light lilac but in the dim light it was hard to tell.

Rumble was terrified, but somehow he managed to move closer. He saw she was wearing tiny button up black polished boots on her feet. One of her hands, now mainly bone was lying to one side while the other was under her body. But Rumble stared at the one hand he could see.

He couldn't take his eyes from the hand he stared some more. It wasn't the hand he stared at so much as the ring that had once been on its finger. It now lay on the ground at the end of the bone that was maybe the ring finger.

The ring had a heavy silver band that was still shiny and blazing with life mounted in the ring was a large red stone. It shone up at him, even in the dim light. He took a step forward and a tiny tinkling sound filled the air, looking down he noticed he had kicked a small silver object; he bent down and picked it up.

It was a small old-fashioned silver baby's rattle. Rumble couldn't be sure in the dim light, but he thought the words written into the silver said 'Baby Sarah' perhaps they did say that and perhaps they did not. Rumble placed the rattle in his pocket and again gazed at the corpse. He could smell it now, the rotting flesh arid and decaying, a heavy cloying smell. It was all around him heavy in the air. Why hadn't he noticed it before?

Again, his eyes moved to the ring lying by the out stretched hand. He had seen that ring before, but where? Then he remembered it was the same ring that Edwards wore on the pinky finger of his left hand. But how can that be? Rumble felt like he was transfixed on the ring, he couldn't move his eyes, or maybe he didn't want to.

As if in a trance Rumble took a couple of small steps closer to the ring. It was just lying there on the wooden floorboards beside the rug and inches from the end of the boney finger.

Rumble bent down to pick it up. He had just retrieved it when the room blazed into life. The door slammed loudly back and forth, back and forth, again and again, as if a giant unseen hand was opening it then slamming it shut in fury. The lamps glowed brighter and brighter, then the whole room was alive with intense white light; Rumble had to shield his eyes.

The furniture vibrated, the drawers in the bedside cabinets and the matching chest-of-drawers flew open and then shut over and over again. The heavy life size portrait fell from the wall staying upright it landed on the floor with a loud thump. The old yellow chenille bedspread flew from the bed, missing Rumble by inches as it landed atop the heavy chest of drawers by the far wall. Rumble was horrified to see the yellowed sheets on the bed were heavy with dried blood, it was caked to the sheets and they appeared to be stuck to the mattress.

Rumble didn't know how he knew, but he knew it was dried blood, and it had been there for a long time. The light was blinding him. It was flashing now brighter and brighter. "Stop," Rumble screamed horrified. Then, he turned and saw the words on the wall behind where the portrait had previously hung. 'You like the dark, I kill the flame,' Rumble screamed again, he couldn't help it and still the activities in the room continued.

Louder and louder.

Brighter and brighter.

"Stop," Rumble screamed shielding his eyes as he saw the words on the wall grow brighter as if they had a power of their own, were they written in blood?

Rumble thought as the ink or blood began to run down the wall from the words. Rumble was only vaguely aware at first of the burning sensation in his hand, but now it was hurting so badly he was very aware that he was holding something hot.

He turned to head for the door, but it was slamming with such ferocity that he knew he would never make it through without getting chopped in half. His legs felt like lead, he could hardly move and his hand was on fire. Still shielding his eyes, he looked at his hand. The red stone in the ring blazed back at him brighter than ever, it seemed to pulsate with a life of its own. Then he heard a deep slow eerie voice, was it in his head or in the room, there was so much noise already and the light... He could definitely hear a voice, it was saying 'you like the dark, I kill the flame,' was it ,Leonard Cohen? Or was he going crazy? Then the burning in his hand grew in intensity until it made him drop the ring.

Instantly the room returned to normal. The bright light went out, and he was again in the dim old-fashioned room with the partly opened drapes. The lamps had also gone out and the portrait was back hanging on the wall with the severe man glaring down at him from within. The room returned to its old, dusty, unused state.

Looking down, Rumble saw the ring on the wooden floor by the corpse of the woman; it was just lying there, with the red stone blazing up at him. It had fallen exactly where it was before – he'd picked it up.

Rumble screamed, a deep guttural scream; it came from somewhere deep inside. Rumble wasn't aware he was the one screaming, it was as if it was someone else, and he was startled by the sound. He had to get out of the room. He willed his body to move, to move anywhere but here. Hoping his legs would hold him and avoiding the corpse on the rug, he hurried to the door; he pulled it wide and raced out slamming it shut behind him. He was moving so fast, he almost hit the banister and fell over to the floor below. But he didn't care anything would be better than being in that room.

He took the stairs two at a time to the third floor and kept on running up the next flight of stairs to the door of his attic. The usual stairs creaked in protest and squeaked loudly under his feet.

Rumble grabbed the familiar doorknob and turned, he wanted to be in the safety of his attic room so badly; he forgot it was locked. Frustrated and out of breath he slammed his shoulder into the door willing it to open, it didn't budge; it was locked tight.

Rumble fumbled in his pocket for the key, nothing, it wasn't there, had he dropped it somewhere? But he was wearing the wrong trousers, why? Then he remembered his key was in his sachet. He grabbed it from his shoulder almost tipping the contents out in his haste. The key, where was it? It wasn't there? "Please," Rumble said aloud as the tears ran down his cheeks, "please," he begged, "the key, where is the key?"

He sunk to the ground and curled up with his back hard against the door; he couldn't open. He was trembling all over, he was sweating profusely, and the tears had blurred his visions. He tried to uncurl himself, he remembered the first time he had curled up crying when he was just a small boy. His mother had found him like that, she told him how disgusting and pathetic he looked, and she'd kicked him hard in the ribs. He still remembered the searing pain. Again, he cried out, "the key, my key, where is the key? I need it." It was the little voice in his head, the one that had been silent for much too long which answered him. *'Remember where you used it last? That is where it will be...'*

Oh no, now Rumble did remember exactly where he had used his key last, 'no,' he said, 'please no...' He suddenly remembered it was still in the lock of the door on the second floor... He then curled up tightly and sobbed, he was gripped in the hand of sheer terror...

Chapter Thirteen

Rumble, curled up even tighter as his trembling continued. He couldn't go down there again, he couldn't… He sobbed gently now, his body curled inward on itself; his head buried in his knees, the tears wet on his cheeks. How long he remained there, he didn't know. He didn't care.

He was finding some kind of primitive comfort by the door. His door. The door to his room. That room was all he had. It was sometime later as the shadows began to descend on the house, that Rumble stirred, for him it was almost like awakening from a trance.

A heavy unworldly trance, which he hadn't known he was in. His body ached as he slowly uncurled his limbs and tried to stand. Once he was on his feet, he gripped the door handle firmly with both hands and tried to turn it. It was no use; it was locked tight. Just the way he liked it, had he been inside.

'You know what you must do?' The little voice commanded and Rumble replied, 'so you're back, now you chose to speak?' The voice ignored him and replied, *'you weren't thinking clearly, you were in your head, too far in your own head for even me to reach you'.* 'Do you blame me?' Rumble asked. *'Okay, you were scared'*, it replied, *'if you go snooping when you're not supposed to,*

what do you think you'll find?.. Yes,' it replied to its own questions, *'things you don't want to see and don't understand.'* Rumble thought for a moment, he wasn't ready to think about the room but the little voice was making him.

He wanted to curl up by the door again. Rumble didn't respond; the images in his head were too vivid, too fresh, he was probably in shock, he thought. The voice replied, *'what you saw wasn't normal, no one should ever have to see what you saw, so what are you going to do about it?'* 'Nothing,' Rumble replied, 'I'm going to do nothing, I saw nothing.' He almost yelled the last words, so wanting to believe them. He waited for the voice to argue but all it said was, *'go and get the key and lock yourself in your room, hurry now, this is not over'.* Rumble assumed the voice was referring to the conversation, but something about the way it spoke scared him, and he felt icy water trickle down his spine.

At first, Rumble's legs wouldn't move, they were heavy with fear. His body wouldn't respond either. Then he knew, it actually was responding, it was doing exactly what he really wanted it to, rather than what he was telling it to do.

He really didn't want to move, but he had to, a part of him knew he had to go down two flights of stairs then turn and walk along to the door at the end. His key would be in the lock.

*'So, **do it, do it, do it**,'* the little voice screamed in his

head when he didn't move, '*now is not the time to think and procrastinate.*' The voice sounded urgent, and Rumble snapped back to the present. Slowly, at first his body began to move back down the stairs from the attic to the third -floor landing and then down the next flight of stairs to the second floor.

His legs were feeling heavier with each step. He didn't want to walk forward, but he knew he must, he didn't want to go anywhere near the door. But he needed his key. He was now walking like a ghost toward the door at the end. He could just make out the key in the lock.

His legs grew so heavy, Rumble thought he was dragging two sacks of potatoes around, heavy sacks.

He was passing the third door and approaching the fourth. There was the key. Just in front of him. He moved toward it, hand outstretched. He grabbed the key. It was hot to his touch. Why? Was it merely his imagination? It burned his hand, and he thrust it into his trouser pocket as he prepared to turn and, hopefully, if his legs would allow, run back up to his attic room.

But there was smoke coming out from under the door; he could see it and smell it. He looked further down the hallway to the end, the part left where he had not yet ventured. Was it smoke or mist?

Yes, it was mist, he thought, just mist, but how did mist get inside a house? As he stared the mist grew thicker, much thicker. Rumble could still see the smoke coming from under the door, he watched it mingling with the mist.

It was all around him, encircling him.

'*Move,*' the voice commanded, '*run and don't look back*'. That's what Rumble tried to do; he made it to the stairs and turned to look back the way he had come. The mist was so thick now, and it was rapidly curling and writhing toward where he stood. Rumble stared. Was it Edwards he could see standing in the mist?

Was it Edwards with his baldhead and snow white hair? It had to be Edwards, he was reaching out to him through the mist his steely eyes locked on his eyes, his arms out stretched and the red stone in the ring, glittered brightly, even though there was hardly any light.

'*Move*', the voice commanded again, '*look forward, don't look back, run fast up the stairs.*' 'But the house is on fire and Edwards will burn, he needs my help.' '*No*', said the voice, '*there is no one there, move, now, **hurry***'. Rumble could clearly see Edwards his eyes locked on him, with his arms out stretched and his hands reaching toward him. When his mouth was visible through the mist, Rumble could just make out his lips moving frantically, they were opening and closing as if he was trying to say something.

Rumble was having trouble seeing anything now; the mist was all around him, he wasn't sure if it was mist or smoke, but he could still breath, so it must be mist. He looked again down the hallway hoping to glimpse Edwards but all he saw was a hazy mist, he couldn't see beyond it.

"Edwards," Rumble yelled, but his voice was damp from the wall of swirling groping mist, and there was no reply. '*Hurry now*', the voice commanded, '*feel your way up the stairs to the attic, hurry, hurry, move,* **do it, do it do it.**' It yelled in his head urgently. Only now Rumble knew he must obey, he could see nothing, and the mist seemed to swirl and move all around like it was damp, clingy, alive and trying to enter his body.

He felt his way up the familiar stairs to the next floor. Until finally, he was on the stairs, he knew the best, they were the narrow ones that lead up to his attic. He could see again, there was hardly any mist up there. Briefly, he recognized the sliver of yellow light coming through the crack between the back of the stair and the tread, but he ignored it and instead looked back down the stairs where he saw a single line of mist swirling up the stairway toward where he stood.

It moved in exactly the same place he had just been, and it was twirling and swirling fast in his direction.

It appeared to have fingers reaching for him, fingers of mist as if they were trying to grab him before he entered his room. Rumble watched in horror as it swirled and twisted toward his attic stairs. '*Don't look,*' the voice ordered, '*don't look back; focus on what you're doing.*' Rumble heard the words and knew the advice was good, but he couldn't help it, he had to look down the stairs as it rose up toward him.

He fumbled in his pocket for the large key. Placed it

in the lock, pulled the door hard toward him and turned the key. Rumble was relieved to hear the usual grinding noise just before it opened. Rumble fell inside, he had never been so glad to be in his attic room as this very moment. He slammed the door and locked it tightly behind him. He grabbed the chair and pushed it hard up under the door handle. Then he reached for a towel from the bathroom, rolled it up and wedged it into the crack at the bottom of the door, the same crack where someone had once pushed notes through.

Finally, he collapsed on his bed and waited. His eyes never left the rolled-up towel pushed into the crack. He began trembling again, the sweat poured from his forehead, and his palms felt slick with moisture. He watched. He waited. When would the mist arrive? It couldn't be far, it was just there, at the bottom of his attic stairs.

Chapter Fourteen

The next morning, Rumble rose as usual when his alarm told him it was time. He'd had a restless night, with little sleep. When he did sleep, the images that floated in his mind woke him instantly, and he would find himself trembling in a bed wet from his own sweat.

Today was Friday, and he knew he didn't need to do any sketching today, but he needed normalcy more than he needed life right now.

He also wanted to buy a flashlight, a strong reliable flashlight. He seldom made any purchases other than his lunch on a daily basis, but he was changing, in his mind, he felt different, some of the little things that once caused him anxiety no longer seemed important. He also thought he may visit a thrift shop and get some second hand clothes, if he tried them on and chose carefully they may just look like new ones. Anyway, to him they would be new. Rumble knew a few more items of clothing were definitely needed.

There was a time, not so long ago, when he would have procrastinated over the purchase of a flashlight until he'd managed to talk himself out of it; but not anymore.

Even though he would no longer be in the house, he knew this was something he needed. But first, he would write a brief letter to Edwards advising him that he was terminating their tenancy agreement, forthwith. He was thinking of posting it this morning, but the little voice strongly advised against it and suggested he mail it from the post box opposite his new lodgings, once he had safely arrived.

The other thing Rumble intended to do this morning was to take his smelly clothes, the ones he always wore, to the dry cleaners. It had been a long time since he had taken anything to the drycleaners if ever, he thought. None of his clothes were worthy of dry cleaning, but the thought of moving into his new room after Ms. Epping had taken such care to clean with clothes that smelt strongly of beer was not the way he intended start his tenancy.

So today, extreme and unusual measures were needed. While his clothes were at the cleaners, he would shop, have lunch or sketch. He knew the latter would take all his attention and keep his mind from thinking of anything else, and he relished the thought.

But first, he must get dressed and leave the room, walk down the stairs and out the back door.

He began trembling at the thought of leaving his room. What would he find? What was beyond his attic door? What waited for him down the stairs? He knew he had seen Edwards in the mist yesterday even though the voice told him, he hadn't. Therefore Edwards must have seen him, he reasoned. '*You saw no one and nothing,*' the voice instructed and Rumble repeated back out loud, 'I saw no one, and I saw nothing.'

Rumble tried to think of anything but leaving his room, but he couldn't find any more reasons why not. He knew he could still catch his usual bus if he left now. His sweaty palms made turning the doorknob difficult, but reluctantly, Rumble persisted, and he cautiously walked down the narrow stairs. Everything seemed as it usually was. *'Don't look behind,'* the voice told him. 'Why not?' Rumble asked, *'oh, don't be so difficult; you must look in front of you. Focus on the future I am always telling you that'*, the voice persisted, and Rumble knew it was trying to take his mind off his walk through the house.

By the time, he was walking down to the second floor Rumble was positively trembling, he was trying hard to quieting his trembling body, but he was unable to do so. The little voice scolded him for doing so several times and told him not to be a baby, but he couldn't seem to stop the trembling that rippled through him.

He tried not to look, he was trying to look straight ahead, and he wanted to keep his eyes focused on the next flight of stairs and his exit from the house. But he couldn't; he had to sneak a peek at the last door at the end of the landing. His eyes briefly flicked toward the door, he could have sworn, he saw it close, had it had been open just a crack; he really did think he saw it gently close. *'You are imagining things; you saw nothing'*, the voice instructed. *'Walk faster why are you walking so slowly? And no, don't look back'*. The voice sounded annoyed. Rumble tried to obey, every part of him wanted to look back at the door, he knew what he had seen. '*No, you saw nothing, because there is nothing to see. Everything is the same as it always is.*' the voice answered his thoughts. '*Walk faster*,' it said until he obeyed.

Once Rumble was outside, he walked briskly toward the bus stop. He felt rather than saw someone watching him, watching him from the upstairs window of the house.

He had felt this before, but the voice told him otherwise. He arrived just seconds before the bus drew to a stop directly at the curb beside him, on time as always. Then as he sat in the rear of the bus it moved off. The voice surprised him by saying, '*the house lives in fear, it wants you to feel its fear, don't give in.*' Rumble reminded the voice that he was moving out tomorrow, away from the house and its fear that he didn't want and didn't need. '*Maybe you are, maybe you're not.*' 'What do you mean?' Rumble asked and he waited for a response. He thought the voice had forgotten they were moving, but it didn't respond, it was silent.

Rumble soon deposited his smelly clothes at the drycleaners on the corner; the old shop looked like they may charge less than some of the fancier looking ones in town. The short grey-haired man with the glasses perched on the end of his nose, promised to have his clothes ready for him after lunch. Rumble reluctantly paid him and realized he may have been able to purchase new clothes from a thrift shop for the same price as he had just paid this little man.

Even though the bus passed by the drycleaners every morning, Rumble had never got off at this stop before. He walked several paces to a pathway leading to a small park hidden nicely behind several small shops. It was leafy and green, and the grass was well-tended. Rumble sat on the park bench and surveyed his new surroundings. In minutes, he had his sketchpad out and was busily sketching several of the quaint cottages that surrounded the park. They stood as if time had passed them by, with neatly tended cottage gardens, bursting with bloom, as each plant jostled for a place to grow taller than its neighbor, toward the sun.

The tiny garden pathways narrowed as the many plants intruded; each one chaotic with growth and a beauty of its own. What a brilliant feast for the eyes with their unique happy jumble of color and greenery.

It was lunchtime by the time Rumble looked up from his work; he had sketched feverishly, loving the new sights and sounds as never before. It was unlike him to wonder outside his daily routine, and he was amazed that he was now, not only doing so, but also enjoying it. He looked closely at his work, 'not bad', he thought, 'not bad at all.

Then he looked again closer this time at the last sketch, the one he had just finished drawing, he'd drawn a figure in the upstairs window of the last cottage in front of him. Yes, there was no mistake, again he looked and saw a tiny figure drawn there, standing inside the small open window directly under the thatch. He couldn't remember drawing that figure, he didn't draw people.

Had he really done that? He looked up at the last cottage and noticed how there was indeed a figure in the attic window. It was just standing there; perhaps it was staring at him?

What a silly thought, Rumble decided as he carefully put his four sketching pencils in their cases and placed them in his sachet. Then he closed his sketchpad and also put that into his sachet. As he got up to leave, he looked briefly at the cottage window, but the figure was gone.

Rumble walked toward the few shops he had seen earlier. He followed his nose and soon found a small bakery. He could tell they were baking and that the food must be good by the number of people milling around in and outside the shop. There were several wrought iron tables on the pavement close to the window of the shop, each table accompanied by two white wrought iron chairs. Only one table was occupied, so Rumble decided to purchase his lunch and return here to the table and enjoy it.

As he listened to the chatter of the shoppers waiting in the shop, he learned that this little bakery made an excellent meat pie, however, the chef could never keep up with the demand. Apparently, they were worth waiting for and a batch of fresh chicken and lamb pies were due out of the oven any moment.

Rumble enjoyed his lunch and decided he would one

day visit this little bakery again.

He strolled back to the drycleaners, but the little man with the glasses on the end of his nose seemed to have disappeared, and a younger lady was smiling apprehensively at him from behind the counter.

He saw his clothes fresh and clean laying across the counter and wondered just how she knew he would be back so promptly after lunch.

"Are you Mr. Rumble?" she enquired looking directly him. She was an average looking woman and could have been pretty without the intense frown line across her forehead and heavy wrinkles around her mouth. She was around the same age as the old man but obviously had taken better care of herself.

"Yes, I am," replied Rumble slightly perplexed, until he realized he had left his name with the dry cleaner earlier, "I'm Pauline Benson, the shop belongs to my brother, Charles Benson."

"Yes," replied Rumble, not sure why he would need to know her name.

"I know this may sound strange, Mr. Rumble, but I see you every morning go by on the bus and this morning when I saw your address I understood who you are," she paused, and Rumble smiled, 'she must be interested in being an artist', Rumble thought, 'that is all.'

"Well, Mr. Rumble, my brother couldn't bear to see you again after knowing where you live. Just the sight of your address made our blood ran cold, it literally did. So, you actually live in that house?" She paused again until Rumble gave her a slight nod in reply. He could see she was uncomfortable or was she just plain scared. Rumble had never been able to read people.

He waited for her to continue.

She changed feet and fidgeted with the pen on the counter, flipping it over and over nervously. She made the end click each time, she did so. Rumble waited for her to continue, he was beginning to feel uncomfortable also; he continued waiting, thinking it would be rude to do otherwise; finally, she spoke again, "Well, Mr. Rumble, I don't know how to say this, but our mother was one of the ladies he kidnapped and took to the house, she had my little sister, Sarah, with her, they both became his victims. She was only a..." Just then the bell over the door rang and a portly gentleman wearing a black suit and bowler hat entered, he had an armful of shirts and several jackets piled high in front of him.

Rumble seized the moment, he gathered up his cleaned clothes, and quickly exited the shop. He kept walking briskly even though he could hear Pauline Benson desperately calling after him.

'Calm down, Rumble', the voice in his head instructed. *'Don't you want to learn more from the woman?'* 'No,' Rumble replied, 'I just want to get away.' *'But, Rumble, the lady in the drycleaners obviously knows something about the house that you don't',* the voice persisted. 'I worked that out myself,' Rumble replied

sarcastically, 'that's why I wanted to get away from her.'
'Aren't you curious?' 'No,' replied Rumble, 'I am not.'
'But don't you want to learn more,' the voice persisted.
'No,' Rumble said, 'she was about to tell me bad things
and don't you think I already know bad things happened
there?' *'Okay',* replied the voice, you win this time.

He turned quickly down the first side street he saw;
now he knew she could not see him from the shop. Soon
Rumble stopped where he was and looked around. There
were not many people on the street, so Rumble knew he
could pause and take several deep breaths. 'I must sit
somewhere less conspicuous on the bus from now on,' he
thought and the voice replied, *'if you don't live there
anymore you won't be using that bus anyway.'* 'Oh, yes,
you're right,' Rumble replied tapping the notice of
termination letter in his pocket.

Rumble stopped, at the first bus stop, he found and sat
waiting for the bus, he knew his bus came through here
every twenty minutes at this time of day.

He was going back to the house, the purchase of a
flashlight and clothes no longer in his head. Instead, he
would pack, even though he knew he could easily pack up
his few possessions in the morning. Thinking over Pauline
Benson's words in his head, he shivered and suddenly
realized he was tired, very, very tired. He just wanted to
lie down and rest. *'You're not contemplating going into
another room, are you?'* The voice asked and quickly
Rumble said, 'No, I wasn't even thinking that.' *'Good,*

because you must leave that house and soon', the voice continued. 'I know,' said Rumble. His shoulders sagging, but he knew it wasn't from the weight of his sachet or his dry cleaning, it was from the enormity of what he had seen and was trying not to think about.

When finally, the bus arrived, Rumble was pleased to see it was almost empty, he took a seat in the third row from the front, it was out of character, he knew, but there was only four other people on the bus so he could take any seat. He felt relieved; he was able to change his routine, and somehow it felt safer.

It was all because he now knew Pauline Benson had been watching him pass by on the bus every morning; he shivered at the thought. Rumble was happiest when he was invisible and in order to remain invisible, no one must notice him, no one.

The motion of bus gave Rumble some small feeling of security, he sat very still and watched the scenery pass by. In no time, he was walking the familiar deserted street. The youths were down the end, revving up an old car, theire cursing and laughter floated on the air. Rumble stayed close to the side of the street, he didn't need them to notice him, and he was thankful once he entered the house that they had not.

The house was quiet, very quiet, too quiet, considering all the secrets it was guarding. Rumble tried to keep his eyes to the floor as he climbed the stairs, he felt so wary; he was hardly able to move up the stairs at all.

Once in his room, he carefully hung his cleaned clothes on the hook behind the door, removed his shoes and lay down on the bed. This was something he seldom did in the middle of the afternoon. In moments, he was asleep.

It was a deep sleep with no nightmares; it was a sleep of sheer exhaustion. For Rumble, it was a necessary sleep. So deeply was he sleeping that the slamming of a door somewhere in the house didn't disturb him, nor was he disturbed by the sound of footsteps softly walking up the stairs, his stairs. He didn't see the doorknob turn nor did he see who placed the single sheet of expensive writing paper under his door, it was folded neatly in half, just once.

Chapter Fifteen

Rumble slept soundly all night. He barely moved other than to pull the bedspread around him. He woke with the alarm the next morning as a weak yellow sun crept toward his window. He felt refreshed but disgusted that he had slept all afternoon and night in his clothes.

His mother's voice came back to him, telling him how he was making more work for her and couldn't he be more considerate than sleeping in his clothes and wrinkling them. Then she would have said he was just like all the other men she had known, irresponsible and disgusting. Rumble shuddered at the thought of her hard, uncaring voice and harsh words.

He was returning from the shower when he noticed the folded piece of paper under his door. No, Rumble said to himself, I see nothing. He was relieved the voice was staying silent. Even though he glanced at the paper a hundred times; he never picked it up, but instead he worked around it, opening drawers and packing his few meagre possessions carefully in his bag. Finally, he folded his bed sheets, blanket, pillow and towels and because they were unwashed, he placed them in a black garbage bag, it was the same one he'd used when he arrived here. He almost forgot his electric kettle and toaster but remembered them at the last minute.

It was still only ten thirty in the morning, and Rumble sat on the end of his bed staring at the folded sheet of paper that someone had slid under his door. This was not a good place to sit, he told himself and instead turned to face the tiny window. He had inched it open during his time here, and it was now open almost ten inches. Rumble had been most pleased with his effort and also enjoyed the fresh air in his room when he arrived home in the evening. He knew it was now time to close the window, and he got to his feet to do so.

It was harder to shut than he would have thought; he pulled on it hard. It closed slowly, almost as slowly as it had opened.

He sat looking through the small grimy window at the treetops and sky. He didn't want to sit here in the house waiting for the minutes on the clock to tick past. His eye kept looking sideways at the sheet of paper, it was just lying there on the floor waiting for him to read it, but he wasn't going to.

'No', he told himself, I see nothing. Then he remembered what Cootes had said about Ms. Epping working on his room; that was several days ago so it must be ready by now.

It was almost eleven o'clock when Rumble was startled by the sound of a loud thump coming from somewhere inside the house. He felt the hairs on the back of his neck rise in terror.

Suddenly, that was all he needed to get him moving. He grabbed his old leather sachet and threw it over his shoulder, and then, with his other hand, he took the other two large bags. Without looking back at his room, he exited the door, locking it behind him. He intended placing the key in the envelope with his letter of termination, before he mailed it to Edwards.

He felt refreshed after his long sleep, so even with the extra weight of his bags, he moved quickly and nimbly down the stairs. Try as he may his eyes wondered once he arrived on the landing on the second floor. He tried not to look at the last door at the end, he really did. But his eyes seemed to move of their own accord until they were looking down the hallway, past the first door, the second door, and then the third door, but they stopped abruptly once they focused on the fourth door.

'No,' Rumble said to himself, 'no,' he couldn't believe his eyes; it can't be, he can't be seeing this? But there was no mistaking what he saw. There was mist, swirling around down the end of the corridor and what looked like dark blue smoke coming from under the door.

Rumble was pretty sure he could smell the smoke, it was mixing with the mist and moving fast toward where he stood, transfixed at the top of the stairs leading to the first floor.

'Move', the voice said startling Rumble out of his trance. 'Move now', it said louder. Rumble couldn't take his eyes from the door and the moving mist, it was darker than the last time, and Rumble knew it was because the smoke had mixed in with it. *'Move'*, the voice said again, and this time Rumble seemed to hear. He was still holding his bags as the mist swirled its way along the landing; it was halfway toward him now. *'Move; go now and fast'*, the voice commanded urgently and Rumble obeyed. His feet moved this time and they kept on moving. Once he was walking past the entranceway he couldn't help but look up. *'keep moving'* the voice said, *'don't look back, go...'* But Rumble had to look up, and he was amazed to see the mist drifting over the banister and down to where he stood, why had it changed course, there was no breeze in the house. Was it after him?

It only took Rumble a few moments to begin to run for the back door, and this time he didn't look back. The smell of smoke filled the house, and Rumble was surprised to find the backdoor doorknob was warm to his touch. How could that be? There was no fire?

Once outside, he locked the door behind him and then retrieved the termination letter he had written Edwards and placed the large key inside the folded letter. Then he sealed the envelope and put it back into his top pocket, so he could mail it later.

Turning away from the door, he breathed deeply, then shivered slightly at the crisp autumn air. Grabbing his bags, he walked briskly toward the bus stop. Being Saturday, there were less buses than usual so he needed to wait. He kept to the trees that over hung the pavement lest

164

the youths should spot him.

They were in the same place as yesterday; only today, they were smashing beer bottles against someone's car that was parked on the wrong side of the road.

Once Rumble was seated on the bus, he let out a sigh from deep inside, he felt a huge relief to have exited the house for the last time. He almost smiled; he never needed to think of the house or speak of the house ever again. Instead, he would endure the haughty Ms. Oh, what was her name? The one that looked like a bird with the dark hair severely pulled back off her face, the one that wasn't so friendly. Oh, yes, wasn't it... Ms. Simons? Rumble asked himself, and to his surprise the voice answered, '*probably*'. 'I wasn't asking you, I was having a conversation with myself', Rumble responded. '*So that would be me, because, I am you*', the voice shot back sounding somewhat offended.

Rumble didn't want to hear the voice, it was ruining the moment he was having, a good moment, and he had them so seldom.

Then he thought of Ms. Primrose Pringle, and he felt his face burn, he knew he was blushing. The nice Ms. Epping, he thought, would be a wonderful landlady and, of course, the one that slapped him on the back all the time, Major... oh, what was his name? Major Watch, was it? No, that didn't sound quite right. Again, the little voice responded, '*his name is Major Winston Bloomington-Tyme*', it said proudly. 'How did you know that?' Rumble asked the voice in his head, '*well he made quite an impression on you, didn't he? And I didn't say a good impression I just said an impression, so I remembered his name*'. 'Right,' was all Rumble said as the bus came to a stop and he grabbed his bags and entered. He would be taking another bus the short distance to Rosemary Lane, it arrived seconds after the last bus left the curb. There were more people on this bus, different people, of a better class, perhaps.

They looked discreetly at his old worn bags especially the garbage bags. Rumble was pleased, he was at least wearing his freshly cleaned clothes. He knew they were pressed neatly even if they were slightly worn and not fancy.

Rumble could imagine the heavy purple door of the cottage, and again he smiled. However, as the bus drew nearer, Rumble noticed many police cars, fire engines and emergency vehicles. Cars were parked haphazardly in the street leading to Rosemary Lane. What is happening? Rumble asked himself as he stepped off the bus, but the moment he entered Rosemary Lane, he stared straight ahead, and he knew.

It was the beautiful cottage; the fireman had smashed the window on the upper floor and some of the thatch was being sprayed down with heavy-duty water hoses.

Hazy smoke surrounded the cottage and people were everywhere, staring. The wail of a distance ambulance over powered the other noises. Rumble walked down

Rosemary Lane until he was closer to the cottage, and the crowd surrounding it. The wailing ambulance sounded closer now, the harsh noise over powered the dim chatter of voices.

Rumble moved toward the cottage as if in a trance, 'oh, no,' he thought, 'oh no, the cottage has caught fire'. As he stood there with a bag in each hand, someone approached him, he saw out the corner of his eye, someone was moving toward him, fast. He turned, it was Primrose, she still wore her nightie, and it was smeared with soot, as were her hands and face. Her curly red hair seemed to have been burnt in places, and she was trying to wipe her glasses with her blackened hands. She was crying and her tears made a clean track down her blackened face.

"Oh, Mr. Rumble," she sobbed. Instinctively, Rumble dropped his bags as she wrapped her arms around him and sobbed hard into his shoulder. *'Well, your clothes are ruined now'*, the little voice said. 'Oh, shut up,' Rumble replied. He didn't quite know what to do with Primrose; he could feel her body pressed hard against his.

Soft and warm her chest heaving, her heart pounding and her full breasts bursting to break free of her nightie. Rumble was blushing deeply, never before had he been in such a situation as this. But he didn't really mind, he just didn't know what to do and he felt so uncomfortable. *'Put your arms around her and comfort her,'* the voice instructed. It was what he instinctively wanted to do and now the voice had validated his inner most thoughts.

So, he did, he wrapped his arms around her and held her close, he felt her wet tears and he smelt her smoky clothes. It began to drizzle and the wind must have changed as they were soon engulfed in the remains of the smoke from the fire. Primrose stayed in his arms for several minutes until through the crowd a bedraggled Ms. Epping appeared, "Oh, Mr. Rumble, oh, dear me, I'm so very sorry. This is just awful, why I've told him a hundred times, if I've told him once." Rumble had no idea what she was talking about as Primrose pulled slightly away from him and hugged Ms. Epping close, she too began to cry.

The wailing ambulance was now upon them, the noise of its sirens deafening. Then the sound stopped. Doors slammed and several ambulance officers raced passed him and into the house. "Oh, dear, oh, dear me," Ms. Epping said as Primrose again started sobbing.

Rumble stood bewildered, he wanted to know what had happened, but he knew now was not the time to ask. Moments later, he watched the ambulance officers appeared from inside the smoky cottage, they were pushing a stretcher and whatever was on it was zipped up tightly inside a large gray bag. Ms. Epping and Primrose raced toward it and Ms. Epping called, "No, no."

"Madam, please, I'm sorry, there was too much smoke, there was nothing we could do, we tried to revive him," one of the officers said as the other inquired.

"Are you his wife?" and Ms. Epping shook her head and turned again to Primrose.

Together they sobbed in each other's arms. Ms. Epping wore a once fluffy yellow dressing gown that was now covered in soot, like she was. The back doors of the ambulance closed, and it slowly moved away, only this time there was no siren wailing. Rumble stood and stared at them both, he knew he should say or do something, but he had no idea what, so he stood where he was and waited.

It must have been those hard, uncaring eyes or the birdlike features that told Rumble Ms. Simons was approaching. Unlike the others, she was fully dressed in a neat brown business suite, she was spotless with hardly a hair out of place.

"Well, I shall be going in just as soon as I am allowed to retrieve my things, you can take this as my tenancy termination. I shall, of course, sue you if there is any damage to any of my belongings..." She never got to finished. Rumble was amazed at the hardness in her voice especially under the circumstances.

It was a fireman standing close by who answered Ms. Simons, "You may not go inside the cottage until such time as it's deemed safe. I doubt there will be much damage to your things, the fire was confined to the upstairs bedroom of the gentleman who is now deceased, ma'am." The fireman said looking directly at Ms. Simons.

Both Primrose and Ms. Epping cried again at his words, but Ms. Simons remained completely composed, "I had one of the rooms at the front, one of the smaller rooms," she paused to shoot a pointed glare at Ms. Epping.

She was about to continue when the same fireman replied, "Well, you shouldn't have much damage then, should you."

"I demand to be let back into the house this minute," Ms. Simons said glaring at the man.

"Madam, you can demand all you like, but until the investigation has been completed, and the fire chief gives the word, this property is deemed a crime scene. No one is allowed inside until it is safe to enter. Should you try and enter before that time, you shall be forcible restrained as necessary."

"Forcibly restrained, indeed? And what do you mean by crime scene, there's been no crime."

"May I remind you, madam, an elderly gentleman lost his life in that fire, until we find out the reason for his loss of life the cottage remains off limits to everyone." Rumble thought she would let it go. Rumble was shocked when he finally realized it was the Major in the body bag.

"There is no crime here, I can tell you why he died. He was smoking in his room like he always does. The only person he has to blame is himself," she said finally moving away, and then abruptly she stopped and turned.

"I shall be staying in a hotel, I shall send you the bill Ms. Epping, and I shall be in touch, probably though my solicitor. This has caused me a great deal of inconvenience."

And she disappeared into the crowd. Primrose and Ms. Epping were still holding each other as the fireman asked, "Does the gentleman have any next of kin?"

"Yes, he has two sons living in London. I shall contact them."

"Thank you, ma'am. I'm sorry for your loss and also your beautiful cottage, but I think you shall find there is not much damage other than the bedroom where the fire began, whoever called the fire department, did so quickly enough to prevent further damage to the rest of the house," he touched his helmet and moved away to roll up the hoses.

"Oh, Primrose, thank you for calling the fire department, so promptly."

"Well, I did call them, but when they answered they said a man had already called, and they were nearly there so to evacuate everyone from the house and wait on the street, that was when I yelled to you all. But I couldn't get the Major's bedroom door open. I tried to get in there, but the door handle was so hot. I tried to save him, I really did, but it wouldn't open," her eyes were huge as she looked from Rumble to Ms. Epping and back again. Then she fell into Rumble's arms again, and this time his arms wrapped around her immediately.

"Oh, Mr. Rumble, I am so terribly sorry, really I am," Primrose and Ms. Epping said in unison and by the look on their face, Rumble knew they meant it. He was truly touched by their concern especially at a time like this. Rumble knew they had both lost a great deal.

"Where will you go, Mr. Rumble?" Primrose asked

the whites of eyes huge and visible in her blackened face.

"I shall be all right, Primrose, but where will you go?"

"I don't know, can I stay with you?" she asked impulsively. Rumble flinched at her words, that wouldn't be at all possible thinking for the first time of the horrid house he must return to. He tapped his pocket to reassure himself the termination letter, and the key were still there and they were.

Primrose was staring up at him, but it was Ms. Epping who replied, "Primrose, we shall have to stay in a hotel, or I have friends who have a rather cozy bed and breakfast not far from here, I know they will help. I do hope you have somewhere to go Mr. Rumble? If not, maybe we can sort something out. I am truly very sorry."

"Oh, please, don't worry about me, Ms. Epping, It is I who am sorry for you and your beautiful cottage." At his words Ms. Epping turned toward the cottage which was still smoldering through the thatch.

A single tear rolled down her sooty cheek, very softly she said, "Rosemary Cottage is my life. I have lived here, and have loved living here since I was a child. And now the Major has died here." Her words were only a whisper but Primrose and Rumble heard. Rumble liked Ms. Epping, and he felt her sorrow, but as usual he didn't know what he should say to make her feel better.

They were all startled when the Fire Chief asked, "Ma'am, is there anything I can get you from inside? I see you are still in your nightie, I cannot go upstairs, but is

172

there anything you need from the first floor?"

Ms. Epping looked down at herself at his words and slowly seemed to realize that she was indeed still in her nightwear. Rumble could tell she was in shock, her mind was moving very slowly, he could almost feel her thinking through the fire chief's question.

"Yes, I would like my handbag, it has my mobile and car keys in it, all my clothes are upstairs, but you can find my handbag on top of the desk in my office at the rear of the first floor. Also, my laptop if you don't mind."

"My pleasure, I'll be right back, Syd hold the water," he called as he moved toward the front door.

Primrose started sobbing again, as she whispered, "My handbag is in my bedroom, so I guess I have nothing. What am I going to do?" Rumble would happily have taken her home with him except...

"Primrose, you'll come with me, we shall go to my friends place they own a delightful B & B. I know we can stay as long as we need to. We will need to clean up and go shopping, and I'm sure in a few days we can at least get back into the cottage and go to your bedroom. It will be all right, I promise," Ms. Epping reassured her as she placed her arms around her. Primrose, no longer wore her glasses, and she was looking hard at Rumble with her pretty green eyes and long dark lashes. Her tears made them sparkle like diamonds. Rumble realized she must have lost her glasses somewhere.

The crowd had almost dispersed, many of the crowd

spoke to Ms. Epping and offered their help or anything else she needed.

Rumble was surprised, she accepted none of it. 'Why not', he thought, 'she really needs all the help she can get'.

Ms. Epping was soon on the phone to her friends. Once she had spoken to the fire-chief and made sure he would secure the cottage, she gave Rumble a quick hug and glided Primrose to her car. Primrose had hardly taken her eyes off Rumble, and he stood where he was and watched her go. His heart was breaking for them, he couldn't believe the tragedy he had just witness. *'Life is fragile'*, said the voice softly, *'it can be taken from you in a moment'*. Rumble didn't feel like talking to the voice. He was watching Ms. Epping and Primrose slowly drive down Rosemary Lane and then turn left and disappear.

Apart from several firemen, busily working around the cottage and an older couple standing to one side and talking in hushed tones, Rumble was alone.

'Well, Rumble', the voice began, *'you know what this means?'* 'No,' replied Rumble, 'I don't.' *'Oh, yes, you do, Rumble, you know exactly what this means'*... 'What are you talking about?' Rumble asked, knowing the voice was always one step ahead of him? *'You,'* the voice began, *'you are what I'm talking about'*. When Rumble didn't respond the voice continued, *'you, who doesn't have a home to go to'?*

Suddenly, Rumble knew exactly what the voice was saying, and he shivered then felt his body break out in a sweat. 'No,' Rumble replied, 'no, surely, I don't have to...' he couldn't finish his sentence, just the thought almost choked him.

"No," Rumble said aloud, not feeling the drizzle turn to rain. He looked up to the heaven and said even louder, "NO."

"Everything all right, sir?" One of the firemen called from across the garden.

"Yes, thank you."

"The rain is a blessing, sir, damps down the thatch, always the problem of secondary flare ups with a thatch roof."

"Yes," replied Rumble feeling foolish. He stood where he was as the cold rain began to fall harder, his clothes were almost soaked through before he saw another younger fireman looking at him strangely, so he retrieved his raincoat from his sachet.

'I don't want to go back there, I can't'. Rumble said in his head. *'Well,'* said the voice *'you could let some moths out of your pockets and stay in hotel or a B&B perhaps?'* 'Much too expensive, why are you suggesting things like that?' *'Things like what, it must be better than the alternative. After all you have been saving for a rainy day your entire life,'* The voice had a point, but Rumble knew he couldn't afford it? 'How long would I be without a home if I stayed in a hotel, all my savings will be used up and what if there is another rainy day?' He replied, *'well, maybe this is your rainy day and maybe it will be your only rainy day. What about the B&B Ms. Epping spoke about? Perhaps you could consider that.'* again the voice had a point, 'maybe this is my rainy day, it was certainly wet enough', he thought with a small smile at his poor and unusual joke. *'Rumble don't try humor, it's just not who you are',* the voice said. 'No,' Rumble replied, 'it's not, neither is a hotel.' *'You're not exactly poor, Rumble, have you seen all those zeros at the end of your bank account. Go on live a little,'* the voice teased and Rumble reminded it again, 'it's not whom I am.'

'Okay, then, you know what the alternative is, Rumble, let's go, let's go back to the place that terrorizes you each time you're there. The house is changing you, Rumble, and not in a good way'. 'No, it's not', Rumble replied; 'I have seen nothing'. *'Okay, that again',* the voice said, 'it's the truth, I have seen nothing, all I do is rent the attic from Edwards, nothing more.' *'Whatever you want to believe,'* the voice said, and Rumble replied instantly, 'oh, do shut up.'

Rumble knew he needed to turn and go back the way he had come, but his legs were heavy, and it was a place he didn't want to go. He didn't want to be there or ever see that house again. Must he go? But his legs wouldn't move, like him, they were fearful. Fear was beginning to creep and ooze into Rumble's soul as he turned to go back the way he had just come. His bags felt like lead and his legs could barely move.

Rumble reluctantly headed back to his attic.

Chapter Sixteen

Rumble moved through the rain like a man in a trance. His body was switched to automatic; it knew the way even if every fiber in him didn't want to go in that direction. Rumble hoped the rain in his face and eyes would wash away the images. Those images, that were in his head now going around and around. Haunting him, chasing him.

The look in Primrose's eyes, he could feel her in his arms, her body trembling, her spirit broken.

He had seen and felt her heavy despair, her guilt at not being able to save the Major, her terror and loss. He knew she was terrified of uncertainty, and he understood, her future seemed to her, most uncertain.

How Rumble would have loved to take her home, and Ms. Epping too. *'You're the one who's always waiting for a rainy day, you could own your own cottage and then you would have been able to take them home. But no, you just keep on saving, what are you waiting for? You're forty-nine years old.'* The voice admonished. Rumble reluctantly admitted the voice, once again, was right... but Rumble said, 'if I had my own cottage, I wouldn't have needed to rent a room, and I would never have met them!' *'Okay'*, said the voice, *'so we're both right, though this should make you think a little, but no, you're not really on the same page as me.'*

Rumble turned the corner of the street and looked back to see the smoldering remains of the fire, it was probably only steam now escaping from the thatch, it was raining too much for it to be anything else.

He heard the sound of his mobile phone notifying him of a text message, he heard the beeping sound but didn't really acknowledge it in his mind; his thoughts were on other things. Now, he had changed direction, and the breeze had also changed, so Rumble became aware for the first time of how he smelt, strongly of smoke, very strongly. He was wearing the same clothes that he had just got professionally cleaned only now they smelled worse than ever.

His mind remembered the old house and the smoke inside, the swirling smoky mist, curling and twisting toward him as he went down the stairs. *'Why hadn't that house burnt down and not Ms. Epping's, life is so unfair'* the voice commented, 'life is seldom fair,' replied Rumble. *'Maybe the smoke in the house was a warning?'* the voice said. 'Whatever do mean?' Rumble asked. *'Well,'* replied the voice speaking slowly, *'maybe it was warning you about the fire today at Rosemary Cottage; perhaps it was an omen, a warning of some kind.'* 'Oh, do shut up,' Rumble said 'and stay out of my head and my thoughts.' Rumble didn't want to hear the voice, it was often too accurate, and it made him think of too many things he didn't want to think about.

'How can I get out of your thoughts and your mind?' The voice replied quickly, *'as I've told you before, I am you'.* Rumble didn't reply, the voice was too logical and it didn't give him nearly enough time to think.

Once Rumble walked onto the bus, he noticed immediately how the other commuters subtly moved away from him. Did he really smell that bad? The short ride was soon over and grabbing his bags he walked off the first bus and waited for the second bus. His nerves were on edge, he was getting closer to the house, the evil place; the place he had tried to call home. He knew the place was full of evil, only now, he was beginning to think the evil was after him. He waited for the voice to answer, but it did not.

Once on the second bus, he saw several other passengers twitch their noses in his direction but unlike the first bus no one tried to move away. Although, Rumble realized you couldn't move far on a bus; Rumble found a seat at the back with enough room to place his bags beside him.

He watched out the window as the scenery became more familiar. His mounting anxiety made his stomach churn, over and over, and, all too soon, the bus arrived at his stop.

Each step he took, bought him closer to familiar surroundings and the house. His legs became heavy, his bags too seemed to weigh more than what they should. And then there it was, looming old and dilapidated directly in front of him. Crumbling with age, unkempt, dirty and unloved with an air of vacancy, forgotten and unwanted – had the house aged while he was away? Could a house age in his absence? Or had he not ever really looked at it before?

Rumble fumbled in his pocket for his key. The key that was not easy to lose, it was so large, old and rusty. It always left a rusty stain in his pocket. But it was not there. He felt the beginning of anxiety well up inside at the thought of losing the old key and having nowhere to live. Then he remembered the envelope in his top pocket. He opened it and retrieved the key. '*You don't have to do this*', the voice said, '*you don't have to return here, there are plenty of options for you*'. Rumble heard the voice but didn't reply; instead he put his bags on the ground beside the back door, before pulling the door hard toward him and inserting the key. It seemed harder to turn than normal but finally the door opened onto the gloomy house, how filthy and old everything was.

Tiny strips of light filtered through from other rooms leaving small patches of yellowish white, which illuminated further the grimy floor. Rumble was now in the entranceway looking at the stairs, leading to his attic. He stared upward as his eyes grew accustomed to the lack of light in the house.

Briefly, he thought of finding a light switch and turning it on, but he had never done this before so why should he do it now? He moved toward the stairway and as he was looking upwards, he felt the unease in his stomach, increase. A movement to his left caught his eye, it was just a change in the light really, but it was something. Rumble stayed where he was and froze, who or what had changed the light.

Rumble felt the temperature in the house drop as he searched the first balcony above him for movement.

Slowly, his eyes became focused in the gloom, he noticed, although he wasn't sure, that several of the doors were open. Not wide open, but they were open about 10-12 inches. This was strange and very odd.

Was his mind playing tricks on him? Were his eyes deceiving him? He blinked, wiped his eyes and looked again; yes, they were still open, why? Was someone there? Had someone been inside the rooms in his absence? Was Edwards here? Yes, that was it, Edwards was here in the house, possibly looking for him,

"Edwards," Rumble yelled although his voice seemed to disappear into his throat. He called again louder this time, "Edwards, are you there?" He stood looking upward, waiting, listening, watching, nothing. No sound, no movement, should he call again, no, there was no one there, he couldn't feel any kind of presence; he felt he was on his own, again. Anyway, he didn't want Edwards to catch him with his bags, how could he explain?

Slowly, he began walking up the first flight of stairs; nearing the first landing, he clearly saw three of the four doors were now slightly open. As he looked, the noise of them slamming shut made Rumble physically jump. The doors shut with super-human force, it shook the very foundations of the house.

Rumble began to tremble; he stood as still as a statue on the landing of the first floor. He stared at the doors, wondering, waiting, watching, listening, terrified. 'What just happened?' He asked himself. Immediately the voice replied, *'you're scared again, that's what just happened and you're not even close to entering the attic and already the house has you scared to death, need you ask what just happened?'* Was the voice, his friend? Wasn't it supposed to be on his side, always in all things? He hated the sound of it in his head, but right now it was all he had and as usual it was right.

Part of him wanted to drop his bags and run toward the doors to see if they would open. However, a larger part of him wanted to run up the next flight of stairs slam and lock his door and hide in his tiny attic room. But what had made the doors slam, altogether, so dramatically. *'Maybe, it's Edwards way of creating effect and trying to frighten you?'* The voice said. Rumble thought about that for a moment, it was an angle he hadn't explored, and he was annoyed with himself for not exploring the possibility; is someone playing mind games with him.

Finally, he asked the voice, 'do you really believe that?' *'Do you'?* It replied, and Rumble said, 'no.' After a moment, the voice answered, *'no neither do I. There is much more to it than that.'* Rumble trembled from head to foot at the words. Then he cautiously asked, 'do you mean a ghost?' *'No, of course, not, it's much worse, even worse than a haunting.'*

Rumble didn't reply, he shuddered again and bolted for the next set of stairs leading to the second floor. His bags felt heavier than ever and his legs increased in weight with each step he took. 'I just need to get to the attic; I must keep moving' he thought. *'Don't even think about looking at the doors',* the voice instructed harshly. 'Why would I?' Rumble replied, he was feeling feed up with the voice. He hadn't been thinking of looking at the doors, until the voice had said that, but now he was.

'Why were they open? Were they asking him to enter? Was someone already in there?' *'Stop the questions',* the voice scolded, *'you gotta stop the questions.* 'Yes,' Rumble replied, 'I know you're right, I must think of other things,' *'yeah, sure like what?'* The voice sounded sarcastic now, so Rumble focused on his climb up the next flight of stairs.

He was aware of the sweat trickling down his forehead, he knew it would soon be in his eyes, and it always stung, but his hands were full with his heavy bags and as much as he wanted to stop and wipe away the sweat, he wasn't going to, not until he was outside the attic door.

Finally, the last flight of stairs, the narrow ones leading upwards to the closed attic door, above him the long electrical wire dangled from the high dirty ceiling amongst the cobwebs, on the end, a light bulb that didn't work, or maybe it did work, he thought, how could he know he had never found the light switch.

He was relieved to place his bags on the ground outside the door on the narrow landing. He held them in place with his knee so they didn't topple down the stairs while he found the key. As usual the door was reluctant to open even as he pulled it toward him like he always did.

He felt for the first time, it was like someone was on the other side of the door trying to hold it shut. What a silly thought, he almost laughed, but the sweat was stinging his eyes now and blurring his vision. Then the door opened, and Rumble almost fell inside. He was so grateful to be home, safe, secure. '*Safe and secure*', the voice said, '*you must be joking.*' Rumble almost slipped as his foot stood on the folded sheet of paper, it was still lying on the floor where it was placed under the door before he left. 'Oh, it's still here,' he thought and the voice replied, '*of course, it is, now that's a good sign surely*'. 'Why?' '*Because it means no one else has been up here in your absence*'. 'Oh, yes, good point,' Rumble replied propping the old chair tightly under the door handle.

He dumped his bags on the bed and even before he sat down he began to unpack. '*Why the hurry?*' The voice asked, '*I thought you were tired*'? 'I just want everything back the way it was. The way it should be, you wouldn't understand,' Rumble replied. '*You do realize you have only been gone since this morning, right?*' 'So, what's your point?' Rumble asked, but the voice was silent. Once the unpacking was complete and his smelly clothes safely in a garbage ready for washing, Rumble attacked the window.

It was indeed an attack as the warped wooden frame around the window seemed to have swollen during the day, and the window refused to budge in spite of Rumbles strong shoulder and heavy hand. Slowly and very reluctantly, it opened a few inches and Rumble decided that was better than nothing, so it would have to do.

The feel of the fresh air on his face was refreshing, and he realized just why he needed the window open. The air inside his room was stuffy, heavy with neglect and age. The whole house smelt even worse than his attic room, and Rumble knew all the windows desperately needed to be open so the house could breathe fresh air and life again. Although, he wouldn't be the one to do it.

Monday was to be Rumble's monthly meeting with Cootes, although Cootes had said he could leave it another week if he was still settling in. However, Rumble liked the routine of his monthly meetings, they were something to work toward. They gave his life purpose, meaning and structure. Rumble had never missed a meeting yet, and he didn't intend to start now.

Anyway, he hadn't changed his domestic situation, he had only tried to, because now he was right back where he was last night, last month and the month before. Rumble didn't have much for Cootes this month not as much as he usually did, but the sketches he did have were good.

He had been using the new watercolors, and he knew

they were some of his best. They had depth, movement and vibrancy, and Rumble was cautiously optimistic that maybe one of them was good enough to be a magazine cover.

Sometimes Rumble's mind moved slowly, he knew, and often it was only able to focus on one thing at a time. But he seldom forgot, he was blessed with a good memory, it was not exceptional, but it was good enough for his sketches, he needed to remember scenes and animals clearly and in detail so he could recall them as needed.

It was now he remembered the beep of his mobile phone, telling him he had a text. It had gone off when he was leaving the burned cottage. He seldom managed to get a signal in his attic room but sometimes he could. He retrieved his mobile phone, and when the screen lit up, he knew today he couldn't get a signal. 'It was probably not important anyway', he thought. The voice answered, 'and how do you know that, you usually don't assume anything and here you are assuming', the voice continued, 'you're changing, who are you and what have you done with Rumble?' Then it chuckled and Rumble said, 'oh, do shut up and forget the humor, if I can't have a try at humor, you can't either, remember you are me.' 'Seriously', the voice said so now you remember this. 'You're simply no fun at all'. Rumble sat on his bed wondering just what the text was about and whom it was from. The voice answered him immediately, 'who do you think it's from? you've only ever got text messages from one person and that's Lucy; so

186

really Rumble who do you think it's from?' 'Oh, cut the sarcasm it's most unbecoming,' Rumble replied, while his eyes were drawn to the folded sheet of paper lying on the floor.

'Just bend down and pick it, how long do you intend on staring at it and wondering?' Rumble was getting annoyed with the voice; he liked to do things when he wanted to do them, and the voice, like his mother was pushing him into doing things he didn't want to do and wasn't ready to do. He remembered his mother pushing him into dancing with her, so he would know how, she had said.

He hated the thought of touching her and tried to say maybe later, but she would have none of it and slapped him hard across the face and told him to wake up to himself. She often said that, and he had never known what it meant, he was sixteen years old at the time. That was the moment when he decided that once he was grown up and independent, he would never be bullied into doing anything that he wasn't ready to do, ever again.

'So how did that work for you?' The voice asked. When Rumble didn't reply it continued, *'I don't bully you just for the record, I encourage you to do things you actually want to do. I mean just look at you forty-nine years old and your still scared to read a letter. Maybe you should rethink some of your beliefs, Rumble, especially the ones that stop you moving forward in life. Not only have you not moved forward or sideways in life you have*

187

actually moved backwards.' 'Oh, do shut,' Rumble replied, placing his hands over his ears and turning toward the wall. At that very moment, a loud thud came from the floor below him, but fortunately Rumble didn't hear it.

Rumble sat where he was rocking slowly back and forth for about ten minutes, until he finally, turned toward the sheet of paper lying on the floor. He bent down and picked it up. Reluctantly, he admitted again the little voice was right, he waited for it to answer in some smart way, but it didn't. Rumble thought the voice was smarter than even he was, it knew when to stay quiet.

His hands trembled, small beads of sweat broke out on his forehead as he held the expensive sheet of stationery in his shaking hands, now all he needed to do was unfold it and see what was written there, this time. He didn't know how long he sat on his bed holding the letter until he become aware that it was beginning to get dark. Suddenly, the voice said loudly in his mind, '*do it, do it, do it!*' Rumble jumped at the disturbance to his solitude. He wasn't about to dignify the voice with an answer and just to annoy it a little more he continued sitting where he was and didn't unfold the sheet of writing paper until he was ready.

He tried to still his trembling hands, but it was more than his hands that trembled, it was in fact, his entire body. He wasn't trembling much, but it was enough to make the paper shake, and his sweaty palms left a damp mark on the edges of the stationery. He was gripping it much too tightly, anyway.

Then all of a sudden, he unfolded the paper. He had expected just a few words, only this time, there was much more…

Chapter Seventeen

Rumble,

I underestimated you; I did not predict your curiosity. I am usually a rather good judge of character, and I assumed your personality would keep you safely out of harm's way. I also assumed you would live by MY rules. I was wrong on both counts. Therefore, I invite you to roam freely about the house, it seems to be what you wish. So, go ahead, meet the other tenants, no more locked doors. You want to explore the house, you are now free to do so. I have nothing to hide, but understand that now you have the run of the house, this will prove to be at your own peril. Sometimes, our dreams are dangerous to ourselves and others. Be careful what you wish for.

Edwards

Under the handwritten note was a squashed bumblebee stuck to the page. Rumble shivered just from the sight of it. But Rumble's hands were shaking even more from reading the letter... so he knew? Edwards knew he had been snooping. He felt like a naughty boy who had just had his hand smacked, but this was much more than that. 'What else did Edwards know? How much of what he had done does Edwards know about?' 'Was Edwards watching him all along'? *'Probably all of it,'* the voice said, and Rumble began to tremble violently. 'Yes,' Rumble thought 'of course, you are right, he knows everything, although I am surprised he hasn't said anything before now.' Rumble sat on his bed, again, he breathed deeply to try and steady his nerves, with slow deep breaths. He closed his eyes until gradually he felt calmer.

'You can't just sit around worrying, its time you went to bed', the voice commanded and Rumble replied, 'who are you, my mother?' *'No, I was just trying to talk some sense in you. You've had a long and stressful day, your back in the house you hate, and I think if you get a good night's sleep tomorrow, Sunday, will be a new and better day'*. 'Oh, a new and better day, will it? all right I'll go to bed, but I'm hungry, I haven't eaten all day.' *'Well, life's not perfect'*, came the immediately reply from the voice. 'Oh, do shut up.' Rumble replied and headed for the shower. In spite of his fear, Rumble realized, he was exhausted and the moment his head hit the pillow, he was asleep.

He didn't hear any of the noises the house made that night. It was his stomach growling loudly that woke him the next morning. He did feel refreshed and much calmer. He didn't have his usual breakfast even though his electric jug and toaster were back under his bed, and he had some bread hidden in his cupboard as he always did.

The fresh air felt good as Rumble caught the bus and headed to the nearest cafe, it would be brunch and not lunch, so to Rumble it felt weird breaking his routine. But this time his stomach ruled.

The cafe was crowded, but finally he took a seat outside at the small table and ordered. His mobile phone reminded him he had a text message so while he waited for his meal, he took it from his pocket. The message was from Lucy to say Mr. and Mrs. Millington and Sykes had been trying to call him. At the mention of Sykes, Rumble smiled and easily remembered the cat he had grown fond of during his time at the Millingtons.' Lucy's message went on to say that when he didn't answer the Millington's message, they had called Cootes's office.

Lucy suggested he call them back immediately as they sounded worried. Rumble replied, 'Thank you for passing on the message' to Lucy and replaced his phone. Moments later, it announced another text message, probably a reply from Lucy, Rumble thought and didn't answer. Just then his food arrived, and he realized just how hungry he was. It was only brunch, but Rumble decided to really break with routine and finish his meal with a cinnamon bun. They were fresh out of the oven, and they smelt so good. Most of the other diners were having one also, so Rumble called the waitress over and said he'd have one too.

He was breaking his routine in so many ways, it confused him. Just why was he able to break his routine?

He had a system in life, it was very basic system he knew, but it worked for him, and he liked it, and if he changed it, just how would he cope, how could he get through each day?

Rumble's mind was beginning again with the 'little thoughts' as he called them, and he must stop them and stop them now. He knew once the 'little thoughts' took over he would be a mass of white noise as they went deeper and deeper into each little thing, until they were micro-managing his life and his many obsessions where again beginning to rule.

Rumble enjoyed his bun, and even though he outwardly appeared to be calm inside his head his mind was battling 'the little thoughts' in a war to make them stop.

Rumble decided to walk several blocks to a bus stop further down the road; he felt as though he needed to walk. But he wouldn't walk all the way home as he would need to walk through the alleyway at the far end of the road, that would put him face to face with the youths, and he knew they couldn't help but see him.

He also knew, they could move much faster than him. Rumble felt calmer than he had in while as he alighted the bus and walked briskly toward the house. At the end of the road, he could see the youths again creating mischief, this time they appeared to be hurling bottles at someone's fence.

Rumble knew by now that most of the houses were

vacant, old, and crumpling into disrepair, so he assumed the fence they were attacking was falling down anyway. Rumble didn't want to appear to be watching the youths, so he did what he usually did. And keeping his head down, he watched them out of the corner of his eye. He knew they had seen him when he turned up the pathway to the back door. He entered as always, and everything appeared to be as it always was. Rumble thought, maybe Edwards letter had merely been in his imagination, because clearly nothing has changed.

Walking briskly, he climbed the stairs to the first landing. He didn't want to look at the doors; he tried to keep his eyes on the floor. '*Well don't look then*', the voice said, 'I'm not going to,' he replied reaching the top of the first landing. He sensed there was something different, he could feel it, but he wasn't about to take his eyes from the floor. And then he stopped, because as hard as he tried he couldn't help not looking at the doors. There was indeed something different, his intuition had not let him down. '*Keep walking, don't look, don't stop*', the voice sounded urgent fearful, and Rumble replied,

'I'm just looking, nothing more'. '*No*', said the voice, '*don't even look, please, don't even look*'. But it was too late Rumble had stopped, and looked, and he did see what was different. Rumble stood and stared, transfixed by what he saw. He didn't answer the voice, he didn't even think of answering the voice. There were four doors and one at the far end, a bathroom Rumble had always assumed. The door at the far end was shut tightly, but the others were all open, every single one of the four doors was open, not wide, but they were open.

Rumble stared and thought instinctively of Edwards's words in his letter, So, I invite you to roam freely about the house and then the words, no more locked doors.

No more locked doors, that was what Edwards had said, and here was the proof Edwards hadn't been lying. *'Do you remember what else he said'?* The voice asked hurriedly, and Rumble didn't answer. He was staring at the doors, each one was open about twelve inches. Each door held its own secrets. Rumble thought, its own hidden secrets and horrors of decades past.

Rumble knew he wouldn't be walking up the stairs to the next level, or not just yet. He wasn't thinking about going upstairs. He surprised himself, as he realized, he was thinking about which door he would enter.

'You can't be serious?' the voice asked, sounding shocked. 'So, what if I am?' Rumble replied, *'and what sort of a ridiculous answer is that?'* the voice said. 'I shall not dignify that with an answer,' Rumble replied and kept right on staring at the door. 'Am I really going to explore?' Rumble asked himself, and he was glad the voice was not crashing his thoughts this time. He asked the same question over in his mind, several more times and then took a few steps toward the closest door.

Then he took another step and another until he could reach out and touch the old wooden door that stood ajar.

He felt as if the door was waiting for him to enter, just waiting for him to explore its depths and learn its secrets. Carefully he reached out and touched the wooden door, he expected it to slam in his face at any second, but it did not. He took another step closer and then without thinking he reached out gingerly with one finger he touched the door, just the merest touch to see if it was actually there, or maybe to see if he was actually doing this.

Then again, he put his finger toward the door, only this time, he gently pushed it. At first, it opened just a few inches, Rumble could see the darkness beyond. He noticed how his fingertip had left an imprint in the dust on the face of the door. Again, he touched the door, carefully placing his finger in the same place, and he pushed a little more. The room beyond was in darkness total and utter darkness.

Rumble gently reached for the doorknob and quietly shut the door. As he turned to walk further down the landing, he turned at the sound of the door opening again, but just a creak this time. He bypassed the first and the second door; until he was at the door at the end of the landing almost in front of the closed door he assumed was a bathroom. The third door was open, the exact amount as the others doors had been. Rumble took another step toward the door, his palms sweaty now. *'Why are you doing this?'* The voice began, *'just walk up the stairs to your attic, don't do this, don't enter any of the rooms, you know this house scares you half to death, so why are you contemplating doing this?'*

'I don't know why?' Rumble replied as he reached out and touched the door gingerly with his finger, it didn't move. He turned to see his footprints in the dust. The dust was thicker at this end of the landing, and Rumble wondered just how long it had been since anyone had ventured along here.

The round brass door handle on this door was badly corroded. It hadn't been touched in years, 'So how did the door open without anyone touching the doorknob?' Rumble wondered and the voice jumped in immediately with an answer, '*so who cares, let's go, walk away, up the next flights of stairs to the attic, lets walk now!*' But Rumble was not listening, he didn't hear the fear in the voice as it spoke, nor did he hear the urgency.

Rumble was now pushing the door open a little wider with the index finger of his left hand. However, it needed more than a push, it was reluctant to open at all. So, he placed his whole palm against the door and pushed. The door slowly opened, inch-by-inch, it needed the hinges oiling, Rumble thought as he kept pushing. Finally, when it was about half way open, Rumble wiped his sweaty palms on his trousers and looked into the darkness. But just like the last room, the darkness within was total. The air smelt heavy and slightly cooler than the air on the landing where he still stood. Rumble knew the voice was speaking to him, but his mind was on other things. Rumble was only able to focus on one thing at a time.

Now as he stood on the threshold looking in, he

wondered if he should move forward or stay where he was or turn away. '*Well, you always stay with the safe option,*' the voice began, '*so why not now, why would you even consider taking a step into the unknown. It's definitely dark in there, and you know from previous experience there is undoubtedly scary things lurking in the shadows, so just turn and walk away*'. 'Oh, do shut up,' Rumble said, but the voice persisted, '*why would you even contemplate going in there, it's just not who you are.*' 'You're wrong about that, it's not who I was,' Rumble replied, and with that said, he took a step inside the darkened room. Immediately his feet were over threshold; he felt, rather than saw, the door was about to slam shut, but he was standing directly in its path. He jumped backwards into the hallway and waited expecting the door to slam in his face. But it did not. Nothing happened, nothing. The house remained silent, the doors remained slightly open, and Rumble stood exactly where he was.

'*Too dark in there for you, is it? You hated the dark as a boy also*', the voice began. 'I am no longer a boy,' Rumble replied, and the voice immediately taunted him. '*If that's what you think, why don't you enter?*' Rumble decided not to answer instead he took several steps backwards and turned toward the stairs at the far end of the landing. 'Why on earth did I choose this door? It's the furthest from the end?' '*Because you're not a boy any more, remember, it's no longer who you are. In fact, it appears you're now seeking out danger.*' Was that a

198

snicker in the voice, did the voice just snicker at him? Rumble felt a momentary flash of anger inside. He would not dignify the voice with an answer, so he merely replied, 'Oh, do shut up.'

Rumble started walking back the way he just came. Looking behind, he saw his footprints in the heavy dust on the wooden floor. He was directly outside the second closest door to the stairs when he heard the voice's words in head, and the snicker within. Rumble turned to the door, and it opened wide.

He looked within, as he expected, there was nothing but darkness. Rumble seldom did anything on impulse, but the snickering in the voice had annoyed him. Without thinking further, he took several steps into the room expecting the door to slam behind him, but nothing.

He couldn't see anything, so he held his arms out in front of him and walked forward. He tripped over something solid but not hard in the middle of the room and after steadying himself again. He took another step, and this time it felt like he was crushing something grainy under his feet.

Rumble felt like he was walking in slow motion, under water, the window could not possibly be this far from the door, but his hands felt nothing. There was nothing in front of him at all. He took several more steps, and some more, until finally, when it seemed like ages had passed. Rumble's hands felt fabric. Not heavy drapes this time but soft cotton fabric. He felt along it slightly until he found what he thought was the middle and then ripped it open with both his hands, fully expecting it to crumble at his feet. But it didn't.

Light flooded the room through the grimy windows the glass long overdue for a wash. This window was indeed further from the door because it was a bay window, complete with crumbling cushions on the window seat. It was dull inside the room, now it filled with an unearthly whitish, yellow light, that only the late afternoon can produce. Rumble blinked several times as his eyes adjusted. Slowly, he turned toward his right, and the first thing he saw was the huge portrait of the man that looked surprisingly like a younger version of Edwards.

It was lifelike in its size and only a few feet from him. It was exactly like the portraits in the other rooms he had visited. Again, he felt the eyes fixed on him, glaring, penetrating and much too real. He stared back, directly into them and after a few seconds of staring without blinking he could have sworn the eyes flickered.

Rumble was trying to tear his eyes away from the portrait. Out the corner of his eye, he could see the door, and it was still open – not wide – but like it was when he had first seen it. It was open enough. He should run from the eyes, and the darkness had unnerved him. He started to tremble, and he felt his palms sweat. '*You need to get out of here, it's happening again. In moments, you'll be terrified, I know you will*'. 'Yes, you're right, of course, you're right,' '*I always am. 'Get out of here, now!*' The voice commanded urgently. Rumble's eyes were again focused on the portrait as he tried to look away, he noticed the red ruby ring on the pinky finger of the man that glared so sternly at him from the wall.

Rumble turned to walk away and then he saw what lay on the floor, a scream that quickly turned to a gurgle constricted his throat, but he was so scared the sound never came out.

Lying face down spread-eagled on the floor between him and door lay the corpse of a woman or what was left of her. Her clothes were partly intact, and they covered her bones. Her skirt was long and made of a light fabric of interminable color; her blouse had long sleeves and still appeared to be tucked in her skirt. Some of her hair was still attached to her skull, and it appeared to be stacked like a blonde birds-nest on her head. Her arms or the bones from her arms were spread out as were her legs, and she appeared to have died with her face on the floor and her body spread out in the shape of an "X" .

Rumble was relieved to notice that her face or what was left of it was not visible. He screamed again, and this time a small sound came from his mouth. He was shaking all over. He needed to get out of here and now; the voice was telling him so over and over in his head. '*Get out, move, go toward the door, now*'. Rumble didn't reply and he didn't move, he couldn't move, his eyes were transfixed on the corpse. Somehow, he felt her pain. Even though he knew little about death; some-how he knew, like the others in the house that this was not a natural death.

He had to walk around or over the corpse to get to the door, and he could see where he had trodden on her leg on his way in, it would account for the crunching noise he had heard, and looking closer, he saw the indent of his foot where he had crushed the bones at the bottom of her leg.

He knew his legs weren't about to take him anywhere so he had a quick look around the room. It was similar but not the same as the last ones. It seemed slightly more modern. He noticed the lamps were not so ornate, and they were definitely not oil lamps, but electric. The chest of drawers was large but also seemed newer while the large bed, was not a four poster but simply a large king size bed. It was covered in a whitish duvet, and it looked like someone had just been sleeping in it. The pillows were thrown haphazardly on top of the crumpled duvet.

Then his eyes roamed back to the corpse on the floor, and, of course, the sparkling red stone in the heavy silver band on her finger.

Or at least it had once been on her finger, now it lay on the floor at the very end of the bony finger where once flesh had covered the bones, they had been alive and moving and living, like the rest of her. Rumble briefly wondered what she must have been like. Was she a younger girl? Was she pretty? Was she happy? *'It really doesn't matter',* the voice yelled in his head, *'she's dead now and you can't do anything to save her so save yourself, and don't even think about touching the ring, you know what happened last time'.* 'Do I know what happened last time, maybe it was all in my mind and what happened had nothing to do with the ring.' *'Oh, don't be so absurd, the same thing happened the time before. Get out of this room move toward the door and leave',* the voice commanded loudly in Rumble's head.

Rumble knew he was stalling, because his legs wouldn't move and because he couldn't bring himself to walk over the corpse.

He wasn't a religious man but it still just wasn't right. *'Well, just cover her then',* the voice said and Rumble agreed this was the best idea. Lying over the end of the bed was a thin blanket, it seemed to be made of cashmere because when Rumble grabbed it, he felt the softness, and he knew it was of very good quality. Hoping it wouldn't disintegrate under his touch, he unfolded it and making his legs move slightly closer to the corpse he tossed it in the air, so it would fan out and cover the body.

It almost worked; the body on the floor was now almost entirely covered by the thin white blanket, but to Rumbles dismay, the boney finger with the ring on it was still showing. The ring blazed a fiery red in the dim light, and Rumble reached over to see if the blanket could be stretched to cover it.

He knew he hadn't touched the ring, but somehow it seemed to leap at him, catching in his hand. It was hot, and he felt his palm burn, he screamed. The door slammed with such force it shook the room.

Then the room came to life, the drawers opened and shut at frightening speed the lamps blazed into life, brighter and brighter until he needed to cover his eyes, the drapes closed and the huge portrait, crashed to the floor, remaining up right, the sound almost shook the room. Then to Rumble's horror, things started flying at him, at first it was just clothes from the drawers as they opened and shut, then the furniture started to move. Flinging itself toward Rumble, he screamed again, unable to move.

Something hit him in the face, and he unknowing dropped the ring. He fell backwards onto the bed, his face wet with blood, sweat and the tears he had not known he was crying, 'help, save me,' he whimpered over and over, his body trembling as he half laid and half sat on the bed. It didn't collapse, so Rumble stayed where he was as more objects flew at him, he managed to duck most of them but several hit him hard in the body or head. Then he felt underneath him something moving. He screamed a scream of sheer terror. He leaped off the bed and grabbed the drapes opening them wide. He looked back to the bed, several round lumpy things were moving under the covers. 'No, please no.' *'Confront your enemy and kill the fear,'* the voice commanded.

Rumble had thought the voice had abandoned him so he was shocked to hear it so clear and concise speak to him in his head again. Without thinking further, Rumble screamed as he moved forward and pulled the covers from the bed. He was aware that the room had calmed down and that he was no longer in procession of the ring. He heard the tiny tinkling sound as the covers began to move, and he saw the tiny silver baby rattle gently fall to the floor.

Once the covers were removed, he screamed again, this time aloud, it was a deep guttural, terrifying sound that he heard come from deep within. He watched them lazily look up at him. Their black beady eyes dark with menace and annoyance at the disruption to their mealtime. Two large black rats and three smaller ones were feasting on something. After looking at him with their fierce and hungry faces, they scuttled toward the far side of the bed and then disappeared down the bed-sheet and over the side. Rumble looked down at the bed and saw what they were eating, it was a tiny corpse, and some of the flesh still hung from the bones. He could smell human flesh; he could smell the rats. The decay of rotting flesh, the filth of the rats, he saw their droppings littering the once white sheets.

He screamed and backed away, as the eyes of the baby stared at him form sunken sockets in its head.

He backed away disgusted, appalled, and frightened beyond words. He stopped when he felt the wall behind him, solid and real. His heel hit against the heavy frame of the painting at his feet. His hands brushed something wet and warm on the wall. With unseeing eyes, he turned and stared at the wall. 'You like the dark, I kill the flame.'

Again, he screamed, his hands moving along the wall away from the wet red paint or blood that was slowly running down the wall. "Leonard Cohen," a voice whispered and, Rumble wasn't sure whether the voice was in his head or his imagination, or maybe he was going mad? Until it continued "is dead..." Rumble knew it wasn't his voice, not the one in his head, it was a deep rasping whisper, and he shivered violently all over, the voice was real, and it was here in the room. He opened his mouth to scream, but before anything came out he saw rats, black fury rats scuttle toward him.

There must have been dozens of them. They ran straight over the corpse on the floor and directly toward him. Then the door slammed and opened several times, the lights blazed into life, and all the drawers began opening and shutting. Rumble realized to late, that the rats had brushed against the ring lying on the floor, and the room in turn had reacted. But there were so many rats, and they were running all over the ring. It still lay where it was, but it was alive, it glowed brilliantly. The room reacted, more violently than ever before to the touch of the rats.

The heavy wooden drawers from the dresser and side table began to hurtle across the room, not directly at Rumble. They moved randomly, smashing against the walls, the lamps toppled to the floor but somehow kept on filling the room with an intense white light, that hurt his eyes. One huge wooden drawer flew directly toward him at frightening speed. He knew the voice was speaking in his head, but he couldn't focus on it, he was in pure survival mode. On instinct and still pressed hard against the wall, he moved slightly to the left and then pushed himself even closer against the wall. The rats were running scared around the room, no longer as one but they now scurried everywhere, squeaking and squealing in terror. Maybe he was imagining it because he was so frightened, but they seemed to be growing in numbers.

Rumble closed his eyes and as he did so he became aware of the wall behind him, moving inwards, until it seemed to give way. Looking to his right, he realized the huge painting had been covering a doorway, not a real doorway but the wall moved when you pressed against it in the right place.

Rumble wiggled his fingers along the wall until he felt the firmness of the wall behind him, and he was holding onto something solid. Somehow, he caught himself just in time; without knowing it, he was positioned over the entranceway, and he almost fell through the space. He felt his body move backwards as the wall moved inwards, but he held fast. The rats saw or smelled the opening, it was only inches wide, but suddenly, and all together they ran toward the small gap, which had been created by Rumble's body leaning against the wall. Chaos as the rats tumbled and climbed over each other squealing in their haste to get past Rumble, and the huge painting propped up against the wall that also sat firmly on the floor.

Rumble felt the cool air come into the room through the doorway as he held fast to the sides of the gap. But as the rats brushed against his feet and trousers, he screamed it was more than he could stand. The room had quieted down. Rumble didn't know if his legs would move, but he needed to move away from the wall. Feeling the wall move slightly into his body, Rumble threw himself onto the bed. He was soaked in sweat and trembling violently; he didn't know how long he'd been sobbing. As he fell on to the bed, his hand touched several small fleshy bones, Rumble knew what they were. Out loud, he cried, "no, no, no, help me." The last thing he remembered before his world went black was the wetness between his legs.

Then he was back in his childhood. A skinny, scared five-year old boy, curled up in the far top corner of his bed, crying as his mother bent over him, he could clearly see the purple patches appear on her cheeks; her face contorted with rage while she beat him with a wooden spoon for again wetting his bed.

He sobbed and told her he wouldn't do it again, he promised not to do it again, he begged her to stop hitting him. He curled up tighter. But she hit him harder and harder over and over again, telling him he had made extra work for her as if she didn't have enough to do, now she had to wash his soiled sheets. She called him irresponsible and dirty; she said he was turning out to be just like every other man. Then she told him how she had once trusted a man, just once, and look where it got her – you're the result – I never wanted you and neither did your father, she yelled. The little boy sobbed loudly, not only feeling the pain of the beating but also learning the pain of rejection.

Then his world thankfully went black. In the morning at school, he would explain away the raised bruises, as he knew he must…

'Rumble, you got to wake up, we got to get out of here, NOW! Rumble, please wake up,' the voice begged, 'I know you're terrified, but please get up.' Finally, the voice stopped pleading, it was no good, Rumble's world was in darkness, and he was in another place and time.

The voice could feel it, but he didn't know where Rumble was. It was somewhere so far away, a dark place, a place of fear and evil. He knew he was in the place the voice did not want to share; it was a place the voice didn't want to go. The voice knew that this time Rumble was almost scared to death. The voice hoped he would come back in time; after all he always had before…

Chapter Eighteen

'Rumble open your eyes, come on, its daytime, the doors open. Please Rumble, wake up. Rumble, can you hear me? Answer me, Rumble?' The voice went on and on, and all Rumble wanted was to do was sleep.

Gradually, Rumble became aware of something sharp poking into his hand. It was hurting him. Rumble knew in order to stop the pain and make the thing stop poking him he had to open his eyes. He didn't want to. He actually hoped he was dead. But hearing the voice go on and on he knew he couldn't be dead because the voice would be dead also.

When he was young boy, and the school had given him some religious teachings, Rumble thought that maybe the voice was actually God, because he spoke to the people and you heard his voice clearly in your head, but as he'd grown, he realized no one other than him could hear the voice, he'd decided it probably wasn't God after all.

Now he wondered again if it was indeed God, and if just maybe he was dead after all and that would be good. Then to his surprise, the voice answered him, *'well, if you're dead that means your mother will be waiting for you on the other side, now do you really want to see her? Are you sure you'd rather be with her than me?'* Rumble shuddered at the thought. '*So, wake up and wake up now, it's time, Rumble, open your eyes and let's get out of here*', the voice sounded anxious or was it scared? Again, Rumble felt the pointed thing poking his hand. Rumble wanted to sleep, he was desperately tired. However, he knew the voice, and he knew the voice wouldn't let him sleep if it wanted him to do something else. Rumble also knew the voice wouldn't even be talking to him if he wasn't in some kind of danger.

Reluctantly, he opened his eyes, the light shone in the window made by a weak yellow sun through the clouds. Rumble felt the sharp object fall from his hand, and looking down, he saw it was a bone, long and pointed; still visible on the bone were pieces of grayish, white skin. Where his head had just been, he saw the sheet was wet with fresh blood. Rumble leapt from the bed, and again he heard the tiny tinkle of the baby's rattle.

He knew what it was, and what he would find engraved on it. He didn't want to search for it; instead, he looked at the remains of the tiny corpse on the bed and, instinctively, knew this was Baby Sarah. His body trembled so much; he could hear his own teeth chatter in his head. '*Get up Rumble, stop being lazy and get out of here now, while you can,*' the voice instructed urgently. 'What do you mean?' Rumble asked confused, then looking around he asked 'and where am I am? Where have you taken me?' '*I haven't taken you anywhere, I told you not to come here. I told you not to touch the door and enter the room. But, Rumble, just get out and do it now'.* 'Okay, okay' Rumble said to shut the voice up, he turned around in the room as he stood beside the bed; then he looked at the tiny corpse and the blood stain on the bed. 'Whose blood is that?' *'It's yours silly, don't you remember, things flying around the room, you got hit several times. I think it was a flying drawer that hit you on the side of the head, it's not a bad cut but then you lay on it as you slept.'* 'Oh,' Rumble said wiping his eye as he felt warm blood trickle in.

Slowly, as he stood beside the bed, the memories came flooding back; they were awful memories ones he didn't want to know.

So, as he always did, he began to block them out. He saw the door, it was open just a few inches; and then as he was about to make a dash toward it, the voice warned him. *'Stop. Look where you're standing, walk carefully, but hurry'.* Rumble's legs felt weak, and he was surprised he could stand at all. Then, he saw the outline of the corpse under the soft white cashmere blanket and the brilliant red stone of the ring close to what he knew must be a finger bone. He swallowed hard and tried to stop shaking.

He heard his own heart beating so fast in his chest; thump, thump, thump. 'Everyone must be able to hear my heart beating so loudly, can you hear it, too?' *'Of course, I can hear it, I'm in your mind, I am you after all. It often beats fast when your terrified, and I always hear it, I think it's normal, you're not going to die or anything, but you got to get out of here or else, you might...* ' 'All right, all right I hear you,' Rumble replied to the voice. He made his legs walk and they did. With each step, he expected the door to slam in his face and if it did, he knew he'd never be able to open it again. Just as Rumble grabbed the doorknob and began to pull it open, it was unexpectedly torn from his grip and thrown wide.

Rumble jumped backwards, the light from outside the room flooded in and made it hard to see, but Rumble knew without a moment's hesitation that he was standing face to face, with Edwards. The man's steely gaze cut into his soul. Edwards stood with the light from the house behind him, and Rumble briefly thought he could see right through him, although he knew the man was real because he could smell garlic on his breath. Rumble stayed where he was. Edward's gaze never left him and Rumble, although shaking from head to toe stared right back. Slowly, he saw Edward's move his head from side to side and then, lifting his index finger, he wagged it briefly but disapprovingly at Rumble.

"You are trespassing in the room of one of my tenants. You have broken the rules, my rules. For that reason, you must know you will never get away. You have become a problem now as you know too much." Edwards stared into Rumble's soul as he spoke. He didn't sound angry, or annoyed or anything. However, his words were enough, Rumble understood the enormity of what he had just heard.

Edwards took a step backwards into the house, and Rumble waited for the door to slam shut in his face. But it stayed opened, and moving closer, he knew he was able to exit the room of horrors. He did so as fast as he could. Rumble was only seconds behind Edwards' departure, but when he looked around, there was no one there, and the only footprints visible in the dust were his own.

Now outside the room, he gulped the air, it wasn't exactly fresh, but it was better than what he'd breathed inside the room, it had been heavy with age, decay and an acid smell of rotting flesh and rats. His legs buckled under him several times as he clung to the railing and looked toward the entranceway below. Everything seemed the same, nothing had changed. 'How can it be so?' he asked, and the voice and the house were silent; there was no movement, and Rumble sensed no other living presence. 'Where was Edwards, where had he gone? And why hadn't he made any footprints in the thick layer of dust on the wooden floor?'

Slowly, he steadied himself and turning toward the stairway, he began to walk up the stairs. Careful not to touch the rickety banister least, it should give way. Once he reached the third stair, he heard the doors altogether slam shut, he thought he felt the house rattle under the force of the doors shutting. He finally breathed out a breath, he wasn't aware he was holding and continued on up the stairs to the attic room, he called home.

Rumble entered his room with shaky hands, sweaty

palms and a heart that was beating fast against his chest. He was exhausted; every part of him ached with fatigue. Once the chair was propped securely under the door handle, he removed his shoes; they were damp from sweat, and then his socks; they were even wetter. He threw them in the corner and fell back on the bed. He grabbed the bedspread, and he wrapped it around him. In the past, he would never have laid on his bed wearing dirty clothes, and now he could smell stale urine.

As he drifted off to sleep, he realized the smell was coming from him. Then he remembered that he had been so terrified he had wet himself. This time, he blocked out his mother's words, he was just too tired. With his eyelids heavy, in seconds, he was asleep.

It was a soft yellow sun and a few birds chirping that woke Rumble the next morning. He blinked at the light and found himself in the same position on the bed he had been when he went to sleep. He had never woken with the sun in his face, something was different, something was wrong. He lay there on the bed rolled up in the bed spread and blinked at the rays of sun that played on his eyelids. Then lazily he turned to search out the time. To Rumble's horror, it was almost four p.m. He bolted upright, 'Oh no, have I missed my appointment with Cootes? I've never missed my monthly appointment,' Rumble said almost aloud feeling the adrenaline curse through him at the thought of breaking his routine. *You haven't missed anything, Rumble. Its Sunday and you don't see Cootes until tomorrow, so calm down and think about stopping that stomach of yours crumbling with hunger; it's driving me crazy'.* The voice said, and Rumble immediately felt it.

Rumble needed a shower more than he did food, and he was running out of clean clothes. He would have to wear his last pair of trousers; they were his oldest pair, and he knew they were beginning to look tatty, but he had no choice. The pair he preferred smelt strongly of smoke, and this pair he was wearing, smelt strongly of urine. He soon found a clean shirt, socks, underpants, and trousers. Then he headed for the shower. He stayed under the water longer than usual. He washed his hair as he always did on Sunday and then stayed under the warm water a little longer, it seemed to steady and relax him.

Once he toweled himself dry and put on his fresh clothes, he felt more like himself. *'Now can we find something to eat and not just dry toast?'* The voice commented. 'Now you're telling me what to eat?' Rumble responded secretly glad to have someone to talk to. *'I can tell you've calmed down by your snappy retorts, Rumble, but let's find some food.'* 'I hear you, and I know I'm hungry also,' Rumble replied.

Rumble filled his pockets with all he needed and headed out the door, opening it just a little at first to peek carefully outside. He expected Edwards to be lurking in the shadows, but so far, he couldn't see him. He carefully walked down the stairs missing the ones that squeaked as he usually tried to do; only today, he took extra care and they managed to remain quiet. The house was silent, as it always was, not a movement, the air stale and still, and the weak rays of sun enhancing the heavy layer of dust that seemed to coat everything. Looking around, he saw the only footprints in the dust were his, and only his. 'How can this be? Edwards was walking around the house I saw him just yesterday'? 'Never mind, Edwards, let's eat;' the voice commanded loudly, although Rumbles mind wanted an answer.

Still moving slowly, he walked down the last flight of stairs through the entranceway and into the grimy kitchen. It really seemed to look even dirtier today than it had last time he was here. He fumbled in his pocket for the large key; it was barely able to fit in any of his trouser pockets. Finally, he located it and was about to place it in the keyhole of the back door when the voice loudly said, '*Stop, Rumble, listen. Don't turn the key.*' 'I thought you wanted food?' Rumble responded the rusty key still in his hand and inches from the lock. '*Just listen*', the voice commanded, but Rumble didn't need to. The door handle turned to and fro right before his eyes, and he felt someone throw themselves hard against the old timbers. It shook but the door held, then the doorknob turned again and again until someone threw their whole body into the door again. Rumble put his ear closer to the door.

"Fucking things locked tight."

"Bloody, hell, it's an old door; it should open easily. Why the whole place is falling down and we can't even fucking get in the back door?"

"Ya, bloody, soft the lot of ya. It's just a door, smash it down, or are ya afraid of ghosts and goblins?" another voice teased, egging them on.

"Well, the place is haunted, everyone bloody knows that Porkey…"

"Everyone – who?"

"Yeah, it's always been haunted," another voice added, and Rumble knew by the accents it was the group of youths from down the end of the street.

"This is the only fuckin house we never been in, in the whole fucking street."

"Probably nothin worth takin anyways, no one's ever lived here."

"Ya, bloody scared or something Sooty."

'No I, I bet you are Scarface." Added another boy,

'Scarface, what kind of a name is that?' The voice asked. 'Oh, shut up,' Rumble replied his ear almost touching the door.

"Stop fighting, you scumbags."

"Who ya callin a scumbag?"

"Yeah, who the hell you callin a scumbag?"

Rumble recognized this as the very first voice he'd heard. So far, he'd counted about six of them.

"Let's burn it to the ground, come on."

"We're not burning nothin until we look inside, it's money we need; maybe we can fuckin sell something from in there."

"Bloody hell, Scamper there's nothin in there worth nothin."

"And how'd ya know? Ya been in there or somethin?"

"Break it up, you two. Let's try another door; this can't be the only way in."

"Yeah, Banger's right, there has to be another way in."

"If we can't bloody well get in, lets torch it boys."

"Banger, you'll torch anything."

"We should be callin him fire boy and not bloody Banger…" Rumble couldn't hear anymore as they moved away.

He could hear their boots shuffling as they walked. 'They're going to burn the house down,' Rumble said alarmed and the voice, instead of calming him replied, '*probably*'. 'I shall race upstairs and pack,' not just wait and see. '*I don't think Edwards will allow some kids to torch the house, do you?*' The voice reasoned, and Rumble had to admit that Edwards wouldn't allow that to happen either.

But again, Rumble was scared. He moved silently toward the front door thinking the youths were headed that way. But there weren't. He stood in the entranceway, waiting. But he heard nothing, no voices, nothing. They must have gone around the back, and he tried to imagine if there was an entranceway there. It would be overgrown, so Rumble had never ventured there. '*But maybe there was another entrance, or two, perhaps a basement?* the voice added.

Rumble decided to wait around a while longer. In the past, he would have run and hidden away, but he needed to know if the house was going to be burned to the ground and if it was he wanted to get out before it happened.

In his mind, he could clearly see Rosemary Cottage, all the fireman and Ms. Primrose's sooty face as she wrapped her arms around him and looked up into his eyes, sobbing. Rumble blushed at the thought.

'I should at least get my sachet'. *'Oh, stop worrying, you think this is the first time anyone's tried to break in?'* The voice said. 'No, of course, not, but I know what those youths can do, I've seen it,' Rumble replied. *'And you've also seen what Edwards can do'*, the voice replied. 'Yes, but how do we know its Edwards who does things?' *'Well, who else?'* Rumble didn't have an answer for this, so he said, 'I think the boys have given up and gone.' *'They've got so much time on their hands, they're not going to give up that easily'*, the voice replied,

Rumble turned to head for the stairs, and the voice called him back. *'Wait, just wait a minute and let's make sure'*. 'Okay, do you think maybe they've found another way in?' *'I didn't say that, I just said wait a while longer and let's make sure they've left.'* 'Do you know something you haven't told me?' Rumble asked walking toward the bottom stair, brushing away the dust and sitting down. The voice said nothing. So, Rumble waited, his ears honed to any new sound, his arms rested on his knees, his hands cupped around his chin.

Rumble was listening intently, and when finally, he heard a strange noise, he jumped, then quickly got to his feet. It was a shuffling sound, and it was getting closer to the front door. Then he heard the doorbell, 'maybe it's not the youths?' '*Who else?*' The voice said, then he heard a loud pounding on the door; someone was using his fists.

"What the fuck did you ring the doorbell for Sooty?"

"See if anyone's home."

"Buggar you, Scamper, stop pounding the fuckin door, the whole neighborhood will hear ya."

"Like what bloody neighbors?"

"And put that damn rock down."

"Real dumb move, Banger, real dumb move."

"Who ya callin, dumb?" Then Rumble heard the boys tumbling around outside cursing and fighting as they always did.

"Anyone try turning the door knob?" Another voice said and Rumble became aware of a movement to his left.

He turned to see Edwards move toward him. But Edwards wasn't looking at Rumble, in fact as Rumble stared at him, he realized Edwards hadn't even noticed him; he was glaring only at the door.

He seemed to be only half alive because this time Rumble was sure. With the dull sunlight from some high up window, Rumble really could see right through him. Instinctively, he moved away. He moved backward watching Edwards all the time, but Edwards gaze was on the front door and never once did he look at Rumble.

"Stop fucking fightin all the damn time and try the door knob."

"Bloody things hardly going to be open when the back doors locked tight."

But Rumble, who had moved behind the door and into the small room that was in darkness, saw the door swing wide. It barely squeaked. Light flooded the entranceway. Rumble peeped around from his hiding place. Where was Edwards, he had been just there inside the door, but he seemed to have vanished again. Then he saw him behind the door.

They watched the first boy, a skinny, black boy who seemed to be too tall for his body. His face glowed like black ebony; Rumble could see tiny beads of sweats sitting amongst his close-cropped black tightly coiled hair. The smile faded when his buckteeth were covered by his large lips. His black eyes flicked around the exterior of the room, and he stood without entering just outside the threshold. No one moved. The boys all crowded together behind the black boy and stared.

"Bloody hell, it's straight out of an old fuckin black and white movie."

"Yeah, plenty of loot here, what ya waiting for, Sooty?" One of the boys said as they pushed him into the room.

However, the moment his foot crossed the threshold and touched the floor inside the house, the heavy wooden front slammed with such force, the old house shook. A high-pitched scream followed from outside.

'Fuck ya nose, Sooty."

"It's bloody broken, help me its hurts bad."

"Holy shit, look at all the blood."

"Look at his nose; it's pushed right into his face."
Then the screaming stopped.

"Is he dead?"

"Who the hell gives a shit? I'm not waitin around 'ere to find out."

"Ya can't just leave him, Scarface. He's one of us, one of the gang."

"Sure, I can. Fuckin watch me."

"Scarface, come back."

"Ya want to wait around for when the cops arrive that's ya fuckin business, but I'm not gettin busted again for nought…" Rumble heard his voice trail off to nothing.

"What the fuck are we goin to do with him, look at all the blood? Shit, we're in for it now."

"Hey, wake up, Sooty. Bloody wake up right now."

"He can't fuckin hear ya Banger."

"Okay, we gotta all carry him and leave him on his mum's door step. Whose with me?"

"Porky, Scamper?"

"Okay, let's lift him. Fuck, he's heavy. Are you guys even holdin him?'

"Yeah, he is heavy and bloody boney too; doesn't his mum feed him nought."

Rumble heard the boy moan and then the others as they shuffled away with their load. *'Told you, Edwards wouldn't let anyone into his precious house'*, the voice said triumphantly. 'Yeah, okay, so you're right again. But maybe the youths will come back, you know pay back and that sort of thing' *'Well, let's get up to the attic before Edwards comes back'*, the voice instructed and Rumble immediately obeyed.

Rumble lay on his bed thinking about all that had just happened, his stomach disturbed his thoughts, and Rumble decided dry toast would suit him fine tonight.

The next morning, Rumble threw his sachet over his shoulder. He didn't have as many sketches as usual, but he was quietly confident that the ones he did have were good, some of his best, this was partly due to the new and vibrant watercolors he was now using and partly due to his own developing skills as an artist. He had been experiencing a heightened awareness of his surroundings, lately. He wasn't sure why this was happening, but it was showing in some of his sketches.

He was out of bed at exactly seventy thirty a.m., and he left the house at his usual time. He caught the same bus, he always did and alighted close to Cootes office, he was ahead of time, just like always.

Briefly, Rumble was aware of his mobile phone, he obviously had messages or texts, but his need for food was overwhelming. He felt he might faint from hunger if he didn't eat soon, so he stopped and quickly ate a chicken burger, he was starving, and it tasted good.

He thought briefly about looking at his texts or messages, but they would probably be from Lucy anyway, and he was almost late for his monthly meeting with Cootes.

He would talk to Lucy on his arrival. He looked around the bustling inner center of Sussex as he walked. People hurrying this and that, all lost in their own heads, probably late or trying to be early for their next appointment.

Housewives quickly shopping or meeting a friend for lunch, grandparents with too much time on their hands and business folk climbing the corporate ladder. It was a ladder to nowhere Rumble always thought, because once you're at the top, you can either fight to stay there or fall down. Either way, it doesn't make your life any happier, and in the meantime, you have missed out on many things you should have enjoyed in life.

Rumble looked at the faces as they walked past him, the heavy faces perplexed by thought, the easy going faces who really didn't care so long as they got paid. The ones that hated the world, and the young faces full of optimism, and just waiting for an adventure.

Rumble was almost at Cootes office; the buildings in front of him, the sleek tall modern glass and concrete loomed large; the inviting lobby with bored bellboys and overzealous receptionists helping you to find your way. Rumble was pleased that Cootes office had stayed the same, he hated change, and he thought Cootes did also, although probably not as much as he did. Change did not fit who he was, and Cootes knew it.

The moment he opened the glass doors and entered the internal office, Lucy seemed to be upon him; she looked at him disapprovingly, with her large eyes and even bigger heavy rimmed glasses. They seemed to magnify her eyes, and he could tell she was not happy with him.

"Rumble, you haven't been answering your mobile, what's the point of you even having one, have you been unwell?" she asked all at once and Rumble stopped, he turned toward her, stared again at the large eyes behind the thick lenses of her glasses. He knew she must have seen his cuts and bruises so why was she asking? He paused as he stared at her, this gave him a moment to think of an answer, but he could not, and she was waiting.

"No."

"You look awful, Rumble," Lucy said, looking closer at him, and when he didn't respond, she continued, "so you have been reading my texts then?"

"No."

"Well, I guessed as much, all you have is your sachet, or do you have another bag outside?" she asked smirking.

"No."

"Well, I expected as much, and I told Mr. Cootes so. Too much for you get your head around, isn't it, Rumble?" Rumble usually liked Lucy, she had never been really friendly with him, but she was usually straight to the point, and he felt they understood each other.

But he didn't know why she was so annoyed and just why she was speaking to him like this. Maybe he should have read his text messages before he arrived, as he still had no idea what she was talking about. But before he could answer the perplexed woman, Cootes office door opened wide, and Cootes called to.

"Rumble, is that you?"

"Yes, Mr. Cootes."

"Well, come on in then," but before he moved forward. Lucy moved in front of him and said to Mr. Cootes,

"You owe me five pounds." And looking very pleased with herself; she retreated to her desk.

"Just two minutes late, Rumble; you really are getting unreliable, but then again, I suppose you were here on time, and Lucy cornered you in the outer office."

"Yes, that she did."

"Well, it does look like she won our little wager, doesn't it, Rumble? Letting the side down, I see." Rumble had no idea what Cootes was talking about, so he moved toward the same large chair, where he always sat, directly opposite Cootes wide desk. It was an overstuffed brown leather armchair, he would never consider sitting anywhere else.

"Mr. Cootes, I don't know…"

"Haven't you got any of your text messages then, Rumble?"

"Well, no I suppose not..." Rumble replied handing over his sachet to Cootes and sitting down again.

"No matter, Rumble, no matter, you've just cost me five pounds indeed you have, just proves a man should never gamble, always a fifty per cent chance one can lose, and I did. But no matter, we're ready for you, Rumble. Probably better like this anyway, doesn't give you too much time to think, and lord knows if anyone can over think a situation, it's you. Oh, I know, you can think it to death and then some," Cootes chuckled at this, and Rumble had no idea why, but what he did know was that he was getting more confused by the second.

What were they all talking about and to Rumble's surprise the little voice in his head replied, '*don't ask me, I'm with you, how would I know.*' Rumble had never had the voice speak to him in Cootes office before, but he had to agree the voice was right, this time. So, like the voice, he waited.

Cootes was flicking through his sketches, but this time, he was doing it slower than usual, he was squeezing his chin between his thumb and first finger. Rumble knew he did this from time to time when he was focusing hard.

In his other hand, he was holding up a sketch Rumble had recently completed, it was of a cottage garden full or brightly blooming flowers, and in the distance, and just visible through the trees, was the ocean.

Cootes nodded and held it closer to his face before placing it on top of the pile and looked at the next one. He hadn't finished looking at all the sketches when Lucy entered and placed a tray holding two teacups on the desk in front of them. Before she left, she turned to Rumble and softly said, "Forgive me, Rumble, for speaking to you as I did; I know you were confused." Rumble was taken aback by her apology, so he only nodded his reply.

"Now, Rumble, what I'm about to tell you does not need to cause you anxiety or concern, and yes, it is indeed outside your normal routine and undoubted outside your comfort zone. But looking at these sketches, I know I have made the right choice; indeed, I do. These are good, Rumble, as I knew they would be, very good, some of your best."

Rumble was secretly pleased, "Thank you, Mr. Cootes." Cootes had not yet looked at all the sketches, but he was sitting back and staring at Rumble from across his desk. He took a sip of tea, Rumble waited and looked shyly back at him and did the same.

"Rumble," he finally said, holding his fingers tip-to-tip and rocking back in his large chair.

"Rumble, I know this will make you anxious, just the very thought of it, will. But looking at your sketches, I also know you're the man for the job. They requested you, and I know you're the man." Rumble hadn't heard a question so he didn't feel a need to reply, he took a large gulp of his hot tea hoping it would quieten his growing apprehension. He didn't know why he was feeling so apprehensive, Cootes hadn't even told him what he had to do.

But Rumble felt in his soul; it was something new and outside his realms of understanding and probably outside his boundaries of doing. He looked at Cootes, he felt his cheeks burn, it was almost as if Cootes knew him so well, he knew what he was thinking. Although Cootes had known him longer than anyone else, so maybe he did.

"Rumble, this will be good for you, an adventure like this. I must say old chap you look like someone has beaten you up or something, but no matter, I know you will tell me about it when you feel comfortable doing so or not at all. Knowing you it shall probably the latter. Anyway, I digress. You see Rumble the way it is; you will get some new clothes, and looking at you, you look as though you need them. I cannot imagine how long you've had those trousers or that shirt, looks like they were secondhand to start with; although they are different to what you usually wear. I had thought you only had one set of clothes, Rumble. Indeed, I did." Cootes paused and Rumble realized that maybe he wasn't looking his best. He had never thought anyone notices, but it seems Cootes notices and Rumble felt slightly embarrassed. Rumble looked away from Cootes, and it was then he spied a folder on Cootes's desk with his name on it. Maybe he was getting fired? Panic was beginning to set in.

Surely Cootes wouldn't fire him? He loved his job, he always had, and he couldn't imagine working for anyone else, at alone having to find another job. He would do anything to avoid being fired.

"Rumble, you're the man for the job, and you're about to have a little adventure. I want you to look on this as an adventure, time away from the awful house where you live, and time in the real world, with real people. Don't look so panicked, Rumble. I know you're the man."

"Yes, Mr. Cootes. I can do it," once Rumble said this Cootes almost leapt from his chair. He came around the front of his desk and leaning back on it he looked closely at Rumble. Rumble was uncomfortable with Cootes show of emotion, and he still didn't know what he had just agreed to.

"Rumble, I see you haven't bought your suitcase then again I'm betting you don't own one. Still Lucy said you wouldn't respond, and you'd come here empty handed. Not to worry, Rumble; I am prepared for any eventuality, to keep my word, to my old friend."

"Yes, Mr. Cootes," Rumble responded; he was becoming more anxious and confused every second, and he had to physically try and hide his growing concern from Cootes who was sitting much to close for Rumble's comfort. He was used to Cootes behind his desk and that's where he liked him.

"In this envelope is cash, one thousand pounds to be exact, it is to cover your expenses. Now I insist that once you get to London, where you will have a six-hour wait time, you catch a cab directly to Marks and Spencer's. Once you're in the store, ask to see a personal shopper by the name of Lee Rinnick. He knows what you need.

Rumble, I spoke to him yesterday, he will be expecting you."

As Cootes took a breath, Rumble jumped in with his question, "I am not going to London, Mr. Cootes?"

"Rumble, you have been asked to cover an assignment for me in Edinburgh, Scotland. It's not a different world; it's just over the border. My friends, the Murrays, will be hosting the Riding of Marches commemorating the year 1513. One of the many family portraits you will see on the walls of the castle will be Randolph Murray himself clasping the Ancient Blue Blanket Banner; he was about to deliver the tragic news of the defeat by the Scottish army at the battle of Flodden. Not a piece of history you will be familiar with and so be it, not important to your assignment as such. However, I do feel you need the need to know. The annual ball has already been held, and I declined your attendance saying you were previously booked with another assignment. I know you would have felt most uncomfortable Rumble at the ball, most uncomfortable, indeed." Cootes handed him a long, white envelope, and as the top was already open, Rumble looked inside.

"Oh," was all Rumble said closing the envelope and taking another large gulp of tea, hoping it might steady his nerves and quiet his anxiety.

"And no, Rumble, this is your expense money; it was provided to you by Lord Riley Murray himself. Apparently, his wife, Maggie, asked if you had suitable attire, and before I thought, I answered no, which, of course, is the truth of the matter, as you know. Well, not twenty-four hours later a courier arrived from Scotland with your expense money; most generous, I would say most generous indeed, and they are also paying for your services, you shall, of course, be staying at their estate as their guest in Cloverdale Castle."

"But…" began Rumble and Cootes cut him short.

"No, Rumble, you cannot save this money for a rainy day; you have saved for far too many rainy days in your life. By the time you arrive in Scotland this evening and are met at Waverley station, you will be suitably attired in every way. I don't want to hear another word about it."

"But, I can't possibly…" Rumble began.

"You can, and you will, Rumble, they have especially requested you, and I'm not about to let them down merely because you have so many phobias and restrictions, that are by the way, all in your mind."

Rumble sat silently, looking at the floor, he was petrified. How could he do this? It was outside his comfort zone, and it would require him to change his daily routine. He wished he had checked his phone, then he could have had a suitable excuse; become violently ill or dropped dead, that would be the best of things to do in a situation like this.

Now Rumble remembered the famous adventurer who once said 'the further from home we roam, the closer to our destination we are.'

"Rumble, are you listening?" Cootes could see

Rumble was clearly not listening, and when Rumble finally looked at Cootes, he could see the concern in Cootes face. Rumble was trying to tell himself he could do this, but a greater part of him was saying he couldn't, he wouldn't, and he didn't want to.

He liked his life just the way it is. Then, to make matters worse, the voice responded, *'you like your life the way it is? How can you? You've got to be joking? Your life is hell you're scared to death most of the time, and now you have an opportunity for something new, an adventure almost, and you're behaving like a child, but then the meaning of adventure was never in your vocabulary was it? What happened to the promise you made to yourself some minutes ago when you said you would do anything to keep your job? The thought of losing it horrified you, but then maybe what you meant was that if you changed your job you would have to change your routine. That's the thing that scares you, isn't it? Just enjoy the adventure for once, you're so dull and boring...'* the voice continued on until Rumble said under his breath 'oh, do shut up.'

"Sorry, Rumble, what did you say?" Cootes asked still staring down at him, concerned.

"I said I've never been on a train, Mr. Cootes," Rumble stammered.

"Well, now there's a first time for everything, won't be a bad experience; you're going first class all the way, once you meet the train at Kings Cross, you'll find the Murrays have also booked you on the Flying Scotsman for your return. They asked if you'd ever ridden the Scotsman, and I was sure, you hadn't. That train is not cheap, not cheap at all. You're a very lucky man, Rumble, it will be quite an experience for you, indeed it will."

"But I don't need an adventure, Mr. Cootes. I like my life just the way it is."

"Well, Rumble, I think the only reason you think you like your life so much is because you don't know anything different. You're almost fifty, and I've never known you to step outside your daily routine, ever."

"Oh, but I do, Mr. Cootes, and I have done so just lately." *'Indeed, you did so just yesterday. Didn't you, Rumble? But it was hardly your choice,'* the voice cut into Rumble's mind, and with it came a flash back of yesterday's horrors, the vivid recollections caught him off guard, and he realized that going anywhere would be preferable to going back to the house tonight.

Rumble must have been silent for too long as Cootes got to his feet, then picking up two folders from his desk, a thick one and a thin one, he handed them both to Rumble.

"Some reading for your journey, Rumble. The thin one outlines Riley and Maggie's estate, some history and what to expect and what's expected of you. Don't let me down, Rumble. They know you like peace while you sketch, so I asked them to have a small table set up for you away from the crowd.

I used the excuse that you are a creative man, and in order to cover the fact you are ill at ease in crowds and people in general frighten you. So, behave and no one will know that's a good chap. And most of all enjoy this opportunity that your talent has provided you with." Cootes was still standing, so Rumble knew it was time to leave. To him, it felt like he was going to prison for all eternity and maybe that would be preferable.

"Rumble, the thick folder makes for very interesting reading, it is all about the history of the old house where you live. Often referred to as hopelessly haunted and gruesome in the extreme. It was apparently used as an experimental lab for over a century. Apparently, Edwards male ancestors claimed to all be scientists, or that was their ruse, scary, mad scientist, and they were looking for the key to eternal life. Some say they found it, but the sacrifices that were made and the human lives lost, is abominable. Anyway, I hope that once you read the history of the house, you won't want to stay there, or maybe somewhere deep inside you're actually a sadist or something," Cootes chuckled.

Rumble was standing with a blank look on his face as he stared back at Cootes, this was all too much, too much for Rumble to comprehend. Lucy hurriedly entered the room, and Rumble vaguely watched her and realized Lucy was always in a hurry. She reminded him of a bird.

"...Rumble, are you listening? I was speaking of my brother, James..." Cootes sounded annoyed. He was leaning closer to Rumble, and Rumble jumped when he became aware of his nearness. Rumble realized he had

236

missed everything Cootes was saying since he spoke of the house.

The moment Cootes stopped talking Lucy added, " Mr. Rumble, your taxi awaits."

Rumble nodded and turned to Cootes. "Remember, Rumble, your meeting Lee Rinnick at Marks and Spencer's and your train leaves at six p.m. sharp, Lee won't let you miss it. He'll take care of it all. Now do try and enjoy yourself, Rumble. At present, you look like the walking dead," Cootes said as Rumble reluctantly got to his feet, and Cootes walked him to the door. Then on impulse, Cootes grabbed his hand and began shaking it wildly for several seconds. Then he quickly dropped it as if he was ashamed of this unexpected show of emotion.

"Mr. Rumble, do you have your mobile phone charger with you? If not, I have a spare. Mr. Cootes said I was to change your plan so you can use it in Scotland should you need to make a call."

Finally, Rumble seemed to come back to earth and answered, "Yes, Lucy, I have the charger for my mobile phone in my sachet. But I have no clothes, no pajamas, no toothbrush…"

"Rumble, the taxi driver is taking you to Marks and Spencer's, and you are meeting with Lee Rinnick. He will take care of everything. Now put that envelope and those folders safely in your sachet. You'll need that money to pay Lee, and the taxi driver and for other things, once you're in London."

Rumble did as instructed. Lucy held the door to the outer office open for him. "Happy drawing," Cootes and Lucy said together and shut the door behind him. Rumble could see the taxi driver holding the rear door open for him. He knew it would be a long ride to London. Rumble also knew if he was going to run it had to be now.

He briefly turned to look back at Cootes' office, and there they were, both Cootes and Lucy standing just inside the doors watching him leave. He now knew what prison must feel like when you are being executed. Every part of Rumble wanted to bolt, but he knew he couldn't. He couldn't let Cootes down, and he really had nowhere to run to, apart from the house and that didn't entice him in any way.

"'ere ya go Gov'nor," the taxi driver said closing the door firmly and getting behind the wheel in the driver's seat. Rumble was sitting in the back seat of the taxi gripping his sachet until his knuckle were white. He willed himself to relax; he didn't want anyone to notice just how nervous and anxious this was making him feel.

"We've got a long trip together, Gov'nor. I just drove all the way from London to collect you. Ya gotta be someone mighty important, like."

"Thank you." Rumble managed only because he knew he needed to say something.

"I can tell ya's scared to death, hate traveling do ya? Or maybe ya get carsick? If ya feel a bit sickish, just let me know, Gov'nor, don't want no soiled taxi or nothin, like," the driver said eyeing him up in the rear vision mirror and looking rather concerned.

"I travel well thank you," Rumble said and immediately saw the relief in the driver's eyes. He felt the driver must know he didn't want to chat, and Rumble could tell the driver was a potential chatterbox.

Finally, Rumble took his sachet and placed it on the seat beside him. He needed to try and enjoy himself and traveling by taxi was much nicer than using the bus. By the time they were on the motorway, Rumble was watching the scenery go by and feeling quite contented in himself; he could easily have fallen asleep from the motion of the car.

Lee Rinnick was a slightly built young man with a mass of black curly hair shaved close at the sides, while the top had been left much longer and piled up on his head. His face was thin with small hazel eyes, a small mouth and a small button nose that turned up at the end. He was dressed conservatively in a light pink shirt and black tailored jacket and trousers. His shoes were very shiny and looked expensive.

He stepped forward and opened the back door of the black taxi for Rumble the moment it drew to the curb. It had been a long ride, and Rumble was glad to alight. He waited for the taxi to pull away and when it did not Lee quickly shook Rumble's hand, introduced himself and whispered to Rumble that he needed to pay the driver.

Rumble hated handing over so much money; he

should have been saving it for a rainy day.

"No tip, Gov'nor?" The driver asked and when Rumble didn't reply, the driver said, "Well, it takes all kinds, and I'd thought we were friends, like." Lee nodded to the driver and closed the door. London was huge, busy, and noisy. Rumble sniffed the air and then added smelly to his list. He could feel the energy of the place and see people everywhere. Most were smartly dressed and in a hurry. Some looked his way with distain and seeing this, Lee grabbed his arm and glided him inside the brightly lit department store.

"Mr. Rumble," Lee began in a cultured accent and a voice much too deep for his body. Lee was now standing a short distance from Rumble and looking him over rather disapprovingly from head to toe.

"I see we have a great deal of work to do; Mr. Cootes was not exaggerating at all." Rumble was not sure what he meant, so he didn't respond, he was now being guided quickly through the department store and up an escalator.

"I just require your shoe size and some measurements, and I shall take you to the spa while I get everything together for you. No suitcases, I see. My, my, you do travel light, sir."

"I didn't know I was travelling at all," Rumble replied.

"Obviously, sir. Don't worry about a thing I have worked extensively for Mr. Cootes in the past. I know where you're going and what shall be expected of you, so while I get together what you shall need, you can just relax for the next two hours and enjoy being pampered," Lee said. They were now in the men's department, and Lee was expertly running a tape measure all over Rumble without touching his person. For this, Rumble was most grateful.

Then it was up several more levels, through a rather plush office building and down a long plush hallway. Two wide misty glass doors stood at the end, and Lee quickly ushered Rumble inside. A pretty girl on the other side of the counter looked up as they entered and smiled when Lee said, "Mr. Rumble for his appointment, Sally."

"Thank you, Lee, we'll take good care of him from here."

"I'll see you soon, Mr. Rumble, enjoy," Lee said as he made a hurried exit. The girl called Sally had spoken softly into her mouthpiece and the moment Lee left two pretty women in matching pale green uniforms glided through some glass doors at the side of the reception desk and introduced themselves.

"Hello, Mr. Rumble, I'm Rhonda and this is Ruth, please follow us."

The next two hours were a blur for Rumble. He had never known anything like it, and he hated anyone in his space, but these girls just smiled at him and took no notice.

Rumble had his hair cut, his eyebrows trimmed and waxed, his face shaved and then covered with a facemask. While he had a manicure, pedicure and a teeth whitening treatment under the face mask. He couldn't move, but he wanted to. From there, he thought it got worse; he had an all over body scrub, then he was wrapped, so he was told, in seaweed that was followed by a complete body and face massage. Although after the initial shock, Rumble had to admit he quite liked it, in fact he almost fell asleep. The girls enquired about the many bruises and cuts on Rumble's body; they both asked him the same question at different times, but Rumble answered neither of them. It was, after all his business, and he knew they wouldn't believe him anyway. As he was scrubbed and washed, he likened himself to a boiled tomato. Then he was handed a set of new clean clothes along with his old ones.

"Please remove anything you wish to keep from the pockets and leave your old clothes behind, sir."

"I don't want to leave my clothes behind, miss?" Rumble admonished.

"Please, sir, you are to put on these new clothes, they also belong to you; this is what we have been instructed to ask you do from Mr. Rinnik."

"But I..."

"Sir..." Rumble noticed she looked like she was about to cry, so he took the neatly folded clothes she handed to him and stepped back into the room. He went through his pockets and only found the old key. Reluctantly, he began by putting on new underpants and socks then there were light tan tailored trousers and a dark green shirt. He had darkish brown ankle boots the likes of which he had never seen, but they fitted perfectly and were very comfortable.

He had a medium brown suede jacket with wool lining. It was soft, and warm, and very easy to wear. Rumble was also glad to see the old key fitted inside the pocket of the jacket. Then, for the first time since his arrival, he turned to look in the mirror. He didn't know who was looking back at him, but it wasn't him. The voice added, '*a better version of yourself, perhaps, I quite like it; you look younger and fresher somehow, and your teeth are whiter too.*' 'There was never anything wrong with my teeth, thank you.'

A discreet knock from the door was followed by Lee's deep voice, "Are you ready, sir? Is everything to your liking?" Rumble opened the door but didn't know what to say, he could see by the look on Lee's face he was pleased with what he saw. A brief battle of wills followed when Lee instructed him to leave his old clothes behind. Although Rumble held tightly to his sachet; he gave into Lee's request, and he made no further comments. Rumble thought it wasteful not to take his old clothes with him as they still had some wear left in them.

Once they were back in the department store, Lee showed him two large suitcases and a smaller carry-on. He then opened them and proceeded to show Rumble the contents. He then informed Rumble the suitcases, and the clothes belonged to him. Rumble noticed his name and Cootes office address neatly written on the tags. This was followed by a run-down of what was suitable attire to wear on each occasion and so on.

Then Rumble had to reluctantly part with some of the 'expense money' he had been given. The clothes and suitcases were over five hundred pounds, and the spa was a staggering two hundred pounds. Rumble hated to part with the money even though it wasn't technically his. His mother would have said he should be keeping it for a rainy day. Although on this occasion, it wasn't possible.

Rumble's head was spinning by the time Lee and Rumble were loaded into the taxi and driven to the train. Rumble almost completely forgot his new luggage; he was so overwhelmed, but Lee laughed it off and said that was what he was there for. *'Now this is what I call an adventure,'* the voice suddenly said startling Rumble. 'Oh, do shut up.'

Chapter Nineteen

The leather seats were soft in the first-class carriage of the train where Rumble sat staring at nothing and trying to focus his mind as to what he had just experienced. It was a blur, maybe a bad dream, maybe a good one, Rumble hadn't decided.

He was exhausted from all the activity and the people; he wasn't use to it at all and having to constantly answer them and follow the conversation was new and tiring to him. Just then the door to his stateroom opened and a neatly dressed steward entered.

"Sir, I hope you've had time to peruse the menu? I am here to take your order." Rumble hadn't even seen the menu, in fact he hadn't known there was one. He looked confused and apparently the steward was used to this so he added,

"Perhaps, sir, you would permit me to order for you? I feel sure you've had a rather long day…?"

"Yes, thank you," Rumble answered, glad to be rid of the pompous youth. Rumble assumed they would serve him a sandwich, so he wasn't prepared when the youth entered a short time later with a tray covered by a white starched cloth.

"Sir, I took the liberty of bringing you the cream of cauliflower soup, to start, should it not be to your liking, I am happy to change it. There is also a choice of cream of carrot, French onion, or ginger chicken."

"Thank you," was all Rumble said, and taking it as a positive, the youth removed the white cloth and left the compartment. Rumble stared at the small bowl of steaming soup, just the smell made him hungry. He never ate at night, so this was a unique experience indeed.

Beside the little soup bowl were two huge thick slices of the freshest bread Rumble had ever seen, they were still warm from the oven and in a white dish beside them was whipped butter. Rumble had eaten all the bread and butter before he even started the soup. He didn't think the soup could be nearly as good as the bread, but it was.

Rumble couldn't believe his luck at getting fed on the train. So far, the ride has been even smoother than the bus, although when he looked outside, he saw the scenery race past at a furious pace.

The only time he was really aware that he was traveling was when the train stopped at a station and started again. He could see the folks on the platform from the huge window in his compartment. But apart from that, he was alone, no one bothered him, and the only person he saw was the steward. To Rumble's amazement, twenty minutes after the youth in the smart uniform had cleared away his dishes, Rumble heard a discreet tap on the door, and the same young man entered with another tray.

"I have already eaten. Thank you; this must for someone else. I believe you have made a mistake." Rumble blurted out. The youth smiled knowingly, set the tray before Rumble, removed the domes that covered the dishes and stood back before announcing.

"Sir, you have baby lamb chops with mint sauce, cauliflower cheese, carrots in honey and sesame seed and new potatoes with parsley. The champagne is Dom Perignon, may I pour?" When Rumble didn't answer, he left the small chilled bottle where it was and continued, "…and for desert I chose apricot crumble. I trust everything is to your liking, sir? I shall return in a while with your order for tea or coffee." He bowed slightly and walked backwards out of the carriage.

Rumble was nothing short of speechless. He was already full from the soup, but he had to admit the meal in front of him was like nothing he had ever seen or smelled before. Then he stopped, as he thought perhaps he would be expected to pay for all this. He felt his palms begin to sweat at the thought before he remembered Cootes had said that from the moment he got on the train everything was paid for. Once he began to eat, he couldn't stop until every crumb on his plate had gone. He was so full; he thought he might burst, but it was by far the best meal he ever had.

While he waited for the steward to return and clear his dishes, he moved further along the seat and reached for the thin file Cootes had given him. He needed to at least read it before he arrived.

The moment he opened it, a full-page photo stared back at him. A tall solid jovial man with a mustache, a grey beard on the end of his chin and a large nose. He had a thinning head of hair much like Rumble's, shining blue eyes and a wide smile. He wore solid boots, a kilt of red and green tartan, and a heavy black jumper. One hand rested on a heavily curved walking stick with a silver handle while the other was behind his back. That must surely be Lord Riley Murray, Rumble thought, and once he started to read his profile, he realized he was right.

There was nothing remarkable in it, but Rumble now knew he liked his whisky neat, not on the rocks; he loved dogs, he liked a person with a fast wit and few words and so on. Then he turned the page and Lady Margaret Murray stared up at him. She had rosy cheeks, small teeth, a straight nose, and wavy greyish hair. She was dressed from head to toe in tweed, and she wore long shiny black riding boots; behind her stood a rather fine-looking horse, beautiful dressed, obviously a thoroughbred.

Her profile said firstly that she preferred to be called Maggie, nothing more nothing less. Also, that she liked Winnie the Pooh and had her own collection; she knew everything about AA Milne. She was a fan and had been her whole life, she even followed Christopher Robin, Alexander Alan Milne's only son. She bred horses some of the finest in the world and didn't suffer fools lightly. She ended her profile with a quote from none other than

Winnie, the Pooh and added that we should all live by his words: *Life is a journey to be experienced, not a problem to be solved.* Most profound, Rumble thought and interesting. It seemed Maggie was probably a nice sort, if slightly eccentric.

Rumble finished reading the information in the folder telling him all he needed to know about the Murrays, the estate, their castle, and the horse show. He fully intended to read the other file, the one he was dreading to open. However, he was cozy, warm, and well fed, and what he really wanted to do right now was to lie down for a few minutes on the soft plush leather seat. He closed his eyes, and by the time the Steward returned to take his coffee or tea order, several minutes later he was fast asleep. The youth covered him in a blanket and turned down the light.

The next thing he felt was the train coming to a stop. The young steward entered and informed him they had arrived at Waverley Station in Edinburgh. Rumble had slept nearly the whole trip. The steward had neatly packed his luggage away in his carriage, and Rumble almost forgot it. He retrieved his sachet and was about to exit when the steward reminded him he had luggage. The steward carried his luggage from the train; once he was on the platform, a tall slim bearded man immediately approached him.

"Now, Laddie, you must be the Master Rumble," the man said in a thick Scottish accent and before Rumble could answer, the man grabbed his bags from the ground and asked him to follow.

They entered an old Bentley, it was a magnificent car and in pristine condition. Once again, the back door was opened for him, and he was addressed as 'sir'. The back seat was most comfortable and covered in soft leather, with silver gray carpeted floors, there was a lot of legroom. Rumble tried to look out the window as they whizzed into the countryside, but it was too dark to see anything more than shadows.

"I imagine you be a wee bit tired after ye long journey, Master Rumble? So, I be takin you straight to the castle, and ye can go directly to ye bedchamber."

"Thank you," Rumble said barely able to understand the man at all. He hoped they didn't all speak like this, because it would make it hard to communicate. He had not expected them to speak another language just because he was in Scotland. If he'd known this, he would have had another reason to decline the trip. Although maybe it hadn't been too bad so far, he grudgingly agreed.

Sometime later, when Rumble was beginning to wonder if they would ever arrive at the castle, the car smoothly drove off the road and turned into a wide driveway with tall trees on either side. They drove on, and then, turning a corner, he saw a glow of light directly in front of him; then around another bend Cloverdale Castle loomed majestically. Rumble couldn't help staring, as there it loomed in all its nightly splendor. Rumble leaned forward in his seat; he had never seen anything like it. He wanted to take out his sketchpad and capture it right away; it inspired him.

As they drew closer, the enormity of the castle became apparent to Rumble and sensing his interest, the driver added to his thoughts, "She be quite somethin? Sir."

"Indeed," Rumble replied. The castle had high turrets, and narrow windows, and moss was clinging to its ancient exterior. Rumble could hardly wait for morning, so he could see it clearly in the daylight, although he knew he would one day draw it from his first impressions of tonight. He was still gazing upward with his nose almost touching the car window when all too soon the car glided to a stop, and the driver opened his door.

Rumble grabbed his sachet and walked up the wide stone steps. Just before he reached the top, he was aware of someone standing there.

"Welcome, Mr. Rumble, welcome. What a delight it is to have you here. My husband and I have been fans of your work for many, many years, and it is indeed an honor that you agreed to come to our estate and cover these events yourself. Oh, dear, where are my manners? I'm Margaret Murray."

"How do you do, Lady Murray," Rumble said extending his hand and shaking hers lightly in his hands.

"It's Maggie, Mr. Rumble, always just Maggie, if you please." Rumble nodded and had to admit she spoke much better than the driver. He could easily understand her.

"My husband, Lord Riley, as he prefers to be called,

apologizes for not being here to greet you. Unfortunately, he had some urgent business to attend to, but I know you shall meet him tomorrow." Rumble again nodded as the driver walked past him with his bags and deposited them inside the castle and discreetly left, tipping his cap at Rumble as he past.

"I know you've had a long journey, Mr. Rumble, and I won't keep you from your bed much longer. I merely wanted to welcome you to our home in person and to say I hope your stay will be a comfortable one. Should you need anything, anything at all, please let me know. This is Milly; she will show you to your room and unpack for you. I bid you goodnight." Rumble watched as she gracefully walked away, her head held high, her back straight. That's class; Rumble briefly thought as he said.

"Good night to you, Maggie."

"Follow me, sir," the younger woman instructed. Behind them, a young boy followed with Rumble's bags, and he made a mental note that he must not forget his new luggage in future. They seemed to walk quite a way, and Rumble wondered how he would ever find his way out.

"Her Ladyship said to put ye in the east wing in the blue room, sir. She said ye must probably want to be close to an exit as she thinks ye be an outdoorsy kind of person. I hope this is suitable?"

"I'm sure it will be, thank you," Rumble replied, as she opened double high wooden doors and revealed a huge room beyond. Surely, this can't be my bedroom? Rumble thought.

"It be one of our smaller suites but her ladyship said ye would prefer it due to the big bay window and access to the outside," Milly said. Rumble looked around at the tastefully decorated room, the huge king-size bed, the high ceilings, and the massive exposed beams. It had a long bay window that was presently covered by heavy drapes, and a blue velvet covered chaise lounge, several chairs, and large TV screen, and telephone.

The carpet was soft under foot, and the room was finished in soft blues. The walls looked like they were covered in pale blue silk, which had swirls through it under the light. Two huge lamps sat on either side of the comfortable looking bed.

"May I run ye bath now, sir," Milly asked standing still beside the bed with her hands clasped in front of her apron. Rumble noticed two other girls' shyly enter the room; they took his suitcases, one each, and began unpacking them inside a large walk in closet that he hadn't noticed. Rumble never had anyone ask to run him a bath before; in fact, he'd only ever had a bath when he'd looked after Millington's cat and lived in the main cottage. He wasn't sure what to say, so he nodded, and she disappeared to what Rumble realized was a bathroom right off his bedroom.

Rumble hadn't moved. He heard the bath water running into the bath. He saw the two girls close his suitcase and place them in a large wooden cupboard by the chairs. Then Milly spoke again, "Mr. Rumble, I have put some Epsom salts into your bathwater, if this is not to your liking, I shall empty your bath and run it again, sir?"

"Thank you," was all Rumble managed to say. Milly curtsied and was just about to leave the room when an older woman entered with a tray and placed it on the table beside the chaise.

"Just in case you are feeling a might pickish, sir. Goodnight." She too curtsied and left the room. Rumble turned around and around not believing his eyes, this couldn't possibly be his own bedroom, could it? Maybe someone else would be joining him, but there was only one bed as large as it was.

A while later, Rumble searched for his pajamas. He didn't recognize them as he'd barely seen them before. There were two pairs, a short sleeve pair with matching cotton shorts in a navy blue that also had a matching robe. Rumble searched further and found a fluffy, burgundy winter pair of pajamas with long legs and sleeves and a long matching robe and slippers. Rumble had never had or even worn a robe before and now he had two.

Rumble headed to the bathroom where a deep gold tub was three quarters filled with steaming water. Rumble looked down at the tub, and then remembered, he needed to brush his teeth, but turning, he saw a toothbrush and toothpaste on the vanity along with moisturizer, deodorant, after shave, and his new electric razor.

The bath was heavenly, and Rumble almost fell asleep

in the warm water as it caressed his body. It was nearly midnight when he peeked under the cloth that covered the tray. There was hot chocolate and shortbread. He raised the lid of the thermos jug and poured. It tasted delicious.

Rumble felt like he was in a dream as he sat and stared around the room. In his absence, while he bathed, someone lit the fire, and it now blazed brightly in the huge hearth. Several large landscapes adorned the walls and everything about him was luxurious. Once he was in bed with the crisp white sheets and soft duvet, Rumble wondered if he would soon awaken from this dream, but within seconds, he was asleep.

The next morning, it was the chirping of the birds, many of them unfamiliar to him, that first stirred his sleep. It was almost six a.m., and the dawn was just breaking outside the window when he opened the heavy drapes. Mist clung to every solid thing as it began to rise into the air and greet the day. Rumble couldn't remember ever feeling this good, he was full of energy and for once in his life, his insecurities and negative thoughts were not present. He searched for something to wear and found everything neatly hung in the large walk in closet or folded neatly in the drawers. He didn't recognize any of the clothes, but he knew they were all his. He briefly stopped and remembered what Lee Rinnick had told him about what to wear. Then he rummaged around until he was dressed in a heavy green woolen sweater, warm corduroy trousers in a paler shade of green, and the same sheepskin jacket that was heavily lined with wool, which he had worn on the train last night. He saw a scarf and cap, so he put them on and then found some heavy socks and wellington boots also in a kaki green that were lined for warmth. They almost came up to his knees, and they were very comfortable as everything so far had been. There were gloves in the pocket of his jacket, but he decided to leave them there.

Rumble grabbed his sachet and exited the room. After several wrong turns, he found a door that lead outside. The castle was just beginning to stir, and Rumble was pleased; he made it through the door without any one seeing him.

Rumble walked to the left slightly when he exited the door, and the ground slopped downwards. Five minutes later, he found himself staring at a huge pond. The water lay still, flat and glassy in the early morning. It looked silver like a huge mirror, and Rumble soon located an old tree with large thick woody roots protruding from the ground. It was drier under the tree, and Rumble sat with his back against the enormous truck.

Rumble sat and surveyed his new surroundings; everything was fresh and clean as it woke, rested from the night. To his right, picturesque rolling paddocks of bright green grass gradually became visible as the mist moved away, and then Rumble could just make out thick woods in the distance. In front of him, the land flowed like a picture down toward the rolling meadows and beautiful large trees that grew outwards as much as upward.

The mist further down the valley, beyond the pond appeared to have a purplish hue, but Rumble assumed the early morning light was merely playing tricks on him. He loved the silence and solitude, and for the first time in a long time, Rumble almost felt at peace with life.

"There ye be, Mr. Rumble, I just knew you be an early riser." A young girl with large sparkling hazel eyes, a small nose, and a rosebud mouth; stood looking down at him. She had long shiny brown hair that curled daintily at the ends. Her body was round and looked too old for her age.

Her hips were plump and round; her waist was tiny while her chest was ample and very round. She wore old leather boots that were maybe once black, along with a gray woolen skirt and a jacket much like his own, although hers had seen a lot more wear. It was unzipped. Rumble looked up at the young girl who had supposedly materialized out of the mist and wondered briefly if she a nymph or something but weren't nymph's only in Ireland and not Scotland?

When Rumble didn't reply, because he thought there was no need to, she held out her hand and continued, "Hi, Nitzy MacDonald, me mam's the housekeeper here, and I'm to be your guide and general factotum while ya be here. I know everything there be to know about anything around here. May I sit?" she said, her were eyes dancing with mischief as she sat close to Rumble who discreetly moved further away.

He thought she smelled of fresh lavender and hay, and she had the most floorless white porcelain skin he had ever seen. Rumble had just retrieved his sketchpad and pencils from his sachet, and he had every intention of sketching, however, he didn't mind this interruption at all.

"I am usually the first up and outside in the morning. I like to feel the crispy dew crunch under my feet and watch the mist as it moves down into the moors and settles over the heather. Usually about this time of the year, ye see a purple haze cos the heather is in full bloom, and once the mist lifts, you'll see nothing but a purple carpet unfold in front of ye, for miles. It be so very beautiful here, don't ye think, Mr. Rumble?"

"Oh, yes, Miss Nitzy, indeed I do," and he meant it.

"Oh, you're so British," she giggled and then she said "I'm just Nitzy, and I'm not yet twenty."

"Oh, I thought you would be younger than that, Nitzy." Rumble immediately saw the downcast expression his words had achieved and felt bad about not thinking before he spoke.

"Oh, dear, did you really? I've got no fashion sense at all ye see, none at all. I just wear whatever is comfortable and clean. All me friends are very fashionable, and they've all got them themselves a fella; in fact, Mr. Rumble, they are engaged the lot of them. But not me; I know I'm rather plain, but I have no idea what to do about it."

"Nitzy, you're really not plain at all. I thought you quite enchanting when you appeared out the mist just a moment ago," Rumble replied honestly.

"Even beautiful, perhaps?" she asked the mischief again dancing in her eyes. Rumble didn't know her, but he didn't want to say anything to upset her either. As she talked, he sketched.

"Of course, Nitzy, of course, you are."

"Oh, thank ye, Mr. Rumble, me mam says beauty is on the inside, and I have no doubts it is, but in order to catch the eye of a young laddie, ye got to have wee dose of beauty on the outside too. Don't ye agree, Mr. Rumble?"

"Well, indeed I have never really thought about it before, but I think you're probably right."

"Why now, I have, of course. Ye see I have me eye on a wee laddie. He works in the village. His name is, Liam Glen," Nitzy said, blushing deeply and giggling as she looked at the ground and twisted her hands together. Rumble smiled at her, she was quite delightful, and he now realized he didn't need to give all his attention to what he was sketching. His hands knew what to do and his eyes knew what to see.

"Do you like him, Nitzy?" Rumble asked but then thought that maybe he should not.

However, Nitzy blushed deeper and answered him directly, "Oh, yes, Mr. Rumble, I likes him a lot. But I don't think he knows I exist. After I've shown ye around, I'm going into the village. I'll put my hair up in a ponytail high on my head, like this," she said holding her hair in place.

"I'm even going to wear a pretty ribbon in it. I have several you know. Then I'll put on a wee bit of lip gloss to make my lips shine and a dab of perfume behind me ears. I'll wear me pretty skirt, the one with the blue flowers on it, and a cashmere sweater in light blue, the one I save for best," she paused to take a breath her eyes and thoughts far away.

"I know you'll look smashing." Rumble ventured.

"Smashing...?" Nitzy replied and giggled, and then she said, "Liam works for the smithie, sorry, I mean the blacksmith, and I have a genuine excuse to visit him. Ye see, Monty, Lady Maggie's favorite horse, has a loose shoe, and the show is in two days' time; everything must be perfect. I know one of the grooms can probably fix it, but I'm sure Liam's far better at these things."

"You have a blacksmith in the village, Nitzy?" Rumble asked amazed at the thought that in this day and age a working blacksmith could still exists.

"Oh, of course, and he's always busy too, many a time he be goin to close his shop but many a time ta folks have proved to him that he's needed. I'll take ye to the village one day if you'd like to see it?"

"Indeed, I would, thank you." Rumble had finished his sketch and tore it from his book. Nitzy reached over and had a look.

"Oh, yes, that is good, I know why you're here ye really are very talented. Is that me, Mr. Rumble?" Nitzy asked clapping together her hands in delight. Rumble had sketched the valley with the moors in the distance right from where he was sitting. It showed a close up, side view of Nitzy, her hands under her chin as she stared out wistfully over the silver pond and the moor beyond. Rumble would later add a purple haze. Two ducks recently appeared on the pond, and Rumble had quickly added them; he could tell Nitzy was very impressed. He hadn't realized he had drawn in Nitzy until she mentioned it, but now, looking at the sketch, there she was. It was his rule to never draw people, but like everything else lately, the way he thought and the things he was doing, were all changing.

He tore the sketch from his sketchpad and after Nitzy had finished gazing at it for what seemed like a long time. Then he opened the sketchpad to the back page. The face of Ms. Primrose stared back at him. He gently touched his index and middle finger to her face as he felt himself blush. Why did he feel like this around her? He really didn't understand. Then he placed the sketch of the pond and Nitzy on top of the one of Ms. Primrose. He was about to close his sketchpad when he decided to place his new sketch under the one of Ms. Primrose rather than on top, yes, that seemed the right thing to do.

"Mr. Rumble, we really should be getting back, breakfast is served in the main dining room from eight o'clock until nine thirty, and I know you'll need to change first."

"I really don't want any breakfast, thank you, Nitzy," Rumble informed her.

"But you simply must. Why breakfast is the most important meal of the day?"

"I had a great deal to eat yesterday, Nitzy, much more than I am used to eating. Anyway, I will need to change for breakfast and then change back again; it does seem like an awful lot of changing clothes to me."

Nitzy giggled and still looking at him hard, she said, "Well, I shouldn't be saying this, but I can sneak you in through the kitchen door, and you can have breakfast with me at the big table. Its rather noisy with all the chatter but the food is the same, and we can get in and out much faster. Oh, come on, Mr. Rumble, I'm starving," Nitzy replied already standing over him. Rumble was really quite happy where he was, and he would have liked to stay here a while longer, but Nitzy was hard to refuse. Grudgingly, he got to his feet and followed her around the side of the castle and in through two huge hidden wooden doors that were round on top instead of square.

Rumble wasn't nearly ready for the sight and noise that greeted him as they entered the large, warm kitchen. People bustled everywhere; others yelled orders telling them to do this or that or hurry up; the stoves had several cooks, all cooking madly, each with a different dish. Nitzy took Rumble's arm and glided him over to the left as they stayed close to the wall to avoid getting run down.

"Is it like this with every meal, Nitzy?"

"Oh, no, this is only breakfast, you should see it at dinner time or when his Lordship is entertaining." Rumble was amazed he'd never imagined so much preparation went into feeding people.

They were seated at a huge, roughly made table. Rumble could see where others had carved their initials into the top of the sawn in half logs that had been placed side by side, four across, to make the table top.

"Ye know better than to bring the likes of him, in 'ere, Nitzy. Why he be a guest of the gentry and that's where he belongs not down here with the likes of us." The woman was short and stout and wore a gray uniform like most of the others with a clean starched apron over it, and she had her gray hair piled up under a white frilly cap that was pinned tightly to her head.

"Cookie, I know all that. But Mr. Rumble didn't want to eat in the fancy dining room with the others."

Rumble noticed the one called Cookie was still looking at Nitzy with a disapproving look on her face, so he added, "I'm sorry, it was my fault."

At his words, her expression softened and she turned to Nitzy and said, "Well, lassie, I'll not be waitin on ye. Ye can look after ye both and be smart about it, I'm not about to be caught with no guest of them in me kitchen."

"Thanks, Cookie, we'll be quick. Mr. Rumble is in a hurry for his tour anyway, and I know tomorrow he'll be busy with Lady Maggie and Lord Riley most of the day."

"Well, ye know where everything is. And don't go

gettin in the way of anyone, ye understand, lass?" Nitzy nodded. Cookie disappeared, and after Nitzy told Rumble to stay where he was, she too seemed to blend into all the commotion and disappear. Several minutes later, she returned with two large plates; she set one down in front of Rumble, while the other was placed where she was to sit. Then she disappeared again. Soon, she presented him with a half loaf of fresh bread from the oven on a worn chopping board, she gave him a knife and placed the butter and marmalade on the table. Moments later, she was back again with a jug of orange juice.

"Coffee or tea, Mr. Rumble?" She inquired, and when he didn't answer, she whizzed into the crowd and returned with two steaming mugs of coffee. Rumble looked at his plate, it was full of bacon, scrambled eggs, sausages, and what looked like a fish of some kind; there was also grilled mushrooms, the largest he had ever seen and tomatoes also bigger than normal.

"I grabbed us the last two kippers; hope you like them? I'll get the porridge later if that's all right unless you want it now?" Rumble shook his head and began tucking into his meal, out the corner of his eye, he noticed Nitzy was doing the same.

Their plates were hardly empty when Cookie appeared from nowhere and whisked them away. Nitzy had lightly toasted a slice each of the fresh bread, although Rumble thought he couldn't eat another bite. The large thick slices of bread were the best he had ever tasted and melted in his mouth. As full as he was he could have managed another slice, however, the moment the last of his juice and coffee was finished, Cookie appeared again. She placed her chubby hands on her wide hips and said, "Out with ye, out of me kitchen, I hear Lady Maggie in the far hall, and she maybe comin this way. I don't intend to get caught with the like of him in me kitchen. Not when he's supposed to be with them folks upstairs. Now away with ye," she shouted, her hands on her hips.

Nitzy grabbed Rumble's arm and almost dragged him to the back door and outside, as he walked down the stairs he could indeed hear Maggie's voice getting louder as she drew closer to the kitchen.

"Come on, we'll start this way. Hope you're up for a walk, Mr. Rumble?"

"Indeed," was all Rumble could say for one so short she walked at a furious pace.

They were going up a slight hill and turning the corner of the castle. Rumble was surprised to see the stables stretch out before him. They were all sparkling clean, state of the art, very modern with many industrious stable hands working together. Rumble saw groomsmen, stable hands, horse handlers and more; the stables were abuzz with activity.

Some horses were being paraded around the courtyard by a handler while others were carefully inspected. Rumble noticed they were all perfectly groomed and impeccably bred. Rumble estimated several million pounds' worth of thoroughbreds, at the very least were housed in these stables.

"Lady Maggie likes her horses, and she's most particular, only the best will do. After all she has a reputation to up hold. Ye must admit these are exceptional stables, Mr. Rumble? Why ye could eat ye dinner off the concrete. These horses are looked after much better than most humans." Nitzy giggled as they dodged a fast-moving horse with a trainer holding the rope.

"This way, Mr. Rumble, we shouldn't really be here; it's probably not safe; some highly spirited horses can get a might snippy. Many of them are highly strung too, and don't mind nipping anyone who gets in their way." Nitzy took his arm, and they moved away from the action of the stables. At the rear of the stables, they headed slightly up hill.

The morning was turning out to be crisp with watery sunlight winning the battle with the clouds. Now blue patches of sky were beginning to show through and with it came a sharp breeze. As they walked, Nitzy pointed out the little cottages hidden all over the estate and told Rumble who lived there and what they did. It wasn't long before he noticed a large outhouse, with steam pouring from the roof and clotheslines strung up at one side.

He pointed in that direction. "That's our laundry facility, that's where they wash, dry, starch, and iron everything from your bed sheets, to your socks, tea towels, evening gowns, and so on. Twenty-five men and woman

266

are employed there, and they work a twelve-hour day and shifts, so it runs seven days a week. It's hard work and usually once the ladies get older or marry, they become under housemaids or kitchen hands. Most of them live above the laundry and some live on the estate with their families.

The laundry facility heats its own water and is completely separate from the castle in every way." Rumble found it fascinating, and as they walked on, Nitzy pointed down the hill to where all the barking noises were coming from. "That's where Lord Riley keeps his hounds; he has rather a lot; do ye want to go down and see them more closely?"

"No, I can see them quite well from here, thank you, Nitzy."

"I can see ye know hounds, Mr. Rumble. Ye can never trust those wee doggies, they often snap or bite or growl and that's not just if you're a stranger. I've seen some nasty wee bites inflicted by some of those doggies over the years let me tell ye I have. But Lord Riley will not hear a bad word said against them; they be his babies, and they all obey only him. He knows most of them by name and there really are a terrible lot of them. He seldom gives away any pups, so their numbers just keep growing. He never takes them all out at once ye understand." Rumble nodded and was glad when they turned away.

As they walked past the tiny cottages, people came out and greeted Nitzy, many of whom she introduced to

Rumble. They eyed him up warily at first, and if Nitzy stopped to chat, they would soon warm to him.

Soon, they were back walking over more pristine paddocks. Fluffy white sheep with long black faces grazed on the healthy green grass, and the occasional herd of cattle could be seen in the distance. Rumble estimated they must have walked for miles everything was so far away.

Nitzy had just told him that the estate has one hundred and sixty-five full-time employees and more that come in from the village as they're needed. Rumble found it extraordinary; he had no idea about any of this, and he was also enjoying learning new things. His mind was alive with new knowledge, and his eyes with the wonders of his surroundings.

Rumble was glad Nitzy was with him as he had no idea where they were or how to get back to the front of the castle.

Around the next bend, they arrived in the middle of the largest vegetable garden; Rumble had ever seen it stretched for miles almost as far as the eye could see.

"This is where they grow all our vegetables. Between the veggie garden and the woods, we have an orchard that supplies us with all the fruit we need. The woods are original woodlands and also belong entirely to the estate. The gamekeepers patrol the woods all year round, as we sometimes have poachers. The ponds where we were this morning are stocked yearly with trout and salmon. In the distance you can see the hatchery's where the fish be created." Rumble would have liked a closer look at the hatcheries, as he'd never seen any before. But just then a tall swarthy man presented himself startling Rumble when he suddenly appeared in front of them. His wide brimmed hat had several large holes in it and his trousers and jacket had both been patched regularly.

"Mr. Rumble, this is Thomas Lyth; he be our chief gardener and occasional grounds man, as the need arises." He shook hands with Rumble who was, by now, getting used to meeting people. Rumble was interested to hear this man's story. He understood the enormity of the responsibilities of being the head gardener. Everyone seemed to have a unique and fascinating story to tell. And then Thomas spoke; his accent was as thick as treacle. He talked so fast; Rumble was unable to understand a word. So, he nodded politely at what he hoped were the right times and let Nitzy do the talking.

Once they bid Thomas farewell, Nitzy explained, "Thomas says a grub has eaten his leeks, and he is just on his way to tell Cookie that leek and potato soup is off the menu for tonight's dinner. Thomas is the best gardener and finding grubs in the leek patch is a huge blow to him and his reputation. Lord Riley, will not be pleased at all." Now Rumble understood the problem and the impact it was to have on the kitchen and the household.

"We'll skirt around the edge of the woods, and end up at the front gate. If we walk fast, we should make it in time for you to get changed and be at the lunch table before the ladies arrives," Nitzy said, moving even faster than she usually did. Even though Rumble walked around every day, it was never at a speed like this and never so far. The Estate was huge, and as Nitzy chatted she told Rumble they had only seen a small part of it. The paddock seemed to go forever, and Rumble was gradually failing to see the beauty as his body told him it was time for a rest. He knew that even if he was living a dream, he was still feeling physically tired.

Chapter Twenty

Finally, they were walking beside the woods. Looking in, Rumble saw the darkness and thick undergrowth, he heard rustling noises, and he couldn't see from where they came. Further in, he could just make out patches of sunshine filtering through the trees and hitting the leafy ground of the hidden dells. Rumble thought Nitzy must have seen where he was looking as she followed his gaze and added, "The foxes, all of them be safe in our woods. The silver fox, the red fox, the larger brown ones, all be safe and sound here. No hunting or poaching is allowed, and His Lordship has this area, and the whole estate patrolled for unwanted guests. He owns thousands of acres around here, Mr. Rumble, and he is a fair but stern land owner."

"Nitzy, I have always wanted to sketch foxes in their own environment, and the woods are wild and natural."

"I could show ye some wee places where the foxes play, but you would have to be a might patient, sit still, remain quiet, and wait a wee while," she commented, still staring into the woodlands.

"I can do that, Nitzy; I need less than ten minutes to capture an outline of what I see."

"I know how professional ye be, Mr. Rumble. I watched ye sketching this mornin, and the way ye captured me hair falling over me face and the light on the pond was wonderful to be sure." Rumble stopped to catch his breath more than to look into the woods, but Nitzy must have thought, he wanted to see the foxes now, so she quickly added, "We don't have time to go in there today, Mr. Rumble. We are already almost late, but one day if there's time, I would be most happy to show ye the foxes," she said with a twinkle in her eyes.

"I would like that very much. You see I don't like to sketch people much, but animals and nature, I really do enjoy."

"Oh, but, Mr. Rumble, ye will need to sketch His Lord and her Ladyship and probably others while you're here and ye will do it so well."

"Thank you, Nitzy, and yes I am beginning to understand that now. Many things have taken me outside my comfort zone since I left home yesterday morning, so I assume there will be more before I leave," Rumble said this in a whisper more to himself than to Nitzy. He could tell she hadn't really heard him as she just nodded in reply.

They seemed to walk for miles beside the woods, and Rumble felt the contrast between the woods, and the bustle, and noise of the kitchen earlier this morning.

As they walked on, Rumble noticed Nitzy had been silent for some time, so it startled Rumble when she suddenly spoke out loudly and with great passion, "Mr. Rumble, you're a man, so please tell me from a man's point of view, am I sexy?"

Rumble almost fell over at her question, he felt his cheeks flush, and he had no idea what he should say. He understood how delicately he needed to handle any questions regarding Nitzy's appearance, but this was really too much. The awkward silence stretched on until Nitzy answered her own question, "Oh, Mr. Rumble, that does give me my answer. By not saying anything, ye are saying a lot. Ye actually don't think I'm sexy at all, and ye probably don't think I'm even attractive. Well, you're right. I've always known it. Liam will never look at me. Why have I been so foolish?" Nitzy was trying to hold back the tears, and when she could not, she ran on ahead. Rumble wanted to go after her, but he was just too tired, he could hardly walk at alone keep up with a nineteen-year-old girl.

Then, to his dismay, the voice that had been so wonderfully silent for so long, startled him by saying, '*now look what you've done, you can't even say the right thing to a young girl, really, Rumble. Why aren't you running after her? Sometimes Rumble, I don't know who you are, and she's been just plain sweet to you. Who are you anyway?*' Rumble had nothing to say to the voice, so he didn't reply. Sometimes he didn't understand himself either.

As he watched, she finally stopped running; even with her back to him, he could see her shoulders shuddering as she cried, she was now composing herself and wiping her eyes. By the time, he arrived at her side, she looked up at him with big hazel eyes that no longer held a sparkle of tears and said, "I'm not only plain and unsexy, but now I'm acting like a child as well." Finally Rumble found his voice, he was never good at talking about emotions or feelings of the heart, he had never had any experience, and he really didn't understand them.

"Nitzy, I don't know much about young boys, but I do know you're a very special young lady, and if Liam can't see that then he doesn't deserve you.

I know beauty comes from within, but I also know, and I've only learned this lately that we need to present ourselves as best we can. Just be yourself. Nitzy, you can't make someone like you, and you wouldn't want to be with them anyway if they didn't." Rumble thought that came out rather well, although looking at Nitzy, she still looked sad.

"You're right, Mr. Rumble, of course, you are. But ye see, we don't have a lot of young ladies of my age here in the village 'tis only a wee place, and Liam is about all there is, plus maybe Mr. Abercrombie. If it's not Liam then I need to go to another village, and they won't know our ways or our doings. Then I might end up a wee bit betwixt and between." Nitzy finished looking up at him.

They were approaching the entrance to the front gate now. They were almost at the same gates the driver had driven Rumble through last night. Rumble needed to say something profound,

"Walt Disney once said, if you can dream it, you can

274

do it. Remember that, Nitzy." He saw her thinking over his words until finally she smiled. Now they were walking up the long driveway toward the daunting and splendid Cloverdale Castle. Through the high iron gates that stood wide and down the long curving driveway where the ancient yew trees stood guard like sentinels.

Those old trees saw it all and knew everything; they looked down and laughed at all those who entered. They laughed as only a tree can, about the mortals' lack of wisdom, knowledge and learning, and their need to understand the ways of the universe if the world was to not only survive, but also evolve.

Rumble could feel their wisdom and wanted to capture it all on paper before he left. All around Rumble, there was history, hundreds of years of history, he wanted to understand it all, but he knew he was here for one task and one task only, and that he would do it to the best of his ability.

"Mr. Rumble, we must run to the castle, the hour it be late, and it leaves ye little time to change and present yourself at lunch. Should ye be late I shall be blamed and I am trying to show Lady Maggie that I am a responsible young lady and a good tour guide. Ye see, Mr. Rumble, ye be me very first charge." Sounding very agitated, Nitzy took his hand and pulled him toward the front entrance of the castle, she kept pulling him upstairs and into the entranceway. With a quick wave, she turned and left through the doors they had just entered.

Rumble was not sure of the way to his room. But he knew the general direction. He closed his eyes and visualized the way they walked last night. Feeling confident, he set off in that direction only to find he was hopelessly lost.

A maid raced toward him carrying an arm full of towels. Rumble stopped her and politely asked the way. She took him to his room and reminded him that lunch would be served in less than fifteen minutes, and perhaps he should hurry so as not to keep them all waiting. Once in his room, he noticed that everything had been tidied. He searched for the clothes he had worn last night, and when he couldn't find them, he gulped down the rising panic that threatened to engulf him.

But looking in his wardrobe, he saw he had plenty more. Again, he closed his eyes and recalled Lee Rinnick words as to what he should wear with what and when. Rumble knew he should have showered as the walking had been more vigorous than he was used to, but there appeared to be no time. Rumble was soon dressed in what he thought was suitable attire. He brushed his teeth, combed his hair, and at the last moment, he added a little aftershave and deodorant. This was his first time using either of these and he recalled Lee Rinnicks words about the amount that was suitable and how too much was in poor taste. He sprayed the aftershave just in front of his face and then walked forward into it, as he had been taught. Most satisfactory, he thought, knowing he had smelled somewhat like a horse after all his walking.

The bed looked so soft and inviting, but Rumble knew he must join his hosts for lunch. He hurried out of his room and down the long hallway. Another maid directed him to the dining room.

On his arrival he found the dining room full of people, and Rumble soon realized every seat had a place card. Nearly all the seats were full, so he easily managed to find his own. He had hardly made it to his chair when Lord and Lady Murray entered the room; everyone stood, until they were seated, no one else sat. Several servants held the lady's chairs for them, and the men looked after themselves.

Rumble watched discreetly to see what was the done thing; and how they reacted. He hated being here with so many people, but he didn't intend to let Cootes down if he could help it.

The first course was mushroom soup, and the three tall crystal glasses in front of Rumble were soon filled with water and then white wine. The second course was pheasant soufflés, and this was served with a different wine. Rumble was learning that the correct wine and cutlery was just as important as the meal. Rumble had just taken the first mouthful of his soufflé when the chatter slowed for a moment, and the man at the far end addressed Rumble in a rather loud, harsh American accent, "So, you're the man they're all talking about the one who scribbles and everyone thinks its art. No one here would have a clue whether you're bad or good, so you are probably a phony." He laughed heartily, and several others politely joined in, all eyes were on Rumble who quickly swallowed his mouthful of soufflé as he tried to find a suitable retort. However, it was Maggie who came to his rescue.

"Thomas, you are really being rather offensive to our guest, and I must ask you to treat him with the same courtesy as you should be treating everyone else."

"Well, now that's the thing, my dear cousin, Maggie, that's the thing; you see I don't really treat anyone with any respect. Not like you English tip toeing around every issue afraid to tread on anyone toes. Attack first and ask questions later, that's the American way, and it's served me very well over the years. All I'm saying is the man is only here because someone thinks he can draw. The devil with it, we can all draw, if we want to, yes, every single one of us. So, what makes him so special?"

"Enough indeed, Thomas," Lord Riley thundered in a loud booming voice that rattled the chandeliers' and bought a hush over the gathering.

"Remember your manners at my table, or you may choose to not grace us with your presence again."

"You're a pompous ass, Riley; everyone thinks so. In fact, I find the English all rather pompous, no secret, and I'm not scared to say what I feel, unlike you lot." No one spoke, Lord Riley's face turned crimson, and he was getting to his feet. Rumble just wanted to disappear. And then gradually one by one, the diners began to clap and then several said, "Jolly good show, old boy, you haven't lost it…"

And another said, "You uncouth Americans are always entertaining, poor taste perhaps but…"

While another added, "I must say, old chap, you do take it to the extreme, the very edge indeed. We don't even know Mr. Rumble, poor choice of a target in my opinion, indeed. Anyway cheers, Thomas." Rumble had no idea what was happening, but soon they raised their glasses in a toast to Thomas. Lord Riley remained seated and did not raise his glass with many of the other guests. Maggie gracefully got up from her chair and came to stand beside Rumble.

"Please, forgive my cousin, Mr. Rumble, there is no excuse for his insolence, rudeness, or arrogant behavior, and I am so sorry if he made you feel uncomfortable," she whispered the words and Rumble knew no one else heard, so he whispered back.

"Thank you, Maggie," and she returned to her seat as the others began to settle back into their lunch. Rumble was unable to eat anything further. Once Lord Riley and Lady Maggie left the table, everyone followed.

Rumble could see Thomas and several other gentlemen were about to make a beeline for him, so he moved quickly to the door. A maid was waiting just outside the door, and she told Rumble that her Ladyship wishes to receive him in the library and could he follow her.

The library was a huge, high ceilinged room with lots of dark wood panels, exposed beams the size of which Rumble had never seen before, and two long narrow windows at the far end of the room that couldn't possibly let in enough light. The walls were lined with many books, some of which were shut away behind glass cabinets. To Rumble, these books looked old and expensive.

In the corner nearest the door was a half-circular glass cabinet, very old and expensive. Inside it sat a rather worn teddy bear with one black glass eye missing, plus some old children's books. Then Rumble remembered Maggie's love of everything Winnie the Pooh, so he assumed that included Pooh Bear, and he understood how precious these things must be to her.

Rumble's eyes had to adjust to the darkness of the room, even though several lamps put out a soft yellow glow. Finally, he spotted Maggie standing beside a high round table.

"Thank you, Mr. Rumble, for joining me. I haven't had much time with you, and I want to outline the next couple of days, and what you can expect, and what we are expecting of you. I have a list of the events, when and where they are happening. I want you to sketch whatever you feel is worthy of your time; please don't allow anyone to curtail your skills that you don't think is deserving. We have the most faith in your abilities to capture the moment."

"Thank you for your confidence in me, Maggie."

"It is much deserved believe me. We have been fans of your work for many years, and it is indeed an honor to have you under our roof. We never miss an edition of *Horse and Hound* and several other of the magazines who print your work."

"Thank you, Maggie, you are most kind."

"Oh, indeed, not at all, Mr. Rumble. Why you make every event you sketch come to life and look like a true adventure?"

"Thank you for noticing, Maggie, that is my aim." She appeared not to hear him, and he wondered what she would say if he told her he did all his sketches from photos on the Internet.

She continued on talking over his words, "You know life is an adventure to be experienced, not a problem to be solved. Do you know who said those famous words, Mr. Rumble, do you?"

Rumble thought quickly over all he'd read about her and soon replied, "Was it perhaps, the creator of Winnie the Pooh, A.A. Milne?" At his reply, her face simply came alive, she beamed at him from ear to ear and clapped her hands. Then, turning, she went to one of the display cabinets and beckoned for him to follow. She pointed to the rather old worn teddy bear sitting on the glass shelf, sharing back at them with one black glass eye. It was the very same bear he had seen as he entered the library.

"Mr. Rumble, this was my first teddy bear. It is an

exact replica of Winnie the Pooh. I really loved him to death as you can tell by his condition. Worth nothing to anyone except me, but to me, this bear, and all things relating to Winnie the Pooh are indeed, priceless." Rumble nodded and noticed the wistful look in her eyes fade as she returned to the high round table. There she showed him a plan of the layout for the point to point and dressage competitions.

She told him that both she and Monty wanted to be sketched before each event and that Lord Riley insisted on a sketch of him with his beloved hounds. Rumble already knew she was expecting him to sketch various parts of the grounds, the castle and also the events. But now Rumble was becoming aware that she also expected him to sketch people and from what she was saying, it would be several people. He did not usually sketch people, and he didn't know why Cootes had not told her so. She handed him several lists and also told him that Nitzy would be at his disposal should he require anything at all.

She asked him if he was comfortable and did he need anything, and if so, to just ask. She then said the framer would be here this Saturday to frame his work, and would he have the sketches ready at that time? He assured her he would, and he knew he would manage it somehow. Then she asked, "Please do not feel the need to hurry away after your work here is done; you are welcome to stay as long as you like Mr. Rumble. You have an open ticket for your return on the Flying Scotsman. Lord Riley and I both enjoy traveling on that train immensely, and we hope you will also."

"You have been most gracious and kind, Maggie."

"Not at all, Mr. Rumble. It is customary for his Lordship and myself to rest after luncheon, and we encourage our guests to do the same. I am keeping you away from your bed. Again, enjoy your time here at Cloverdale Castle, Mr. Rumble. Good afternoon to you." Maggie graciously turned, and walked across the floor; her heels clicking loudly on the old wooden timbers beneath her feet. She softly opened the door and left. Rumble liked her lot; she was a real lady. As the door closed behind her, he realized he needed to also wish her a 'good afternoon', but it was too late; she would never hear him now.

After several wrong turns, he managed to find his own way back to his room without the need to ask anyone. Parts of the castle were now becoming familiar to him. Even though the fire in his room was not yet lit, the room looked cozy and inviting. Sunlight streamed in the large windows that had been partly opened. The sheer curtains danced lightly in the breeze. Once Rumble closed the door to his room, he realized he was dead tired. He should have been working on this morning's sketches, but the comfort of the bed beckoned. Rumble seldom lay on his bed during the day, although in the small space of his attic room, which he realized was smaller than the walk-in closet in front of him, there was not much choice of being anywhere else. He only had one chair and kept that propped under the door knob. That, to him was most important, more important than using it to sit on.

If the others were resting, maybe he would also, he was quite tired after his long walk with Nitzy.

For one so small, she certainly could move. Rumble wondered just how the gentry would approach the afternoon rest time, not in their clothes, surely, nor in their pajamas, either. Rumble wondered into this large walk in closet and then spied his robe hanging on a hook on the wall. That's what he'd wear. He thought he'd simply wear his robe. He removed his clothes and left his underwear on. Then he wrapped the soft burgundy robe tightly around him. He couldn't help but run his hands over the fabric; he had never felt anything so soft before.

Then he remembered the hundreds of pounds he had parted with at the huge London department store. It made him feel sick. But no, he wouldn't dwell on it like he used to. He was having a wonderful time, and he had learned so much from Nitzy this morning. He lay on his bed, not intending to sleep, but instead he wanted to think about his day so far. He pulled the blanket from the bottom of the bed up over him, and as his mind drifted through all he had seen, and learned. His eyelids drooped, and in minutes, he was fast asleep.

Sometime later, Rumble became aware of a gentle tapping; it went on and on, until finally, he opened his eyes. The sun was no longer illuminating the room, and the shadows from outside were beginning to close in. He should have worn that watch, Lee Rinnick had for him, but he kept forgetting. He turned to look at the time on his clock radio that stood on the bedside table. He was startled to see that it was almost five forty-five in the afternoon; no wonder the shadows were long. How could he sleep for so long? The gentle tapping on the door continued, and then he heard a soft voice ask, "Mr. Rumble, are ye in there? Are ye all right? May I come in?"

Rumble jumped out of bed, the thought of a woman seeing him in his robe was enough to send his anxiety level through the roof. But he had to answer the door; otherwise, he knew she would enter anyway. He wrapped his robe tightly around him, walked to the door, and opened it. Two very young maids stood outside; their eyes downcast as they moved past him into the room.

"We be so sorry to be disturbing ye afternoon, sir, but we be a needin to light ye fire before the wee drafty be comin down ye chimney."

"Thank you," was all Rumble managed; he had no idea what they were saying, but it appeared they wanted to light the fire, and Rumble had to admit. He too could feel the chill in the air.

"It be nearly five, sir. I see ye not be dressin for dinner, will ye not be joinin them then?"

Rumble took a moment to work out what they were asking him, so he simply replied, "No." With the fire now lit in the hearth, they curtsied and backed out of the room shutting the door softly behind them. Rumble had completely forgotten dinner; he was so unused to eating more than one meal a day. Well, now, they knew he wouldn't be present at dinner; he didn't need to go down stairs at all.

Soon, he had put all his sketches on the table, although his eyes kept drifting to the one of Ms. Primrose. He wanted to add some color to the one of Nitzy by the pond, and he wanted to draw and color some others he was about to do from memory. It was after six when someone next tapped on his door.

So engrossed was he in his work that he jumped at the intrusion. Two maids entered but not the same ones as last time. They each carried a large tray, and seeing, he was using the table they stood turning around in the room looking for somewhere to set them down. Rumble was not about to move his work, so he ignored them and kept sketching; he was almost finished anyway.

Finally, still holding the trays, they left the room only to return several minutes later, with a luggage stand each. They then went and got the trays and placed them on the luggage stand and left the room. Rumble had just finished adding color to the sketches including the new one of the grounds he had just done from memory.

Ms. Primrose almost came to life with the colors he added to the sketch; he could hardly take his eyes from it. Finally, he placed it and several others in the back of his sketchbook. Then he went again to the back of his sketchpad and removed Ms. Primrose's sketch from the bottom of the pile to the top; now every time he looked in the back of his book, she would be the first thing he saw.

The delicious smells coming from under the covers of the trays were most distracting, so Rumble was glad he had finished for the evening. He was trying to turn on the TV when, again, a knock came from the door. This time the maid wanted to turn down his bed and asked if she should run his bath now or later. He said maybe later and asked her to show him how the remote for the TV worked. Sometime later, he was sitting in front of the TV enjoying a vivid look at flamingos, their habits and habitats.

Rumble had never watched TV on such a large screen before, although he had seen these large TVs in shop windows and the like. The Millington's had a small TV, and he often watched it when he was in their cottage looking after Skye, their ginger cat.

He had again eaten an excellent meal of roast venison, with new peas, roasted Brussels sprouts, and roast potatoes. The meal had started with smoked salmon on lettuce, capers, and a light sauce with a touch of spice that Rumble didn't recognize. He was so full; he didn't want to look under the dome covering his desert, but when he did, he knew he had to squeeze in the strawberry shortcake, somehow. It was like the whole meal, the best he had ever tasted.

Once the dinner trays were removed and replaced with the tray containing the hot chocolate and shortbread, Rumble changed the channels on the TV tentatively until he found what he thought was the beginning of a movie.

It was Pretty Woman with Richard Gere and Julia Roberts. Rumble sat transfixed as he shared the emotions with the two stars on the screen. Lying in bed that night with the TV off and the dying embers in the fire creating a moving orange pattern on the ceiling, Rumble realized he had learned more tonight from watching that movie about romance, than he had ever learned in his whole life.

It had been James Coote's, Mr. Cootes, younger brother and Rumble's school friend, who, along with James's other brothers, who had taught Rumble all he knew about the fairer sex, and he understood now that wasn't much at all.

As he drifted off to sleep, he thought of Primrose, he hoped she was safely back in Rosemary Cottage with Ms. Epping, and he hoped, she hadn't suffered too much as a result of the fire. He knew her guilt was extreme over not being able to save the Major. This said a lot about her heart and character and proved she was indeed a kind and caring person. Rumble knew that if he had not taken the time to watch Pretty Woman tonight, he wouldn't have understood her at all.

Rumble rose early the next morning and showered before dressing. He was again sitting under the huge old tree by the pond as dawn battled the night for another day. He was sketching feverishly, and he didn't notice Nitzy beside him until she spoke.

"No wonder you're a famous artist, Mr. Rumble. Oh,

I'm sorry, I didn't mean to startle you," Nitzy said, looking concerned as she sat beside him. He had just finished three sketches, and he handed them to her to look at.

"It's all right, Nitzy. I forget you're an early riser like myself."

"Oh, yes, I love it at this time of day. I sit here for hours watching ye mist rise off ta water and hearing the wee birds, ducks, and animals wake up in the mornin." Nitzy seemed to be her usual happy self as she sat looking at the detail in his sketches. I can even see those flower petals that have fallen into the pond and their reflection. You really are very good, Mr. Rumble."

"Wait, 'til you see them in color, Nitzy. That's the deciding factor as to whether or not they're good."

"Oh, you color them, too?" she asked as Rumble again opened his sketchpad and starting to sketch her. He had decided that if he must sketch people, he might as well get some practice.

"Well, aren't you going to ask me then?"

"Ask you what, Nitzy?" Rumble said only half listening,

"No one else really cares, so I was hoping you would, Mr. Rumble. Ye see me mam's, always too busy running the house, like…"

"Your mother runs the house?" Rumbled questioned.

Now the outline was done, and he had tuned into what she was saying again. "Yes, Mr. Rumble, I told ye that before, did you forget? Well, any ways me mam's the housekeeper; she's in charge of everything. She had to take the job after me pa and brother died. Because suddenly, we had no income and soon we wouldn't have had anywhere to live, neither. So, when the old housekeeper Mrs. Petrie retired, me mam applied for the job and her ladyship was good enough to give it to her. Me mam and me don't know whether it was out of sympathy, kindness, or she really did think me mam was capable. Anyway, we're lucky ta be here," Nitzy said and Rumble noticed several large tears running down her cheeks. He wasn't sure what to say, but he knew he needed to say something. Finally, he decided on a little kindness. He hated seeing Ntizy sad.

"Nitzy, I'm sorry to have upset you. I should never have asked you something so personal." When finally, she looked at him, her huge eyes shone like diamonds as the last of her tears fell onto her cheeks.

"It's all right, Mr. Rumble, I like ye, and ye be a kind man. I be happy to share my life story with ya." He thought she sounded so wise for her young age. Then she bowed her head again and continued, "I miss them both so much, Mr. Rumble. Me brother and me we was so close; we told each other everythin. He was only sixteen months older than me. I was nearly in the car that night with them, so it could have been me also that died. It was a freak accident, me mam says. My pa was the only solicitor in the village; he had his own practice and me mam was his secretary. That's how they met. Anyway, it was late one night when he needed to go back to the office; apparently, me mam had forgotten to bring home some important documents for his court case the next mornin. He was a wee bit angry with her before he left the house, so me brother went with him for the ride. Well, he took longer than he should have at ta office; he couldn't find all the paperwork he needed, so by the time, they headed home, ta fog had rolled on in off ta moors makin visibility on the road, poor. The runaway horse was spooked by the sound of ta car. The horse ran into the road, and they didn't have any chance of seeing it or time to stop. They all perished, ta horse included. It be one of Lady Maggie's prize horses; she had only purchased it that very day. No one was knowing how it got lose. But one of the young stable hands was fired, they said he be responsible, like. It be sad all round, Mr. Rumble, it surely be." Nitzy hung her head and sobbed softly.

Rumble felt her sadness but said nothing. Several minutes passed and the silence engulfed them, Rumble felt time seemed to stand still. Rumble looked off into the pond as he tried not to intrude on Nitzy's grief. *'Rumble I thought I taught you something about empathy, but apparently not, and just when I thought you were learning too'*, the voice suddenly scolded and Rumble physically jumped, 'and I thought I only needed to hear you when I was scared or in danger,' Rumble replied annoyed. *'Feelings, Rumble its sometimes about feelings and I had to step in when you're hurting Nitzy's feelings with your silence. She's been nothing but nice to you,'* Rumble had to admit the voice was right again, when he didn't answer, it added, *'So...'* 'Oh do shut up', Rumble responded while trying to think of what to say to Nitzy.

Instead, he watched two female ducks digging their light brown bills into the soft earth and grass at the side of the pond just above the water line. Over and over, they dug their bills deep into the earth, and each time they came out with a worm wiggling on the end of their bills or an insect that Rumble couldn't see.

Finally, Nitzy look up at him and smiled weakly, then removed her backpack and proceeded to lift out two hot thermoses, two bowls, two spoons, and two plates. She laid them on a flat piece of earth, uncapped the thermos and poured out the hot tea followed by what Rumble assumed was porridge. She handed him a bowl.

"I already put some fresh honey and a little cream in the porridge; I didn't know how to carry them separately."

"This is perfect, Nitzy, thank you."

"I thought you'd like it, Mr. Rumble, this way Cookie won't be hovering over us if we sneak into the kitchen."

Rumble was hungry, and the small bowl of porridge was hot and sweet. They ate in silence until the last of their porridge was gone. As Rumble began to drink his tea, Nitzy searched deeper into her backpack and bought out another package, this time, she handed him buttered toast, and it was still warm.

"This is a wonderful breakfast, Nitzy, thank you," Rumble said, not knowing just how to express his gratitude for her thoughtfulness.

"I'm leaving my back pack here, and I'll pick it up later. I know you'll be havin a busy day, 'cause I heard Lady Maggie talkin. But yesterday, I forgot to show you the bee hives and the rose gardens. Don't worry, they are not being too far away, and I'll have ye back before the last of the breakfast has been served to the houseguests?"

More walking, Rumble thought, stowing his pad and pencils carefully in his sachet. Nitzy was again her happy smiling self as they began their adventure, she skipped every so often like a young girl, and Rumble found her enchanting.

"Well, Mr. Rumble, you still haven't asked me?"

"Nitzy, I'm really no good at guessing games, you're going to have to give me a hint." No sooner had Rumble spoken than the voice reminded him where Nitzy had gone yesterday. So, before she answered, he quickly said, "I was only teasing, Nitzy, sorry. Of course, I want to know how your visit to the blacksmith's went. I hope you saw your young beau Liam yesterday?"

"Oh, Mr. Rumble, you remembered, I knew you would." Nitzy simply jumped in the air and clapped her hands at his words; her eyes were positively shining again, so Rumble knew she must have had a good afternoon in the village.

"Well, I think I looked pretty, and I remembered what ye said, so yes I really did feel pretty also. As I got closer to the village, I wondered if Liam would actually be there,

293

but he was. Oh, but he's a bonnie laddie that he be. Me heart goes all a flutter and me palms get a wee bit sweaty and that's just at the sight of him. I stood lookin at him for a wee minute, before he even knew I was there. This time, he actually stopped his hammering and came over to greet me. I thought I'd surely faint clean away, really I did. He looked me in ta eye and asked me 'Now what's a young lassie with the likes of ye, doin in the smithie's shop? Ye be gettin ye pretty dress all dirty like,' that's what he said, Mr. Rumble, and he looked at me the whole time. I seemed to have lost my tongue, hard to believe I know, but I couldn't think of a wee thing to say."

"So, what did you say, Nitzy?" They were now walking briskly up the slop to the side of the castle and over the meadow beyond.

"Well, I just couldn't think of nought to say for ages, and we just stared at each other; it was magic, Mr. Rumble, pure magic. Then, finally, he says he has to be a gettin back to work, so I says I thought he was very bonnie; he blushed like and that made him look a wee bit more bonnie. Then he winked at me and walked away." Nitzy was simply bouncing around in front of Rumble as she spoke, and her excitement at recalling the encounter was simply bubbling out of her.

Personally, Rumble didn't think it was much of an exchange, but he guessed that at her age, it must have been enough.

Several men on their way to work raised their caps in

their direction; Nitzy waved and Rumble touched his cap in reply. Then Nitzy fell into step beside him and said, "Well, I told me mam last night, I had ta tell someone, and ye know what she said?"

"No, Nitzy, I don't," Rumble replied trying hard to keep up with her.

"She said, Nitzy, ye got ta check him out, gal, everyone's related about these parts, and ye don't want to go a marryin anyone ye related to."

"Oh, are they really?" Rumble asked.

"Well, Mr. Rumble, ye see that the cabin yonder, well, the Glions live there. Mrs. Glions brother is Albert Timmons; he be the apiarist, who keeps the bees. He married Lee Turner's little sister, who be the cousin of the grounds keeper, Thomas Lyth, you met yesterday. Thomas's older sister works in the laundry, and she's married to the Glions younger brother. Their first cousin married, Mable Crozier, well now no one be a knowin who Mable's father be, some say he's dead and some say her father lives right here on the estate. All we knows is that Lord Riley has always been mighty kind to her, and he be giving her an allowance and everythin, but I'm not saying nought more…"

"Oh," was all Rumble said, he really didn't understand.

"Well, ye can see how we're all related like Mr. Rumble, so me mam's got a point. See, Liam be Mable's son. Mable was sent off to university in Edinburgh; no one ever goes to university around these parts unless ye be the gentry like. Well, Mable worked for me dad after she came back to the village from university, and then left suddenly and me mam got the job. No one saw her for several months. Then she came back and Allen Macdonald, Thomas Lyth's first cousin married her really fast; they only dated about a month. That's what I want to do with Liam. I really be a hopin we're not related. Me mam wasn't nearly as excited as I thought she'd be to hear about me possible fella."

They had stopped walking at the top of a small hill. Stretched out before them was the rolling slopes of the paddocks and pastures, dotted with sheep and cattle and to their right was a man with fancy head gear and a small puffing machine that was spraying out smoke into the bee hives.

Then he removed the trays of honeycomb. 'Mr. Rumble, I be most sorry like but we can't go close to them bees today,' Rumble didn't mind, he, found everything new and fascinating all around him, especially the pockets of mist as they rose into the morning air. Rumble just wanted to sketch the moment and keep it forever.

All too soon, they were off again, this time arriving at the Rose Garden and flowerbeds. All beautifully tended, and inside the greenhouses, Rumble could see many brightly colored spectacular blooms bursting forth. A young man came toward them, having seen them arrive, he was better dressed than most of the others Rumble had met, and when he spoke, Rumble released; he was also better educated.

"Mason Abercrombie," he said extending his hand to Rumble. He had a firm grip and cultured accent.

"I'm the horticulturist on the estate, Mr. Rumble, and ye are no doubt the famous artist we've all been eager to meet.

"Hardly famous Mr. Abercrombie but thank you. These flowers are beautiful indeed."

"These are all my own breeds and cross breeds of several different geniuses they would make for a great sketch, if you have time?"

"Speakin of time, we're already late, sorry," Nitzy said grabbing Rumble's sleeve and dragging him away.

"Nice to meet ye, Mr. Rumble, I hope I'll see ye again," he called, and all Rumble could do was reply with a wave as Nitzy hurried him over the hill and down toward to the castle.

"We really must be a hurrying, Mr. Rumble, I know ye have a busy day, and ye will need to be changing before ye meet with Lady Maggie."

"Oh, yes, I suppose I shall. I would like to speak to Mr. Abercrombie some more; he seems like a rather nice chap, and I can easily understand his accent," Rumble said and Nitzy laughed.

"Well, Mr. Abercrombie is the one they think I should marry."

"Oh," was all Rumble could think to say.

"But you know it must be more than that, Mr. Rumble. There has to be chemistry and that's somethin, ye can't fake, or find, or learn. It's either there or it ain't. And it maybe there for him, but for me, it ain't. He be a might too perfect for the likes of me, no mystery like. I still don't fully understand the world of love and romance, but I know it's all about what ye be feeling inside and who makes your heart beat faster and your palms sweat. You be understanding, Mr. Rumble, don't ye?" She said as she giggled and smiled with the mischief again shining from her huge hazel eyes; she then opened a side door to the castle and almost pushed him inside. As the door closed, she promised to see him tomorrow.

This was a new part of the castle Rumble hadn't been in before. The hallway was narrow, the carpet thick, dark and old, and the way seemed unfamiliar to him. Although there was only one way he could go as directly behind him loomed a tall wooden door that was shut tight. So, he had to walk forward. To Rumble, the hallway went on and on, but suddenly he came to a heavy curtain covering his way. He reached out and touched it, and it moved easily. A shiver briefly rippled over Rumble as he recalled other heavy curtains he had touched. Rumble really believed Nitzy would not have knowingly allowed him to get lost in the castle when he was running late, so this must lead somewhere...

Chapter Twenty-one

Rumble was delighted to find he was just down the hallway from his bedroom.

He walked through the curtain into the brightly lit modern part of the castle and was soon in his room. A moment later, a light tap came from the door.

"Mr. Rumble, we be thinkin ye want a lunch tray in ye room as there isn't being any time for ye to make it to the dining room they be already seated, sir," the maid said curtseying. Rumble had forgotten he was expected to attend yet another meal, so it was a relief, he had unknowing missed the luncheon call.

"Thank you, a tray will do nicely." Without any further talk, she quietly closed the door and left. Now Rumble had to work out what he would wear. Just as he was thinking hard about what Lee had told him to do, there came another knock on his door. They are certainly efficient with the lunch tray Rumble thought, and he called for them to enter. But it wasn't his lunch tray but some of his clothes, not that he recognized them. In fact, it appeared to be a lot of his clothes; no wonder he couldn't find them yesterday.

"May I hung these, sir; they be clean and pressed," she bowed as she passed him and disappeared into his walk-in closet, minutes later she reappeared.

"I shall return later and collect what ye be a wearin now, thank you, sir; sorry to be intruding." And she was gone. Rumble was astounded that so many people paid so much attention to what he was wearing and cared about his clothes. He smiled a slight smile, pleased; he was suitably attired, and it would have been rather embarrassing otherwise. It seemed Cootes was right again.

Rumble ate his lunch as he thought about what Lee had told him to wear, finally as he finished the last morsel of his delicious food, he remembered. He looked at the time, and it was already after one, he was supposed to meet Maggie at the stables at one thirty p.m. sharp. Quickly dressing, then throwing his old worn leather sachet over his shoulder, he realized that getting dressed was the easy part, finding his way to the stables would prove not so easy. After several wrong turns and asking a few staff as he pased, he reached the stables with five minutes to spare and rather out of breath.

"Mr. Rumble, how delightful, you're on time as I knew you would be." Maggie beamed on seeing him.

She was dressed in full dressage gear, and Rumble thought, she looked very smart indeed. Her horse also had been saddled, brushed and braided, his coat was simply shining in the sunlight. Even his horseshoes were highly polished.

He was a handsome looking horse with a thick dark tail and main, his lower body was a light brownish red, and he had a dark stripe down his back, which continued on to his tail. His face was narrow but well-proportioned, and Rumble knew he was a thoroughbred and worth more money than he would see in his lifetime.

Maggie walked around to the horse's head and stroked him softly; she was obviously very fond of this horse, "Rumble, this is Monty. One of my favorites, he stands almost eighteen hands tall, and as you can see, he comes from very good stock. I would like a sketch of me standing by Monty's head, and then one of me mounted. We shall then bring out Chester and do the same. Then, I would like one with several of my other favorite horses, and by that time, I feel sure his Lordship shall be demanding your attention." Rumble nodded, he was checking the light, so he could begin. "Yes, Maggie I understand. Can you please move Monty to the left, I want the light directly on his face," A groom immediately appeared and moved Monty the few steps he needed to the left while Rumble got set. He knew Maggie would know the pose she wanted him to capture.

Rumble remained silent as he worked and Maggie appeared to respect his deep concentration and total focus. Rumble did some excellent work even though he didn't like sketching people; he found that in these surroundings it felt natural and not forced.

Maggie, indeed, owned some of the best horse flesh Rumble had ever had the good fortune to sketch, and seeing a horse and its rider in person was nothing like sketching it from a book or off the internet.

Half way through the afternoon, Rumble had to admit he was enjoying himself, even the attention he was getting and the positive feedback everyone was giving him, began to lift his spirits.

Before he finished with Maggie and her horses, and just as she had predicted, a groom arrived with a note from His Lordship requesting Rumble's imminent presence, to sketch him with his hounds.

Rumble was a little anxious as he remembered Nitzy's warning, but he soon found he didn't need to be. The hounds obeyed Lord Riley to the letter and didn't move without a word from him. Rumble knew it would be quite a different thing if he was alone, but with His Lordship in attendance, everything went smoothly. It was almost dark by the time he was finished, and Lord Riley asked if they would be seeing him for dinner. Rumble graciously declined saying he must add color to the sketches, so they have time to dry and are ready for framing. Lord Riley only nodded his approval.

Rumble was exhausted, and he was glad; he had a genuine excuse to retreat early. Whether Lord Riley believed him or not, he wasn't sure, but he was glad to get away with it on this occasion.

Lord Riley was a big authoritative man with a booming voice and a persona that said he must be obeyed. Several times Rumble had to explain why he wanted him to sit or stand in a certain place due to the placement of the light; he argued on each occasion but reluctantly gave in once Rumble explained why it must be so. Rumble had to admit that Lord Riley was quite a handful and not easily controlled.

Rumble enjoyed another delicious meal in his room that evening, and as he said he would, he completed the sketches, and he was most proud of him, he thought they were some of his best work. He hoped the Murrays would feel likewise.

He was excited about watching TV again tonight, so after his bath had been run, and he'd soaked in it for much too long, he climbed into bed and turned on the TV, but Rumble had been mentally focusing all day, and soon he was sleep. The TV was still on in the morning as the first light of dawn brushed the windows. Rumble's morning clothes were nowhere to be found, so it took him longer to dress than yesterday.

He had only just got to the tree and taken out his sketchpad when Nitzy arrived with a large wicker basket, which Rumble assumed, was their breakfast. Today was the point-to-point, and Rumble knew it would be another busy day. Maggie had instructed Rumble that later today, her personal kilt maker, Gordon Nicholson, would be measuring him for a kilt to wear to the celebration of the Riding of the Marches. She said even though the ball was held last Saturday, several more celebrations happen at this time of the year, and on Saturday night, the men would all be in kilts; she didn't want him to feel out of place.

Rumble thanked her for her thoughtfulness and secretly dreaded being touched and measured for more clothes, surely, he had enough already.

The day passed, and he managed to again not sit at the dinner table as Gordon the Kilt-maker was running late.

"I, Mr. Rumble, I be happy to wait while ye sup, sir, that I be."

"Oh, no, Gordon, I know you are a busy man, and I would not dream of keeping you waiting."

"I ye be a good lad, but it be fair, I be kept a waitin as I be the one who was running a wee bit late," Rumble persisted and soon they were in his room, and he was getting measured for a Kilt; it was much more involved than he could have imagined. And when Gordon asked him whether his preference for his sporran was leather or fabric, Rumble knew he was totally out of his depth. He had no idea what a sporran was. He barely understood the man anyway.

Gordon talked endlessly, and Rumble found it quite stressful focusing on what the man was saying. Finally, as he left, Rumble's dinner arrived, then his clean clothes, followed by the girls lighting the fire and soon after they turned down the bed. They ran his bath and delivered hot chocolate. Once that was done, he was finally on his own.

He worked on his day's sketches, and there were many of them, he worked until after midnight.

In the morning, it was someone tapping on his door that wakened him. It was after nine, as Rumble had done every morning when he woke in the large cozy bed and huge room, he pinched himself. Today like the other mornings, he found, it still wasn't a dream he was really here. Soon, they were bringing him breakfast in bed.

He had missed his time with Nitzy, and he felt disappointed. Today would be the point-to-point, and later the jumping championships for which Maggie's horses usually took all the ribbons. Rumble felt tired; his eyes were heavy with sleep as he sat on the side of his bed looking at the silver dome covering his breakfast on the breakfast tray. A large knocking came from the door, and before Rumble got to his feet, Gordon the Kilt-maker burst into the room

"I, well, I've caught ye I have. Ye see, Mr. Rumble, a kilt is somethin that takes a good many hours to make, as does the rest of ye outfit. We be workin all night long at the request of Lady Maggie. I be needin just one more wee measurement, and we should have it done on time." Rumble got to his feet, embarrassed that anyone would see him in his pajamas and straight out of bed, although Gordon didn't seem to notice.

He seemed to be in a feverish hurry, so Rumble did as he instructed and, quickly stood in the middle of the room. Just as Gordon finished running his tape measure expertly over Rumble, his chatter was interrupted by a soft tapping from the door.

"Mr. Rumble, sir, they will be leavin in about thirty minutes; Lady Maggie asked me to remind ye, they meet out the front, sir." The maid must have looked at him and Gordon, and decided he needed help to get ready as she asked, "May I lay out ye clothes, Mr. Rumble?"

Rumble was about to say 'no' when Gordon answered for him, "A fine idea that be lassie ye see I been a takin up all his time, and now I made the lad late for his work and how very sorry I be, sir. And top of the morning to ye…" Gordon said, bowing slightly and leaving the room hurriedly after gathering up his things. By the time Rumble was focused again on getting dressed, he turned to see his whole outfit for today laid out on the bed.

He was pleased, as he would never have chosen what the maid put out. It was much dressier than Rumble thought he needed. But he realized she knew better than him. The maid said she would wait outside for him to dress and show him the way, so he didn't keep everyone waiting. Rumble managed to eat only half a slice of toast, before she knocked again at the door.

Rumble wasn't aware of why he had to hurry until he entered the front entranceway and saw everyone being ushered into waiting limousines. Maggie and several others greeted Rumble who was soon seated in the back of the same Bentley that had picked up from the train station on his arrival. He was seated with two smartly dressed women who obviously knew each other and another gentleman who introduced himself as the husband to one of the women.

Looking them over Rumble realized he was dressed

just right for today's activities. The women didn't stop chattering the entire drive, and Rumble appreciated that no one needed to talk to him.

The man also sat in silence. The scenery was spectacular as they drove the short distance, and Rumble would have dearly liked to capture it on his sketchpad. However, the day had begun in all its glory, and it proved another busy one.

Today Rumble didn't have a list of what to sketch as he had been given previously, but he was instructed to capture all Lady Maggie's horses in action and anything else he wanted to sketch. Rumble had never sketched so fast and furiously in all his life as he had in the last two days.

He realized, this was not a holiday and nothing was free; and this was the time he needed to prove himself worthy of being here. The day pasted in a blur of horses, people, champagne, chatter, and sketching, and all too soon Rumble arrived back at the castle. It was a hive of activity, and Rumble had to push his way through the crowd in order to get to his room.

It was already after five, and Maggie had said formal cocktails in the ballroom at six, sharp! Rumble was thinking of what to wear but upon entering his room, there was Gordon, tape measure around his neck dusting some invisible specks from the newly made kilt laid out on the bed. 'Surely, I don't have to wear that?' Rumble thought. He didn't like showing his knees; they'd never seen daylight and, much like the rest of him, they were as white as snow.

Once again Rumble was caught up in the moment, only this time, Gordon was part of it. He chattered away in his heavy accent, and Rumble barely understood a word.

Gordon had stripped him down to his underwear in a wee Scottish second, and Rumble was feeling most uncomfortable. Now he was dressed in a green, black and yellow tartan kilt, with a black leather sporran complete with feathers. The jacket was made of black wool, double-breasted, and very fitted. Four elaborate gold buttons closed the jacket, and under it was, what Rumble thought, a frilly girl's blouse. Heavy black woolen knee-high socks and shiny shoes completed his outfit. Gordon walked around Rumble talking all the time, he sounded pleased. But all Rumble could think about was how silly he looked and the fact his knees were cold. The kilt just covered them, but he still felt like everyone could see them.

"Traditionally, Mr. Rumble, we wear nothin under our wee Kilts, but as ye be no a true Scot, I don't think ye need to follow tradition, and we can leave ye wee undies on." Rumble wasn't sure if he heard the last part correctly. But if he had, there was no way he was removing his underpants tradition or no tradition. Once Rumble looked in the mirror, he knew he looked even more foolish than he thought he would. He was feeling anxious and his anxiety was steadily growing inside him. He didn't want to attend this function, he hated people and even though most of them had been kind, he felt foolish and knew he would look out of place.

However, there was no way for him to get out of attending. Gordon said he was leaving and would walk with Rumble down the stairs, as he wanted to have a wee look see at the others. Rumble felt again like a condemned man, he tried to quiet his nerves, and he even hoped to hear from the little voice in his head, but he didn't. He told himself he would exit as soon as no one was looking; he knew no one would miss him.

There were people, photographers, TV cameras, everywhere and even a red carpet where everyone stood as they entered to have their photo taken or to be interviewed. Rumble cringed inside as his heart pounded in his chest. Rumble wanted to remain invisible as was his preference. But Gordon would have none of it. He was proud of his work, and he wanted his photo taken with Rumble in his new kilt before he left.

Rumble was relieved to see all the other men looked equally as foolish as he did, they were all in kilts and the ladies in long formal gowns. Several people he had met since his arrival wanted him in their photos, and Rumble knew he must oblige, but he felt most uncomfortable, nevertheless. Rumble was handed a cocktail and ushered with everyone else into the ballroom. Rumble could feel his heart beating and his palms sweating; there were so many people and so much happening all around him. After half an hour in which time Rumble tasted the cocktail and almost spat it out; the crowd was asked to hush.

"Ladies and Gentlemen, please be up standing for your hosts, Lord and Lady Riley Murray." The large doors that were previously shut now opened wide. Lord Riley entered with Lady Maggie on his arm. He was resplendent in a red and green tartan kilt and, just like Rumble's, it had all the trimmings, and then some. Maggie was wearing a full-length pale lilac satin ball gown, complete with a bejeweled tiara and diamonds sparkling from her ears, throat and wrists. She also wore a sash made from the same tartan as her husband's kilt, it was held in place by a huge bejeweled brooch. How had she got ready so quickly? Rumble wondered, and then he remembered that both Lord Riley and Lady Maggie had left the jump earlier than everyone else.

Finally, it was time to be seated, and search as he may, Rumble was unable to find his place name beside any of the place settings. Once everyone was seated, he stood alone at the back of the room. Rumble felt his cheeks burn as all eyes looked at him. Looking around, he saw Maggie discreetly beckon for him to come toward her. He felt like he was approaching royalty and maybe he was.

"You have your own table, Mr. Rumble, as my dear old friend Sebastian Cootes suggested, you may prefer. You can sketch in seclusion without interruptions. If this is not your preference, and you want to be seated at the one of the large tables please let me know."

"No, thank you, Maggie, this is perfect," he

whispered. "But I did not bring my sketch pad. I shall fetch it now."

"Oh, Mr. Rumble tut, tut, you forgot your sketchpad. I shall have someone fetch it for you, forthwith." And with that she turned away and spoke in Lord Riley's ear. Maggie then discreetly beckoned to one of the manservants standing at attention close behind her. Rumble knew she didn't suffer fools lightly and even though she was charming the two 'tut, tuts' showed him she was displeased. Also, the way Lord Riley looked at him out the corner of his eye.

This was indeed worse for Rumble than having to wear a kilt; Rumble's social graces had let him down, and he felt most embarrassed. Rumble moved slowly over to the small table at the far corner of the room, it was set for one with his name clearly printed beside the place setting.

Of course, he was here to sketch how could he have forgotten his sachet. In less than five minutes, a servant dressed neatly in a white shirt, black bowtie cummerbund and black trousers, moved discreetly toward him and placed Rumble's sachet beside the table. The speeches were now beginning. Rumble looked up to see Maggie nod discreetly in his direction, so he nodded his thanks, noting Maggie's approving glance and got to work.

Rumble sketched all night long, he only stopped long enough to eat. The smoked trout was superb, the haddock and mussels, even better and so on through the whole ten-course meal. Rumble declined the last three courses, the wine and the desert, saying he was working and needed to concentrate.

Most everyone left him alone, apart from Thomas the American, who he had met several days ago at the only luncheon he'd ever attended.

"Only kids draw, Rumble, bet you play in the sandbox when you get home too?" He said smirking happily and obviously quite drunk, the lady who Rumble assumed was his wife drew him reluctantly away as he said, "I haven't finished talking to him, I've got more to say…"

"No dear, I think you've said quite enough," and then turning she whispered to Rumble, "Most sorry, Mr. Rumble, he's drunk again…"

Rumble stopped what he was sketching and started a new page. He expertly drew a most unflattering caricature of Thomas. He'd once enjoyed doing these as a teenager but hadn't done so in years. It depicted a grotesquely ugly Thomas in all his glory, stumbling around an ugly look on his face and slopping his drink over the lady's formal dresses.

Rumble smiled briefly, knowing it would stay in his sketchpad and got back to work.

That evening after he excused himself, he noted it was nearly midnight before he got to his room. The formal cocktail party was still in full swing downstairs; once in his room, he opened his curtains and his window so he could hear all the activity below. Rumble stood listening to the laughter and gaiety going on down stairs.

The crisp night air refreshed him enough, so he could color the sketches, and they would be dry by the time the framer arrived in the morning. Getting out of his kilt proved harder than he'd thought it would be, and once he was in his pajamas and dressing gown, he breathed a sigh of relief.

Rumble worked until almost three in the morning; he had drawn a lot of sketches, and looking at them over, he knew that overall, he had enjoyed himself. The last sketch he picked up was the caricature he had drawn of Thomas. He was about to throw it into the fireplace when he decided to color it instead, he already had all his colors out, so he may as well. As tired as he was, once it colored its grotesque ugliness brought a smile to his lips. Rumble intended to get up early the next morning and hopefully see Nitzy by the pond. But when he opened his eyes, the sun was filling his room, and it was already high in the sky.

No one had knocked on his door or disturbed him, how strange? Again, he pinched himself to make sure he wasn't dreaming. Looking at the clock beside his bed, he couldn't believe his eyes; it was almost eleven o'clock in the morning. How could that be? Rumble had hardly finished shaving and was just putting on his shoes when he heard a tap at the door. Come in, he called thinking it was the maid with his breakfast tray.

"Mr. Rumble, please excuse the intrusion, so early in the morning; I know the household was celebrating until late last night." Rumble had never seen this man before and had no idea who he was. He walked into the room and extended a business card toward Rumble. Once Rumble took the card, the man quickly grabbed his hand and shook it heartily.

"Daily McDougal, Mr. Rumble. Daily framing from Edinburgh." Now Rumble knew who he was. The man was already looking around at all the sketches that were scattered round the room and carefully drying.

"I wasn't sure where you would want me to set up, but I see this is the chosen area. And may I say these are rather good, very good indeed. Has her ladyship seen them yet?" When Rumble shook his head the man continued, "Oh, my... she made a good choice in you, indeed she did, she will be most pleased, indeed she will." Rumble noted he was English and enjoyed hearing the familiar speech.

When Rumble didn't answer, he continued, "Her ladyship has a complete wall cleared, re-painted and ready for your sketches. I'm sure she showed it to you. These will look perfect, it is a big wall, and I didn't think you would have had the time to do enough sketches to compliment the wall, but I must say, she won't be disappointed..." A tap on the door interrupted Daily; a girl entered carrying Rumble's clean laundry. Behind the laundry girl, a maid entered to make the bed and tidy the room. Rumble was not sure what was expected of him. Was the man going to work right here in his room?

From the way he was removing pieces of framing equipment, it did look like it. Finally, Rumble decided to take his sachet and leave, there was too much activity in the room anyway, and he had a few more sketches to do before his departure.

Rumble found a spot under an old Yew tree, one of the ones that lined the driveway. He was sitting beneath it, just inside the iron gate, where you entered the property. He had done several sketches of the castle and was just packing up to move, so he could sketch the castle from another angle, when Nitzy called to him from somewhere to his right.

"Oh, Mr. Rumble, I saw ye here, and I've missed ye down by the pond the last couple of mornins, is everything all right?"

"Yes, indeed, Nitzy, I have just been working until late, and I slept in."

"Well, Cookie said you hadn't had ye breakfast, so I packed us a wee bite for luncheon, and I thought I might take ye to the woods, maybe we can see some of those sly old foxes if ye be a wee bit quiet."

"That sounds perfect, Nitzy, lead the way." Again, she walked fast around the back of the castle, past the flower gardens, the bee hives the vegetable plot, past several cottages with smoke coming from the chimneys and cheery waves from the occupants, then on across the paddocks. 'No wonder, everyone eats so much,' Rumble thought, 'if they all race around the grounds all day like this.' He was getting tired keeping up with Nitzy, until finally she slowed as the woods drew near.

They walked deep in to the shadows of the woods until they found a sunny dell, it had moss all around, and Nitzy spread out a chintz tablecloth and started unpacking the basket. Rumble didn't know he was hungry until he smelled the food.

There were chunky slices of warm bread, smoked trout, cold lamb chops, fresh peaches, several cheeses and orange juice. It was a delicious lunch, and they relaxed in the sunlight after the meal was cleared away. Rumble leaned back onto a tree trunk, and Nitzy lay in the sun. Then, he began to sketch.

First, he captured Nitzy, and this time she had a face. He was just finishing sketching her laying on her stomach on the mossy ground in the sunshine when he saw a movement. Slowly, he turned his head to see a small red fox nervously sniffing the ground; the smell of their lunch had clearly wafted through the woods, and this young fox had come to investigate.

While trying to remain very still Rumble began sketching; he was almost finished with his outline when another fox joined the first. Nitzy was still lying on her stomach, she was almost at eye level and stared straight at them.

It was magical, even though they were timid, they were perfect in their natural beauty. At that moment, he knew the trip was worth it just to be here in the woods and sketching these handsome wild foxes. Rumble was careful about moving, but he knew he must do a third sketch. He must capture the two foxes, and Nitzy illuminated in the glow of the afternoon sun. It was exquisite. This sketch Rumble would keep forever.

As they walked back to the castle later that afternoon, Rumble handed Nitzy the sketch of her by the pond, he had another, so he didn't mind parting with it. She was thrilled and threw her arms around Rumble and kissed him on the cheek. He then told her he was leaving the following evening.

"Maybe I will see ye at the pond in the morning, Mr. Rumble"? she asked hopefully.

"Maybe, Nitzy, but I don't think I so. I shall have to pack and prepare to leave."

"But, Mr. Rumble, the maids will pack for ye; it is what they are paid to do. Ye don't want to offend them by doing it yourself'; they may think their work is not up to ye standard," she replied eagerly.

"Oh indeed, I hadn't thought of it like that," Rumble responded.

"No one is having dinner tonight in the dining room, it is always the way after we have a party the night before, everyone dines in their rooms. Ye do know that after luncheon tomorrow ye wall of sketches will be unveiled, why ye simply must be present, Mr. Rumble. They simply would never forgive ye if you left before then."

"I shall be Nitzy, my ticket is booked on the Flying Scotsman, but it doesn't leave until five forty p.m."

"Oh, good, Mr. Rumble, all the staff will be at the

unveiling of your work, and I will be there also, ye are a big event here at the castle. And in the village, why everyone is excited about havin ye here. What do ye plan on doing this evening?" she asked, as he was about to enter the castle.

"Maybe enjoy my wonderful bedroom, Nitzy, it is the nicest room I have ever stayed in," Rumble said honestly.

"So ye home is not bein quite as grand as ta castle then, Mr. Rumble?" Rumble shook his head not wanting to discuss his home further; he was relieved when she continued,

"Anyway, I thought maybe ye would like to visit the village with me, this evening? It may not be as sleepy as you'd expect," Nitzy asked hopefully. Rumble would very much have liked to visit the village but his stay had been a whirl of activity, and for Rumble's normal slow pace of life, it had been exhausting.

The thought of having to meet more folks and talk was just too much for Rumble, so he graciously declined. Nitzy looked sad for a moment. Then smiled up at him and waved, as he entered the castle by the side door, he had used yesterday.

Rumble didn't want to leave, but he knew it was time. He'd done good work, and he hoped everyone would like it. He hoped they would, but as always, he felt apprehensive. His concern and anxiety rushed around in the pit of his stomach, just the thought that they may be disappointed with him.

He knew from the previous evening when he couldn't locate his seat at the party, that Maggie didn't suffer fools lightly, and he hoped never to hear the edge in her voice directed at him, again.

Finally, Rumble knew the way to his room from the outside, now he was leaving. It had all been rather like a fairytale even though he had done more sketches since his arrival than he would usually do in a year. The last week had put a new perspective on his life, opened doors to many new possibilities.

Just as he was about to open the door to his room his mobile phone notified him of a text message.

He looked around at the cozy fire blazing in the hearth, the pretty lilacs that had been placed on the table and the lack of sketches; they were all gone, every last one. The room was tidy, his bed was made and no doubt his clothes had arrived back from the laundry and were hung in the closet.

He retrieved his phone and seeing the flashing battery, he knew he needed to read the messages fast; he had forgotten to charge his phone since his arrival. There were several missed calls, but he didn't recognize the number, so he would check for messages later, they were probably wrong numbers, anyway. There were two text messages both from Lucy, the first informed him that Cootes wanted to know when he planned to return as they had more work for him. The second message was also from Lucy, only this one was longer, and it stated that he hadn't returned the Millington's messages, and they had called again several times.

They needed to know whether or not he wanted to rent his old room again, as it was now vacant, if he didn't, then they would advertise, but they wanted an answer from him first. Lucy then berated him for not contacting them.

Rumble could see his phone was about to die any second, so he hastily replied, 'Yes, he did want his old room back at the Millington's.' He had only just sent it and was replying to the first text about his return date when the screen went black. He hurriedly found the charger and plugged it in. In a short time, he knew the phone would be up and running again, and he would make sure his answers had got through. He hated it when Lucy was angry with him, it reminded him of his mother. He quickly shut out any further thoughts of her.

Rumble felt like jumping in the air with the thought of getting his own room back at the Millington's. He had now forgiven them for making him leave, although on reflection, he realized, that in order for him to get his room back, there must have been a death in the family. 'It would be just like old times,' he thought, Sykes, of course, would remember him and everything would be, as before, he couldn't wait. No more changes.

He had been coming to terms with the fact that he couldn't spend another night at the house. In fact he didn't want to return there at all. He knew Edwards rules, and by the time, he got to the house after he arrived in London it would be the middle of the night. Rumble clearly knew the rules about entering the house after dark – but what could he do? At the very least, he needed to clear his things out of his room, but did he? All too clearly, he remembered Edwards warning about how he would never be free. He couldn't remember the exact words, but the thought of Edwards voice and half presence was enough to make him shudder.

Rumble was feeling depressed at the thought of Edwards and the weird house. He knew in that moment he wouldn't return to the house again, he would stay perhaps in London in a hotel after he returned on the train then call the Millington's in the morning and go straight there, and he would be home.

The thought of staying away from the house permanently cheered Rumble, and he realized he'd been actually happy since his time in Edinburgh, it was a rare and unexplored feeling for him, but he liked it very much. A light tapping on the door took Rumble from his thoughts, and he called for them to enter. It was his dinner tray, carried by two young maids, they placed it on the table and asked Rumble if he wanted them to serve, to which he replied, "No, thank you," they bowed politely and left. Rumble had to pinch himself; he was being treated like a prince, like someone famous, like someone!

He pinched himself – how could he, Rumble be getting treated like this? This was another world one Rumble was not familiar with – one Rumble hadn't known existed. And yet here he sat in this huge beautifully appointed room, with a delicious dinner laid out before him, new clothes in enormous closet and a fire burning in the hearth. It was like a dream, Rumble had to sketch it, sketch it all, the room, the bathroom, the view from his window, everything; he felt obliged to sketch, otherwise how would he remember it.

Then he remembered he had a camera on his phone. The phone was charged enough to be alive and if Rumble left it plugged in, he could take some photos of his room.

He had never used the camera before, and he should have. He quickly worked out how to use it and snapped several photos of the bedroom, the view and the bathroom. He saw the bars on his phone diminish, so he decided to take no more.

He needed to sketch the view from the window while the light was right; the sun was almost over the horizon, so it had to be now.

Fifteen minutes later, he had the outline and that was all he needed; he turned to the room and also began sketching that. He then got a whiff of the smells coming from under the dinner tray. He could sketch anytime, but he couldn't eat like this anytime. He lifted the covers. Today he had roast chicken with mushrooms, the large ones, like he had never seen before, baby green peas, parsnips, and roasted potatoes. There was a small jug of gravy on the side and a small bowl of what liked Pumpkin soup to start. Rumble peeked under the last dome, and it was a huge serving of bread and butter pudding with treacle, clotted cream and a side of ice cream that was beginning to melt.

Thirty minutes later, Rumble was so full he could hardly move; he was just reaching for his sketchpad when the tap at the door announced the maids had arrived to collect his tray. He told them it was delicious, and he thought they said they would pass on his compliment to Cookie. They then told him they had heard he was leaving tomorrow after noon. He confirmed this, and they bowed and backed out of the room. Rumble had never thought to tell anyone what he was doing, and now he realized how everyone in the castle worked together, and they all needed to know what was happening. It was a new concept, and Rumble thought about it for some time.

He had told the maids he didn't wish for a bath this evening. He had a huge shower he had hardly used, and he was over due to wash his hair and try out the new hair and skin products he now owned before he forgot how to use them. Then he intended to go to bed and watch TV – what a wonderful evening and what a treat. Tonight, he wasn't about to think of his return to the house.

The next morning, he was up bright and early feeling refreshed and invigorated, the country air was to his liking, and he felt younger and fitter than he ever had. Nitzy and Rumble arrived at the tree by the pond at much the same time. But one look at Nitzy, and Rumble knew she wasn't at all happy,

"Nitzy, whatever is the matter?" Rumble asked concerned.

"He don't be a likin me; he didn't even be a noticin me. I'm just too plain, Mr. Rumble. Why I'll never get a wee laddie of me own," she said her eye sad as she tried to hold back the tears.

"Oh, Nitzy, what happened?" Rumble asked.

"Well, I went into the village on me own the evenin last and met with some girlfriends, one of their fella's knows Liam, and he asked Liam what he thought of me. Well, Liam said he didn't even know me," Nitzy said as a sob escaped.

"Oh, Nitzy, why that means nothing, nothing at all. All that happened is that he doesn't want to discuss you with his friends. Now cheer up how could he not notice you, Nitzy, just give him time."

"I be almost twenty, Mr. Rumble. I don't have me much time. All me friends are to be married this very year, all of them, except me."

"Oh, Nitzy, life doesn't run to time. Look at me I've never married, and I'll be fifty next week and no one ever notices me, either." Rumble realized he shouldn't have said this, as it took the focus off what Nitzy was saying, but it did seem to make Nitzy forget herself and her worries.

"Oh, Mr. Rumble, ye are funny, why any lassie would be happy to have ye, why ye can have a choice of them any time ye want to. I think you be most handsome and you be talented, and you be rather nice to boot. What else can a gal look for in a fella." Rumble blushed at her words, and somehow he knew she really meant them. Nitzy was a gal who wore her heart on her sleeve, and he liked that about her very much.

Soon, they sneaked into the kitchen like two wayward school children and enjoyed a huge breakfast. Then they went for a short walk directly around the outside of the castle, it was huge and old, with moss growing on the sides that didn't get any sun. In places, you could see where the stone had crumbled away with age, while in others places, you could see where it had been roughly repaired.

All too soon, it was time to go, and Rumble reached into his sachet and handed Nitzy a sketch of herself with the foxes. She loved it even more than the last one of her by the pond; she said she now had a pair and would frame them when she could afford to. She gave him another tight hug and a kiss on the cheek. He blushed, but he didn't pull away, he liked her a lot.

"Mr. Rumble, me Mam's buyin a wee car for me twenty-first birthday, so if I don't have a fella by that time, can I come and see ye and maybe stay with ye for a while? I've never left the village, and I want to see the world. I've always wanted to go to England, and now I know ye I'll have an excuse." Rumble laughed and gave Nitzy his mobile number.

"You'll get your fella Nitzy, I know you will. He'd be a silly young man to pass you by," Rumble replied honestly.

He liked seeing the sparkle he created return to her eyes; he said farewell and slipped inside the castle to change for lunch.

He was relieved to see his clothes had been laid out for him on the bed. These were some garments he had never seen before, and he wouldn't have thought to wear them. But like all the others, they were of good quality and fitted him well; he also knew they made him look good, or about as good as he could expect to look.

He had to admit that maybe clothes really do, make the man. Lunch was served in the formal dining room that day. But as some of the guests had now left after the horse trials, there was not so many of them. Rumble was disappointed to see Thomas and his wife or partner were seated in their usual seats. He would try not to let the arrogant man get under his skin.

"So, it's the boy with the pencil and the purse full of money, is it?" Rumble blushed but didn't reply. To his amazement, it was Lord Riley who spoke up on Rumble's behalf, again.

"Thomas, your rude comments are getting very tedious, and they are unfounded and most uncalled for. May I remind you Mr. Rumble is a guest at this table, he is here at our request, whereas, you are not."

"Oh, Riley, really, I'm just having a bit of fun..."

"Yes, at someone else expense as usual, and in very poor taste indeed. Now that's enough..." Lord Riley concluded firmly and everyone was quiet around the table for some time. Rumble remained quiet and slowly the chatter started. A few of the other guests said how excited they were to soon be seeing his work. Then another guest added that they had stayed on just to see the unveiling. Rumble nodded at their compliments and enjoyed his lunch.

By two o'clock, they were all assembled in the huge drawing room with the big windows that overlooked the flower gardens. Rumble noticed even the servants, or some of them were present.

He spied Nitzy at the side, and she gave him a wink. Lord Riley made a short speech and thanked Rumble again for gracing them with his presence and all the work he'd done since his arrival; then they all counted down to the minute when Maggie would pull the chord, and the sheet covering the wall would fall and reveal the many hung sketches underneath.

Five, four, three, two, one… they all clapped. To Rumble's horror, there was the caricature of Thomas framed and sitting in the very middle of the wall, Rumble had completely forgotten he had done it and never meant for it to be displayed.

Everyone walked slowly passed the many sketches hanging in rows on the wall; they all made the right noises of liking his work. As they passed, the one of Thomas, most everyone giggled. All except Thomas, who went very red in the face and exited the room. Maggie winked approvingly at Rumble when she saw Thomas exit the room, embarrassed. Both Lord Riley and Lady Maggie laughed as they surveyed the caricature hanging in the center of the wall.

Lord Riley and Maggie then made a short speech and presented Rumble with an envelope containing what they said was a little bonus to show their appreciation for a job well done. Everyone clapped, and Nitzy cheered. Rumble was most embarrassed. He mumbled a thank you and placed the envelope in the top pocket of his smart navy sports jacket, which he hadn't worn before. He was also wearing gray flannel trousers a pale blue shirt and new highly polished dark gray Italian shoes. Rumble stayed behind and looked over his work hanging on the wall. He thought he was alone until Maggie whispered in his ear.

"Jolly nice work with the caricature of Thomas. I must say, neither Lord Riley nor myself thought you had it in you, Mr. Rumble. Nice retort indeed."

"Thank you, Maggie," Rumble mumbled still feeling rather embarrassed that it had been seen at all.

"My husband always likes a dry wit and a subtle come back, and I must say, Mr. Rumble, he was impressed with both of yours. I was delighted to see my cousin slink away, to avoid being ridiculed. And you did it all without raising your voice, most impressive indeed. Thomas is only a cousin through marriage, Mr. Rumble. And I must say he has taken rather a lot of liberties and advantage of our generosity and hospitality, I do apologize again for his uncalled-for and arrogant behavior.

Also, thank you, for doing justice to Monty as anyone could, of course. He's a piece of fine horseflesh, he certainly is. You also made me look rather good, Mr. Rumble, and I must say I had lost some sleep over how you would capture me. But I think you caught a younger fresher version of myself, and for that I am most grateful.

Thank you again for gracing us with your presence. I had hoped you would stay on a little longer, but I understand you are in demand, and it has been an honor meeting you. Mr. Rumble, I hope you shall come back again when next we need your talent."

"Of course, Maggie, it would be my pleasure. I appreciate all your hospitality and kindness, also."

"Oh, indeed, come now, Mr. Rumble, it is nothing more than you deserve."

"Well, thank you again to both you and His Lordship."

"I shall bid you farewell and retire to my bedchamber, us ladies need to nap in the afternoons, must try and fend off the ravages of time as long as possible. The car shall be outside at four o'clock sharp, Mr. Rumble; I shall not detain you any further." With that she shook his hand and gracefully exited the huge drawing room.

Rumble stayed where he was and surveyed the wall. He had never seen his work presented like this before, although he knew it had been.

He liked the way his nom-de-plume trademark the

tiny bumblebee sat at the bottom right hand corner of each sketch. Cootes had been right all those years ago, it stood out and stood him apart from the rest.

Although the thought of having to change his name to Bumble still made him cringe. He walked slowly along the wall and looked at each of his sketches as they stared back at him from behind the glass inside their frames. Somehow, he thought they looked more formal, less free and wild, and Rumble wasn't sure whether he preferred them in the raw or in frames. He was astounded at just how many sketches he'd done since his arrival. But he had to admit they were good, each was full of movement and had not only captured the surroundings but also the feeling of the scene and moment. He took out his phone and was busy taking photos of the wall when he heard voices.

They were rapidly approaching, there were loud angry voices, it was Thomas's voice that was the loudest.

"...I'm going to have it out with him that's what..." and then his wife replied softly, but Rumble couldn't hear her. He quickly moved to the door and exited to the right in the opposite direct to Thomas's arrival. He just made it as he heard Thomas move around the corner of the hallway seconds after he disappeared.

Once in his room, Rumble removed his smart clothes and dressed casually for the trip home. The envelope Rumble had been presented with fell from his pocket. He peeked inside intending to look more fully at it later and was amazed to see a hand printed thank you card and a banker's cheque for five thousand pounds; he couldn't believe his eyes. How very generous, and they had obviously written the cheque before they had even viewed his completed work on the wall. He knew he should also send them a thank you card after his return; it was the right thing to do. All too soon Rumble's adventure was drawing to a close and the nightmare that had become his life, awaited his return...

Chapter Twenty-two

The staff were lined up outside the front entrance as Rumble followed his bags and the same young youth who had carried them in earlier, to the car. Cookie came forward with an enormous bag of food and hugged Rumble and wished him a safe journey.

Nitzy too, hugged Rumble, she had a tear running down her cheek, but Rumble didn't think for a minute, it was because he was leaving. Nitzy told him to stay in touch and that she was only a phone call away.

As he got into the car, they all clapped and as he drove away and turned in his seat they were still waving to him as the car drove down the drive. Rumble really thought these people liked him, but why would they? He didn't know?

Seeing the Scottish scenery in the fading light of the evening was pure delight to Rumble; it was magnificent, and he secretly made a promise to one-day return and sketch this perfect place with the picture-perfect rolling hills and brilliant green paddocks.

The Bentley rolled to a stop at the station as Rumble's bags were removed from the boot. The driver tipped his hat and handed them to the smartly dressed steward waiting on the platform. The Flying Scotsman was like no train Rumble had ever seen.

It stood tall and grand and it was in perfect condition considering it was far from new. Its red and green paint gleamed in the fading light, and it looked much too posh for Rumble to ever consider boarding.

Steam seemed to be coming from under the carriage in several places, and Rumble thought this only added to its charm. Rumble again was shown into his own compartment, and it was even grander by far than the train he had traveled down from London on. The steward wore a very smart uniform complete with hat, gold braid, gold buttons and white gloves.

After the train was out of the station and gliding silently into the night, dinner was served, and it was almost as grand as it had been at the castle.

Soon Rumble began to relax, until he realized where he was headed. He quickly retrieved the thick folder he had not had time to read and opened it on the first page.

A photo of the house loomed up at him and his blood turned to ice. His mobile tinkled, and he knew he should check if his messages had been sent, so he checked and found the first one was gone, but he replied again just to be sure. He then told Lucy he was on his way back. And then he decided to check his voice messages, probably wrong numbers, but he would clear them anyway.

The first and second messages were from the Millington's as he's expected. He was glad to have their phone number again, as he had discarded it long ago when he'd left their cottage. Now he could call them. He would first listen the other messages and delete them, so he was up-to-date.

At the first sound of her voice, he knew who it was, his heart missed a beat, his palms began to sweat; he could feel the blush slowly creep over his face and down his neck.

Rumble had two messages from Primrose; the first was with Ms. Epping, saying how sorry they were it hadn't worked out, but he could move in any time he was ready. And please let them know when. Primrose said she was happy to help him move and to call her; she was looking forward to seeing him.

The second message was just from Primrose, she had apparently found out the address of where he lived from Lucy at Cootes office. Seeing that they hadn't heard from him over the last week; she was going to visit him tomorrow, Saturday.

She hoped it would be a pleasant surprise. "Oh, no," Rumble said aloud.

"No, no, no! Not Primrose, not her coming to the house. NO!" Rumble was beside himself with worry; he was still a long way from London and home. There was nothing he could do; he was trapped on the train. He had to relax, he had to stop his mind from thinking... He sat there flipping through the file but not really seeing it.

He saw photos of the red shiny ring with the silver stone. Apparently, it was believed to have belonged to one of the ancient Egyptian Pharaohs, and it supposedly had magical powers. Because it had apparently been stolen, it was thought the ring would create evil rather than eternal life and happiness for the Pharaoh and his princess.

He read briefly how the house had been used as the house of terror; it was believed that Edwards had kidnapped many women, and soon they had become pregnant with his child. Each time, Edwards really believed he would achieve everlasting life once the birth happened.

The next page had photos of many of the woman who had gone missing, and were never seen again. At least some, if not all of these were believed to have come under Edwards spell.

They were all young and pretty with blonde or auburn hair. Then as Rumble stared down at them, he suddenly really looked at them. To Rumble's horror, he realized they all looked somewhat like Primrose.

The train was flying along but to Rumble it felt like it was standing still. Then he received a text, it was from Ms. Epping, and apparently, she too had left him messages. Once he had heard Primrose's message, he hadn't listened to any others. There was no point. Ms. Epping said Primrose had set out to visit Rumble late yesterday afternoon; Ms. Epping just wanted to know they were together, and she would stop worrying.

Only Primrose was not answering her mobile, and it was now Sunday evening. Apparently, Primrose really wanted Rumble to move into the house with them. Ms. Epping had said if they didn't hear from him soon, she must place an ad in the newspaper next week. She said she had tried contacting him all week.

With shaking hand's he called Ms. Epping he quickly told her he was on the train from Edinburgh and wouldn't be home for several hours. Ms. Epping replied immediately, saying that if they didn't contact her before morning she'd call the police.

Rumble gave her the address of the house, even though he assumed she already had it. Then he changed the time she was to contact the police to two in the morning. That would give him lots of time to get home, and if there were trouble, at least the police would investigate, sooner rather than later. Ms. Epping wished him 'God's speed' and said she would pray Primrose is all right.

A few minutes later, Ms. Epping texted again, she suggested that perhaps someone else at his lodgings had let Primrose into his room to wait? Rumble didn't know what to reply to this, so he merely said, perhaps.

He didn't want to alarm Ms. Epping, but this was not sounding good, and Rumble didn't know what he would find when he arrived at the house or if Primrose was even there. But in his gut, he knew she would be, there was no other explanation. Rumble cursed himself for ever going to Scotland he cursed himself for not leaving yesterday, and he cursed himself for forgetting to check his phone yet again. Then the voice spoke, '*so how does this help, feeling guilty is not going to let you think clearly or be at your best.*' 'So what do you know?' Rumble asked the voice, and it was silent. "WHAT DO YOU KNOW?"

Rumble yelled out loud, and the steward quietly opened the door to his compartment and asked, "Sir, excuse the intrusion, but I thought I heard you call. Is everything all right, sir?"

"Yes, yes, quite all right thank you. How far from London are we?"

"Sir, we shall arrive exactly on time at Kings Cross station as we always do in a little over an hour's time. Will that be all, sir?" The steward enquired looking strangely at Rumble. Rumble knew his face was red, and he was sweating profusely, but he didn't care, he roughly replaced the file folder, and its contents that were spilling out over the seat, into his carry-on luggage.

As he did so several small pieces of newspaper fluttered to the floor. At first, Rumble wasn't going to pick them up. But then reluctantly he bent down and retrieved them from the spotlessly clean carpet at his feet.

'The first article was about a woman called Pauline Benson; he had heard that name before, but where?' Rumble searched his mind and could not recall. Then the voice spoke, '*she worked at the drycleaners*'. Rumble only heard the word drycleaners, so he replied, 'do you think I'm thinking of cleaning my clothes at a time like this? Why Primrose could be...' then he stopped horrified at what he was thinking. The article was a plea from Pauline and her brother to anyone who had seen their mother. According to the article, Pauline's mother was a widow. Then she told the story…

One day a debonair gentleman came into our shop, my mother was behind the counter.

We knew him merely as Mr. Edwards and, of course, we had the address of the house where he lived. My mother and Mr. Edwards stepped out together several times, and my mother seemed to get more and more smitten.

But for my brother and me, something didn't seem quite right. Mr. Edwards hardly noticed us; he seldom if ever spoke to us even when he stayed to dinner. His sole attention was on our mother. He had a steely gaze, which seemed to go right through you when he looked at you. My brother and I decided he gave us the creeps, and we asked our mother to stop seeing him. But by this time, she said she was in love and how she intended on marrying him. It had only been several months, and we were shocked. Several days later, she told us she was pregnant, together they would be telling everyone that weekend over dinner. While she was out with Mr. Edwards that evening we called a family meeting, in our gut, we knew this wasn't right. But our mother never came home that night, and we never saw her again. We visited the address he had given us, as did the police, and the house looked empty like it hadn't been lived in for years. We are still searching, and we ask if anyone knows anything, please contact us.

That was all it said, Rumble checked the date it was written over forty years ago.

Rumble crumpled the small newspaper clipping and threw it on the floor. Then he began pacing again. Outside, he could gradually see more and more lights as the huge city of London approached.

He felt like a caged animal, these feelings were all new to him. He hadn't really felt anything for a very long time, and he thought it strange just how strongly he felt about Primrose.

He knew his experiences in Scotland had changed him, but what he was feeling now was clouding his head and occupying his thoughts.

The train seemed to pull into the station, rather too slowly. Looking out the window, Rumble saw clouds of steam and not much else. The steward sensing his anxiety, was in his compartment with his bags in hand before they stopped, "I sense you're in a hurry, sir?" the young man asked politely.

"Yes, yes, I am indeed."

"Will it be a limo or taxi, sir?" The steward then asked, Rumble was hardly listening, in his haste to get off the train.

"Whatever moves the fastest?" Rumble replied and didn't see the young man smile.

"I shall get you a limo, sir." Rumble didn't hear, he was following the young man off the train, urging him to go faster. The bustle of people, luggage and porters crowded the platform as Rumble and the steward pushed their way through. Rumble didn't know quite how he ended up in a limousine, and on the motorway, but he had, and he was glad he had, only he hoped he had enough money to pay the smartly dressed driver.

Rumble was trying not to think of what may have happened to Primrose, he was trying to quiet his beating heart and racing pulse. But most of all, he was trying to focus. The hour was late, and it had been dark for some time, so just by entering the house, Rumble knew he was breaking the rules. 'Well, I don't care, what could possibly happen to me'*?* Rumble muttered aloud as the voice replied, *'You've seen what Edwards is capable of, and you ask that?'* The voice said. 'Oh, do shut up,' Rumble replied. *'No, I won't, we're in this together, you die, I die, and I don't want to. You have to focus and not race in like an idiot'.* 'Are you calling me an idiot now?' *'I'm just saying that you are not use to doing things outside the law or anything where people are concerned. I don't know if you can call Edwards an actual person, but I know he's dangerous'.* The voice replied and Rumble could hear the concern 'All right, I hear you, but I am a different person now.' *'Sure you are, your fearless and brave and ready to fight for your girl...'* the voice said sarcastically. Rumble almost answered, then realized the voice was again playing with him 'my what...?' Rumble asked but not waiting or wanting an answer he quickly added, 'oh, do shut up.' Then Rumble repeated 'my girl?' *'She must be special,* *look at the state you're in?* 'The rational voice added, 'I don't think she's my girl,' Rumble said and the voice didn't reply.

Rumble was hoping he had enough money left to pay the driver. He fumbled around for the envelope Cootes had given him, there was still several hundred pounds left inside, surely that would be enough. Thirty minutes later, Rumble instructed the driver to pull to the curb. He asked him to stop several houses away; he didn't want to draw attention to his arrival at this time of night. It was already after midnight. He had enough money to pay the driver with still some left over.

Again, he almost forgot to take his luggage. He realized this was the first time he had actually wheeled his own luggage. As he crossed the road and walked to the house, he could tell the driver couldn't wait to get out of the neighborhood; he'd seen the shock on his face when Rumble had instructed him where to go. Fortunately, the limo engine was quiet, because the driver pulled away from the curb, fast.

Rumble was alone in the darkness, there was one streetlight that glowed a pale yellow and illuminated a small patch of road. It was the only one still working in the street, but it was some way further down. Darkness and silence surrounded him as he looked up at the old house. Its windows black with darkness, and its demeanor unloved and forgotten.

Soon Rumble drew closer to the back door, he

gradually became aware of shouting in the distance. Looking down to the far end of the street, he saw the youths, they were still awake at his time of night, and they had a small fire blazing in the street. Rumble briefly wondered whose belongings they were burning now, and then a bottle smashed, and he knew they were drinking. So long as they stayed away from him, he didn't care.

Rumble rolled his suitcases quietly to a stop outside the kitchen door. He stood them close to the wall, one beside the other.

Then he took the shoulder strap of his sachet and placed it over his head, so he didn't need to hold it on his shoulder. He fumbled with his new and unfamiliar clothes in the darkness until he found the old key. It wasn't hard to find, but the clouds were covering the moon, so he needed to find the keyhole with his finger -tips. *'Quietly, now, don't be in such a hurry, you'll make too much noise'*, the voice warned, and Rumble had to admit it was right. The door was always reluctant to open, but tonight, it seemed more so.

Rumble had to physically push his shoulder against it. He knew if he opened it too fast, it would moan and groan as it always did, and in the silence of the night anyone or anything would hear it. So, as the voice suggested he pushed it open, slowly.

He didn't try to shut the door after he entered; he didn't intend to stay. When it was open just enough to squeeze through sideways, he did so.

He stood still and listened once he was inside the cold dark kitchen, to the stillness, and silence. But he somehow knew the house was not sleeping, it was just waiting. The usual musty, grimy smell clouded his nose, and he walked slowly from memory through the kitchen and into the entranceway. The floors were gritty and unwashed, and for the first time, Rumble was aware that the dirt beneath his shoes made a crunching noise, so he slowed his pace and moved with sleuth. His senses were honed and with the lack of light his mind had never been more alive.

Keeping close to the wall, he climbed the stairs, slowly, placing just a little of his weight at a time on each tread, to make sure it didn't protest. Keeping close to the wall, he could barely see the stairs under his feet. He had his flashlight in his pocket should he need it, but he was reluctant to show himself. The first -floor landing approached and when Rumble was at eye level with it, he noticed the soft beams of moonlight play on small parts of the dusty floor. 'The clouds must have shifted', he thought. Then Rumble stopped, the hairs on the back of his neck prickled. He stared at the dust on the old wooden floor.

He knew this dust, he had looked at it often. He was quite sure of what he saw someone had been walking here. He could see their footprints, small footprints smaller than his own. Then the dust was disturbed even more as if in a frenzy of activity, which stopped outside the first door. The door stood open. Then the moon must have disappeared behind a cloud, as everything was enveloped in darkness.

Rumble finished climbing the stairs, now he knew someone was here. Someone else was in the house, and from the way, the footprints were pointing they hadn't left. Rumble's heart was beating so fast and loud, he thought everyone must hear it. He willed it to stop; he needed to steady his shaking, and he wanted to feel calm. Rumble felt his own sweat hot and salty, run down his forehead and into his eyes. He blinked it away, but it stung as it entered his eyes and his vision went momentarily blurry.

'She has to be in that room, she has to be, Edwards has her...' Rumble thought as he began shaking more valiantly. '*And how are you going to help her in this state, all that will happen will be; he'll have you both. Don't linger around the door, move around the side of the hallway, sit on the bottom stair and get a grip. You're not use to anyone like this. And I for one don't want to go down with you...* ' Rumble knew the voice was right, he had to get a grip, 'She has to be in there, but if she is, why is the door open, and if the door is open, why hadn't she made a run for it? Primrose is young, fit, and probably fast.' Rumble thought. '*Concentrate on the things you know not on the things you don't. Only certainties Rumble, will get you through.*' The voice was right again but Rumble was hardly listening, soon it continued, '*This could be one of the most important nights of your life. Now slow your breathing and close your eyes,*' the voice instructed. 'No, I'm not closing my eyes.' '*Okay, then don't, just take deep slow breaths and count in your head, or don't worry about counting, I'll count for you...'* the voice had only counted to six when a scream ripped through the stillness, it was somewhere below them and sounded slightly muffled.

Another scream that stopped as if it was cut in half, as Rumble listened closely he heard Primroses voice begged... "No, leave me alone, please, No."

Rumble was about to jump to his feet when the voice said loudly, *'WAIT.'* The next moment Rumble heard shuffling outside the front door. Then the unmistakably voices of the youths down the street. Even though their words were slurred, their voices were loud, and their intent clear.

"Fuck ya all, hold it you arseholes."

"Bloody hell, who ya calling a fucking arsehole?"

"Shut up, Sooty, the doors probably locked tight, we gotta all ram it together, like."

"Yeah, we bloody, know what to do."

"Maybe the doors open, like last time, like."

Rumble had to listen hard to what they said, he hadn't moved. He got to his feet and leaned closer toward the wall, he peeked around to the first open door. Primrose must be in there and those youths will surely torch the place. Rumble was just about move out of his hiding place toward the door. When the apparition that was surely Edwards seemed to float hurriedly through the opening in the first door. It didn't go down the stairs but straight over the railing to the entranceway below.

Rumble was transfixed; the thing that must be Edwards was definitely transparent. It didn't seem to know he was there; its whole focus was on the front door and the boys outside. *'Now,'* said the voice, *'move now, go into the room, hurry. **Do it, do it, do it'**.* Rumble was surprised, his feet could move; he was so scared. *'Hurry-move faster'.* The voice commanded and suddenly at the thought of Primrose his feet had wings. He tried to tread quietly as he moved quickly from his hiding place and in through the open door.

The room was in darkness. Quickly Rumble eyes adjusted to the pitch-blackness. Then he saw it. The huge painting on the wall was turned slightly sideways and a trickle of deep yellow light came into the room. Rumble remembered the door behind the picture. *'Hurry, you haven't much time, while Edwards is down in the entrance way,'* Rumble could hear the muffled voices of the youths. He moved toward the light in the wall, once he was there and hadn't fallen over anything, he gently pushed the wall. It turned slightly, so he pushed again. More light flooded the room it wasn't the bright white light of today, but the dark yellow light of yesteryear.

Rumble looked inside, he heard the voice of Leonard Cohen, Tower of Song almost coming out of the walls; and then he saw a dim narrow stairway leading steeply downwards. On the walls hung many old small-framed brownish photos. In each photo was a man that looks somewhat like Edwards. These men were all wearing lab coats and stood over a victim on a slab. *'Move Rumble, you don't have time to sight see'*, said the voice, urgently. The room was long and narrow, and Rumble could just make out other stairways like the one he had just descended. In the dim light, Rumble saw a long narrow table in the center; on the table were many Bunsen burners and other old-fashioned instruments.

The Bunsen burners bright flames touching the undersides of the glass containers, the colored ingredients in the glass jars bubbled and steamed. Under his feet, something crunched; looking down he saw a small pair of wire-rimmed glasses. They were almost ground into the floor, the glass now in tiny pieces but still mainly inside the frames. He had seen these glasses before, he briefly thought.

Then Rumble heard a noise, and turning to the left, he could just make out the form of Primrose. She was shackled to a narrow slab, her clothes almost ripped from her body, and with a gag in her mouth. She was trashing around as best she could trying to get his attention.

Rumble ran to her, grabbing the gag; he pulled it free. Her face was streaked with tears, her hair matted and wet.

"Oh, Mr. Rumble," she said through dry parched lips. He tried to pull her up and then realized the wide shackles on her ankles and wrists were holding her down.

"The key, it is on the table, hurry, please," she sobbed as Rumble retrieved a huge ring of old keys from amongst the bubbling potions.

"It's the little one, hurry." *'Yes, Rumble, hurry',* the voice said urgently *'hurry'*. Rumble found the smallest key. He inserted it in the lock on her ankles, and it turned smoothly, the shackles fell open. Then he did the same on her wrists. She almost fell off the bed into his arms. Just the nearness of her made his heart beat, but it was not with fear this time. *'Hurry, Rumble, HURRY!'* The voice screamed in his head. Rumble didn't want to be locked down here for all eternity.

'Quickly up the stairs and then close the door to where it was, this will give you more time'. Rumble already had Primrose on her feet.

Before they began to climb the narrow stairway, Rumble grabbed a photo off the wall and tossed it roughly on the table. The burners crashed as did the containers and their contents rapidly ran over the table, dripping onto the floor. The contents on the table instantly ignited;

Rumble knew whatever the bubbling colored potions were inside the glass containers they were very flammable.

He hurriedly pulled Primrose up the stairs. Several more containers crashed to the floor, the contents caused little explosions as they met other liquids, more flames followed, and Rumble knew they needed to get far away and fast.

He could feel Primrose was weak, he was almost dragging her along, but he felt strong enough for them both. He peeked through the door at the top of the stairs as flames licked the stairs below and smoke entered the room before them.

It made their eyes smart, and Rumble moved faster remembering the advice of the voice. He placed the door in the wall back in exactly the same place as it was before.

The huge portrait gazed down at him accusingly. Then Rumble heard the deep gravelly voice of Leonard Cohen clearly echo around the room, 'You like the dark, we kill the flame.' Rumble saw the glow of light, go out down on the stairs through the gap behind the portrait, but the flames burned brightly behind him, and they were headed directly for them.

Rumble could hear yelling from the hallway and glancing down he saw the heavy front door give way, only to bounce back again. He saw the thing that was Edwards easily battling the youths.

He stayed close to the wall and pulled Primrose down the stairs, being sure to stay away from the banister where they might be easily seen. Rumble knew her energy was nearly spent. Rumble never took his eyes from the apparition of Edwards, but noted its focus was not on them for the moment. Staying as quiet as he could, he was relieved when they made it to the bottom of the stairs. Then turning, they vanished into the darkness of the kitchen. Rumble turned and looked upwards before they entered the kitchen to see smoke bellowing out the door they had just exited. Flames licked the edges of the doorframe and Rumble knew with the dry timbers of the old house, it wouldn't be long before it went up in flames.

Rumble could feel the grime underfoot, and he hated to think what it must feel like to Primrose without any shoes, but she said nothing as they moved.

Finally, they squeezed out through the back door. *'Close the door'*, the voice instructed, and Rumble did so just as a loud explosion ripped through the house. Primrose was grabbing his bags as he pulled the door shut.

"Leave them," he whispered.

"No, you must take them. I know what it's like to lose your belongings," she whispered back taking the two large bags and trying to grab the carryon. Rumble didn't care about the luggage, only his sachet. But he knew they needed to get out of here and fast. He grabbed the two big suitcases from Primrose, and she took the carry on.

Rumble looked into the darkness and noticed the youths scattering up the street, why aren't they going home he wondered. Now the only exit for them was down the end of the street. He thought there was an alleyway there that took you through to the main road on the other side. However, he had never used it and knew it was probably used only by the youths, and they would therefor claim it as their property.

He had no choice but to go in that direction if he didn't want to see the youths. They were screaming and yelling at the top of their voices.

"Run, Primrose, run," Rumble said, wishing he could hold her hand and help her. Primrose surprised him by moving faster; they were running together down the center of the street trailing his luggage behind them. They were now approaching the streetlight halfway down the street. Rumble noticed a porch light go on to his left as they passed.

Primrose must have noticed it also as she ducked into the shadows. Another explosion ripped through the night. Rumble turned to see flames shooting through the old roof and up into the night. They were now approaching the end of the street, they passed by the low burning fire the youths had started earlier, and it began to rain, not heavy rain, but it was more than a light drizzle. Entering the alley they heard the first of the sirens and flashing lights turn into the far end of the street.

Rumble knew they were safe from view. Rumble was worried about Primrose's feet and the broken glass that was scattered everywhere, he could hear it crunch under his shoes.

He wasn't sure what to do so finally he said. "Primrose, sit on the suitcase and keep your feet up. I shall pull you."

"But your suitcases is not strong enough, I shall break it," Primrose replied and even though Primrose didn't want to break his suitcase she did as he asked. He could see her feet were dirty and bleeding, and he remonstrated himself for not doing something sooner.

The suitcase must have been tough as it held her weight and still easily moved on the four wheels over all the obstacles in the alleyway. Rumble wanted to use his torch to see what was on the ground, but he thought the light might be seen.

Several minutes later, they arrived in the main street.

Overhead streetlights illuminated their way, and Rumble left the suitcases and put his arms around Primrose. The moment he did so, she seemed to collapse into him. Rumble looked up to see single car come toward them, it was a taxicab, and he hailed it down. From where they had just been the sirens wailed, and you could see the many flashing lights reflect into the sky along with the flames from the house fire.

Once his luggage was stowed into the taxi and they were in the back seat, Primrose briefly gave the address of Rosemary Cottage to the driver and then fainted into Rumble's arms.

As they drove through the night, Rumble sent Ms. Epping a text to say they were on their way and safe. She responded immediately. Rumble gathered Primrose tightly in his arms. He imagined the white picket, the large purple front door of Rosemary Cottage with the elaborate handle the neat expansive gardens, and what would be the newly woven thatch roof.

But more important than the cottage was the fact that they were both safe, and the house of horrors was burning to the ground. He had escaped and life was suddenly good, very good indeed. *'Well done, Rumble, proud of you, didn't think you had it in you'*, said the voice, surprising Rumble as he held the limp body of Primrose close, and a small smile moved his lips. Then he replied 'Oh, do shut up.'

Epilogue
Nine months later.

From the moment Primrose and Rumble arrived at Rosemary Cottage, Primrose never again left his side. She stayed in his room at night and spent all her days with him. Gradually, she recovered although seldom spoke of her experience in the house.

Rumble too was trying to block the horrendous experience completely from his mind although often Primrose would have nightmares and she would call out. "The mist, the mist, get it away from me," her words haunted Rumble, and he looked forward to the day when her nightmares would stop.

A week later, they celebrated his fiftieth birthday. It was the first time, since living with the Millington's that Rumble had celebrated a birthday, had a birthday cake or shared it with friends. Soon afterwards on Primrose's instruction, it was also the first time Rumble had ever visited the dentist. He hated anyone touching him and the thought of a stranger poking around in his mouth made him feel physical sick. Internally, he wrestled with the idea. He wanted to please Primrose but was unable to come to terms with the prospect of the dentist. After all, he hadn't needed one all these years; he'd never felt the need.

Rumble had always known his teeth were one of his best features. But finally, his love for Primrose prevailed.

He wanted to please her so the appointment was made. He cringed inwardly at the sight of the white coats, and the smell of the dental rooms. And then he had to tightly close his eyes to avoid running, screaming from the chair. He felt trapped, like a caged animal ready for the slaughter.

However, he enjoyed the praise when they told him his teeth were in very good shape for his age and that he only had two small cavities. He was not about to get them fixed, but he did agree to have his teeth cleaned and whitened and his chipped front tooth fixed.

When they handed him the mirror, he had to admit his white teeth made him look younger, fresher somehow. He'd visited the dentists reluctantly, but it was another thing he did now, for Primrose.

She was the center of his entire world, and he loved the feeling of being part of a couple; although inside, he was still secretly scared and thought he may wake up one day and find it was all dream.

One month after arriving at Rosemary Cottage, Primrose and Rumble were married. It was Primrose's idea as everything was, and Rumble didn't object. 'It is not who he was,' he thought 'but it is now whom I am; most profound' he thought as the day approached. Their wedding was a small affair in the back garden of Rosemary Cottage. With Cootes, James Cootes, Lucy, the Millingtons and the occupants of Rosemary Cottage.

Rumble had paid for Nitzy to ride up on the train to attend his wedding.

This was the biggest adventure of Nitzy's life and she simply bubbled with excitement from the moment she arrived. These were all the people Rumble knew.

Primrose had a lot more friends and family. Soon after the wedding, they went house hunting and were delighted to stumble across and buy a rather cozy three-bedroom cottage of their own. To Cootes's delight, and in order to purchase the cottage, Rumble needed to let some moths out of his very deep pockets. However, Rumble did so, before thinking too deeply, and immediately purchased the cottage on Primrose's instruction.

It was fully furnished and came complete with a red mini cooper "S" in the garage. The couple that owned it had been transferred to South Africa, and they were in a hurry to leave and wanted to take nothing with them.

The cottage was only sixteen-years old and had been completely renovated. It was a modern thatched cottage, and they moved in the moment the paperwork was completed. Primrose had her drivers' license and loved having a car; slowly but surely, she talked Rumble into getting his drivers' license also.

He drove only locally, and he remained rather tentative on the road, but he was pleased of his achievement, as was the voice, which he seldom heard these days.

Nor did Rumble think of the negative beliefs his

mother has instilled in him as a child, most of which had controlled his waking hours for his whole life. Now happy, he had managed to block them out.

His money had bought him enjoyment, and he still had enough in the bank for a rainy day, so her words controlled him no longer.

~

Nine months later, Rumble lay in bed in the darkness of their bedroom. Primrose was curled up close beside him. They had just completed turning the third bedroom into a nursery, and any day now, they would be filling it with their new baby daughter.

Rumble lay watching the shadows play on the ceiling as he listened to Primrose's rhythmic breathing close beside him.

Every so often, she would murmur in her sleep as she tried to move. Her stomach heavy with child, now she was too big to go anywhere and could no longer see her feet. But the worst part for Primrose was not being able to drive.

There simply wasn't enough room behind the steering wheel. However, they were both excited about the imminent birth. Since turning fifty, Rumble knew it was now the best time of his life, and each morning, he pinched himself to make sure he wasn't dreaming. How could anyone like the beautiful Ms. Primrose be interested in an ordinary, boring someone like him? He knew love really must be blind.

However, as Rumble lay in his bed that night he was

secretly anxious. Primrose had given up her job several months ago, and Rumble worked from home most days, never wanting to leave her side.

Primrose had thought she was too old to have children, and she wanted three. But right now, he was questioning his feelings, what were his concerns about having a child? What was causing the anxiety and fear he felt, why was he lying awake feeling nervous about Primrose and the impending birth. Or was it something else troubling him, something he couldn't quite grasp – was something clawing at the fringes of his consciousness?

He couldn't believe he was married, nor could he believe the delights of making love to Primrose. Of course, she had needed to teach him everything and they had both read many books.

But what a wonderful loving and caring life they had created for themselves in such a short time; Rumble knew he was truly blessed.

He loved having Primrose around however if he thought too much he had to admit becoming a father scared him to death. But overall he knew he had never been happier. He had never thought of marrying, and he had certainly never thought of having children.

So many changes, and they had all happened so fast. But then, if they hadn't happened fast, Rumble knew he would have talked himself out of letting any changes happen, ever. No, it had all worked out for the best, and so long as Primrose was happy and healthy, then he was happy also. She was his life; although now he knew it must change because it would soon be Primrose and their beautiful daughter, they would both be his life.

He wanted his daughter to look and act just like her mother, everything about Primrose was perfect.

He watched the shadows dancing on the ceiling and thought of how life had changed and how he had grown and evolved with it. He blocked out all the horrors of the past and focused only on the good things and his future.

It was a loud thump coming from the kitchen – it was a noise he'd not heard before? He felt icy talons run down his neck, and he felt the heat of his sweaty palms. *'Danger'* the long-forgotten voice startled him. Rumble knew the voice wouldn't be speaking if there wasn't danger, because the only times he had ever heard it was when he was scared or in danger, and here it was talking to him again.

He wondered again, where the loud noise had come from. Then he heard again in his head, the voice he hadn't heard for so long, the one he thought he was rid of, loud and clear, it replied to his question. *'In the house silly, it's a noise that shouldn't be inside your house,'* for a moment it was more the sound of the voice that startled him rather than what it said, until finally he listened to what it was saying, *'be very careful and don't wake Primrose,'* it instructed. Then another heavy thump followed by a crash, were they being burgled? *'no, it isn't a burglar. Someone who wants to wake you more likely.'* It was more of a thud, than a crash, really.

Rumble's fear increased, he began to shake violently, his heart pounded and his palms and forehead sweated; carefully, he moved Primrose's arm from his chest and slipped out of bed leaving behind the warmth and comfort of his wife, as he moved, she stirred and groaned in her sleep.

He stood where he was and waited. Then he watched in the darkness as she settled into sleep again.

Another thump. Rumble threw on his robe and slippers, then on his way out of the bedroom, he grabbed the baseball bat they kept behind the door. Pale yellow light glowed from the kitchen door. Softly Rumble crept down the hallway. *'Shouldn't you be calling the police and the ambulance,'* the voice instructed, 'Maybe' Rumble replied moving silently toward the kitchen, then he added, 'Why the ambulance? What do you know?' The voice didn't reply. He was now at the kitchen door.

Carefully looking in Rumble saw on the kitchen bench, a candle glowed. Where had it come from, why was it here? *'You have more important things to think about apart from a candle...Danger. Be very careful.'* The voice almost whispered.

Rumble moved into the room and then he stopped dead. Lying on the kitchen table and glowing fiercely was the blazing red stone in the ring, it jumped on the table several inches into the air, and it seemed to move toward Rumble. *'Don't touch the ring, move away, it holds evil.'*

He couldn't take his eyes from it until he heard the soft tinkling sound, and there on the table lying beside the ring was an old- fashioned silver baby's rattle which he knew would bear the inscription 'Baby Sarah'. Rumble had seen it before; he knew what was written on it without looking. But what he didn't know was, why it was here?

"I have been watching you from the start, we have all been watching you. I know you felt us watching you," came the thin raspy voice. It came from everywhere but nowhere.

"You have proved yourself to be like the other tenants. You have disobeyed my rules." Rumble knew that voice, as thin, distorted and raspy as it now was; there was no mistaking, he knew that voice. *'Danger, you are in grave danger, get out NOW!'* the voice yelled in his head.

Rumble turned to see the shape that was once Edwards, huge and almost transparent in the corner of the room. It loomed above him, its face, distorted and grotesque.

Coarse long white whiskers protruded from his ears, nose and eyebrows. With deep-set steely eyes and thin lips; Edwards seemed an intense enigma from another place and time. *'Run, get out, this cannot end well, even I'm scared.'* The voice instructed and Rumble replied, 'I can't get out this is my house Edwards is the intruder,' *'Who cares who belongs where, get out now!'* 'Primrose, I can't leave her' *'Save yourself, she may be all right, run, leave now,'* the voice replied urgently, 'Maybe all right?'

Rumble replied and knew he wasn't going anywhere. '*Go, run, leave now*' the voice continued, but Rumble's attention was focused elsewhere and he was terrified, all he managed to reply was, 'Oh do shut up.'

Edwards steely gray eyes penetrated Rumble's soul with an intensity that was not of this earth. His shiny bald head shone transport under the light and the snowy white hair that surrounds it, glistened where the light from the candle danced in the air. Finally, Rumble found his voice,

"Why are you here? What do you want? Get out, get out of my house now." Rumble wanted to sound authoritative, but he knew he didn't, because Edwards didn't move, he just continued staring at him. Rumble felt weak as he stared back into the hollow eyes, his hand unknowing searched to support him; they continued staring, the air between them hung heavy with an unspoken challenge. Rumble was aware that on the table the ring moved toward his finger and every so often the rattle tinkled, all on its own.

"I take what I want. I shall leave when you give it to me!" The apparition replied its gaze never leaving Rumble's eyes.

He watched terrified as it grew in size until it was almost touching the ceiling. It was more than a shadow but not quite a solid form, and it seemed to float before his eyes. '*now you realize why you should have called someone. I'm scared too,*' Rumble didn't hear the voice he was petrified; he hated being this close to Edwards. He could smell the garlic on his breath, a strong overpowering smell in the small kitchen. Rumble remembered Edward's single-minded focus, and he was horrified to realize that intense focus was now firmly on him.

Edwards moved closer, his shadow upon Rumble now; Rumble felt the deep chill of the shadow on him, he could smell the mist as it creeped in under the back door. *'maybe it's not too late to run, please get out. I don't want to die'.* The voice whispered sounding very scared, but Rumble didn't respond.

Rumble moved backwards until he was against the door. When Rumble had first met Edwards, he was a short stout man, but looking at him now that was no longer so.

The baseball bat that he gripped so tightly flew from Rumble's hand and smashed through the kitchen window. Again, the rattle tinkled and Rumble asked, his voice nearly gone with fear, "What do you want?" The blackness of Edwards was creeping slowly upon him now, he felt the ring on his finger deeply burning into his flesh, he tried to scream with terror and the searing pain, but no sound came from his open mouth. Again, the rattle tinkled.

Then Rumble noticed the mist had almost encircled him. More and more gray mist swirled and twirled toward him, the small kitchen was nearly full of mist. It slowly crept in his direction, its focus too was on him. Turning and curling, with long talons. It reached out completely focused on touching him, engulfing him. Rumble could smell it, and instinctively he knew it was the same smell that always lingered in Edwards' old house.

"I need her in order to live. Don't you understand? Why doesn't anyone understand? I will take her…"

Rumble tried to scream but nothing came out, or did it? Then he realized it was Primrose screaming and her screams tore at his heart.

"Rumble, where are you? The baby's coming, help me Rumble…" *'And that's why you should have called the ambulance…'* the voice whispered but Rumble didn't hear.

The darkness of Edwards was beginning to engulf Rumble; The freezing mist encircling him now, he felt the life seep from his soul; again, in a mere whisper he asked.

"Why are you here? What do you want?" he must know he couldn't have Primrose surely, he must know? But deep inside, he knew Edwards could take anything he wanted. He must have come for Primrose, and he could hardly bear the thought,

"I take what I want?"

"You shall not have her," this time as darkness almost completely engulfed him; he felt as if he had become part of Edwards.

Rumble repeated. "You cannot have her. Primrose is mine," Rumble replied the tears hot on his cheeks, his heart pounding in his chest. He heard Edwards laugh, it began slowly, a shallow, disconnected rattle.

Rumble was startled by the urgent voice so loud in his head, *'he sounds like dead dry leaves on a cold winter's day, be very careful you are in grave danger. You realize I am you and I for one am not ready to die yet. Do something Rumble, do something!'* the laugh continued from somewhere deep inside the apparition in Rumble's kitchen. Rumble still couldn't believe this was happening, Edwards was here in his home, the voice was back, the baby was arriving, and Rumble was still a coward and scared out of his wits.

"Rumble, please come to me, I need you the baby is coming and I am scared I need you now…Rumble…Please" Primrose called, but to Rumble she sounded a long way away. His heart ached that he could not get to her, not move.

He could smell the mist but even stronger now was the garlic heavily all around him, in him. All the while slowly creeping as Edwards' soul continued to become his. Then Rumble heard another voice, 'You like the dark, I kill the flame.'

Before Edwards replied, darkness engulfed the kitchen; impenetrable blackness, inky thick and heavy within the mist… Was this death? Rumble questioned briefly, *'I don't want to die, hold on, be strong, you can do it. **Do it, do it, do it,***' and somewhere far away, he heard Primrose screaming and calling for him, only this time she added that she was coming to find him. "No." Rumble tried to yell but only a crackle came from his lips; she needed him, it was his job to protect, to protect her and his child, at all costs.

He knew he must not die, but he could feel Edwards dominating him, inside him. He was wrapped heavily inside the clinging, clawing mist, unable to speak or see.

Again, he heard Primrose scream in pain, only she sounded closer, she must not come into the kitchen, he tried again to warn her, only this time his mouth felt full of dust, he croaked in silence.

He needed to call to her but try as he did no words came from his mouth. Edwards was again speaking to him, but Rumble had no idea what he said or what he wanted, he only knew Edwards would take whatever he chose to take. Rumble must speak, he must tell Edwards, but he was becoming weaker.

It was the sound of Primrose's voice so close now, just outside in the hallway that bought a whisper to his lips.

It was indeed a mere whisper as he pleaded, "You cannot have her, you cannot have Primrose. Why are you here?"

This time Edwards was all around Rumble and when his voice spoke it was close to Rumble's ear. Rumble held tightly to reality as gradually he knew he was slipping away, slipping into Edwards. "I do not want you or Primrose, but you belong to me. I told you, you cannot get away from me or the house, you know too much," Edwards voice was a mere whisper. '*But the house burned to the ground, why is he saying this?*' the voice suddenly asked and Rumble immediately asked Edwards the same questions. Edwards voice was gaining in strength, as

Rumble felt he was slipping into him.

"You cannot destroy my house. I will always live, I will live on forever, I just relocated everything, it is all exactly the same, nothing has changed. You cannot destroy me, why doesn't anyway understand, but I need something in order to live and Rumble I need it now." He only just managed to hear Edwards thin voice, he sounded so far away. Rumble new Edwards voice was now stronger but he could barely hear him. He was now no more than a hollow distant whisper, Rumble asked again, "Then what do you want?" Before Rumble fainted into oblivion he heard Edwards reply.

"I take what I want. I take what is mine.

It is not Primrose nor you I want. Its Baby Sarah."

The End

More fiction books you may enjoy – from Mary Barr

Wild Dog Canyon (Same Genre)

Hagar's Curse

Browning Amble – The Sect. (similar Genre)

Mrs. Dolymauchers Daughter's

The Grasshopper File

Dahlia's Choice

How to Buy a Husband

Ms. Barr also writes:
Short stories
Novella's
Young adults
Juvenile
Children's books

<u>WWW.Mary-Barr.com</u>

'Remember, adventures in life are all around, live in the moment, there are no second chances.'
Mary Barr